dance lessons

dance lessons

a novel | Áine Greaney

SYRACUSE UNIVERSITY PRESS

Syracuse University Press, Syracuse, New York 13244-5290

First Edition 2011
11 12 13 14 15 16 6 5 4 3 2 1

∞ The paper used in this publication meets the minimum requirements of the American National Standard for Information Sciences—Permanence of Paper for Printed Library Materials, ANSI Z39.48-1992.

For a listing of books published and distributed by Syracuse University Press, visit our Web site at SyracuseUniversityPress.syr.edu.

ISBN: 978-0-8156-0984-1

Library of Congress Cataloging-in-Publication Data

Greaney, Áine.
Dance lessons : a novel / Áine Greaney. — 1st ed.
p. cm.
ISBN 978-0-8156-0984-1 (cloth : alk. paper)
1. Widows—Fiction. 2. Irish Americans—Fiction. 3. Americans—Ireland—Fiction. 4. Family secrets—Fiction. 5. Domestic fiction. 6. Psychological fiction. I. Title.
PS3607.R4283D36 2011
813'.6—dc22 2011001692

Manufactured in the United States of America

Áine Greaney, born and brought up on a remote farm in the west of Ireland, now lives and writes on Boston's North Shore. Her literary works have been published in Ireland, the United Kingdom, and the United States. Previous book-length publications include a novel, *The Big House*, and a short-story collection, *The Sheep Breeders Dance*.

dance lessons

Prologue

August 1986

THE KITCHEN PHONE is ringing again. This time, everyone ignores it until a young man named Liam from County Offally pushes through the party crowd to pick it up. His voice is husky from sleep. He is not long awake and up after sleeping off his night shift in a Back Bay hotel. He stands there shouting above the music and the voices, pale, skinny legs under his boxer shorts. He gives directions to their triple-decker apartment house on Springvale Avenue, Dorchester.

"Yeah, we're going barbecuing out on the balcony," he says. "I heard there's a new fella arrived. He's here somewhere. I know he brought us rakes of Galtee sausages and we're doing burgers, too." He's about to hang up the wall phone when he remembers something. "Hey!" he says. "Bring crisps. And beer."

Earlier, while Liam was still asleep, someone new arrived on the Sunday flight from Shannon, Ireland. Now, the newcomer's luggage sits in a corner of the living room, abandoned while he's drinking ice-cold American beer and being introduced around to the apartment roommates—always a changing lineup of young Irish tenants and subletters and their assorted guests.

Almost a year ago, Fintan Dowd from County Mayo was the latest new arrival, another young immigrant full of bravado stories and how he told his lies and kept his cool at the airport immigration. He was the latest new squatter sleeping on the couch and wandering the city looking for tidings of an under-the-table job. Now Fintan works in a bar, the Paul Revere

Tavern, where his weekly tips are more than anything he ever earned as a bachelor of commerce graduate, first class honors, from University College, Dublin.

For the past five months, Fintan has been dating Ellen Boisvert, a girl from New Hampshire who has just graduated from Saint Bonaventure College.

This summer, Ellen is working her usual summer gig at a seafood restaurant on Cape Cod, where she has asked for Sundays and Mondays off so she can take the Hyannis bus north to stay with her new boyfriend in this apartment of six, eight, or ten tenants.

In the living room of shag-pile carpet and garage-sale couches, someone has set an old, rusted fan on the windowsill. It seems to make the room hotter. In the distance, the John Hancock building is a blurry-grey daub on the Boston skyline.

Each new party guest comes walking up the hill from the T station with six-packs in hand, junk food in a brown paper bag. There are screechy exchanges from the balcony to the sidewalk.

Fintan and Liam from County Offally share a bedroom. On their Sunday nights together, Ellen and Fintan have this bedroom to themselves until 8 A.M. while Liam works his night porter job. In the hot Boston mornings, the lovers huddle closer as they listen to Liam climbing out of his hotel uniform and creaking into bed.

Now Ellen Boisvert is pushing through the loud, hot rooms where the Irish accents compete with the music from a boom box. Someone has just collided with her in the living room, and her T-shirt stinks of spilled beer.

The music follows her down the hallway to the shadowy bedroom that smells of men's socks and fusty bed sheets. Liam's bed sits unmade, the covers just rolled back. The window blinds are drawn against the heat.

She's standing there in her bra when she hears three girls who are queuing for the one bathroom at the other end of the hallway.

"Jesus, if I don't go soon I'll piss me knickers," one of them says. "Are they having a shaggin' baby in there or what? Who the feck is it anyways?"

Another girl answers, "I think it's yer woman. What's her name? Eileen is it, or Ellen? The Yank."

In the bedroom, Ellen knows that she should pull on a clean T-shirt, then go stand in the doorway and announce herself.

Now there's a different girl's voice. It's a girl that Ellen has just been introduced to out in the living room. Her name is Sheila McCormack. "Oh, yeah. Right. I was just actually talking to her. That little dwarfy one? A bit of a drip, isn't she? Fintan's Yank girlfriend? His green card."

The toilet flushes. The bathroom door opens, then shuts again, and the Irish girls' voices go on—gossiping about who else is here and who left with whom from a different party the night before.

Standing there, Ellen curses her own cowardice.

Another flush. Then there are footsteps down the landing and past the bedroom door. Then silence.

At last, Ellen pulls on her T-shirt and leaves the bedroom. She pushes back through the hot, screechy partiers to find Fintan. There he is, standing inside a window in that packed living room, drinking a can of beer. As usual, he is standing half in and half out of a giggly, drunken conversation.

He beckons her over.

In the Irish pubs, she's heard the term before—more than once. It's their term for when someone is dating an American, not one of their own.

"Hey," he starts to say, taking her arm, flashing his collusive boyfriend smile.

She takes him aside. *Fintan's green card.* "Your insult," she says. "Your people." Then she nods toward the huddle of girls who have started to dance around the boom box. One, a brunette with a 1980s poodle-style hairstyle, is Sheila McCormack.

There is something about this girl called Sheila, her raised arms, her jiggling bottom, that startles him. He looks petrified. "Look, the girls are just jealous, mad jealous, that's all. Let's go for a walk out to Carson Beach until this madness dies down."

Fintan Dowd takes her hand. His grip tightens as he leads her through the sweaty people, through the blaring music and down the two flights of stairs where he says, "Sorry," "Excuse us," "Yeah, see you later."

Outside on the sidewalk, he stops to kiss her while the boys on the upstairs balcony whoop and screech, "Yoo-hoo! Yee-ha! Dowd, you boy ya!"

His arm around her waist, they walk down the hill to the sound of the boys laughing and banging their beer bottles against the balcony railing.

In this hot, August afternoon, Ellen Boisvert looks up and smiles at her Irish boyfriend. “I really love him,” she thinks.

Ellen

1

May 2002

ELLEN BOISVERT is munching on a lobster salad and scanning the real estate ads in the *Coventry Daily Gazette* when she feels someone watching her. The Risen Planet Café is packed with the usual business crowd—the gallery owners and bankers and real estate agents that comprise Coventry-by-the-Sea's year-round commerce. Earlier, when she walked around town, some Friday tourists were strolling among the shops and galleries. And there was the usual dribble of bicyclists with their maps and helmets and spandex.

Ellen looks up from the *Gazette* to see a woman in a pink T-shirt and blond highlighted hair giving her that puzzled, do-I-know-you look. At the table inside the window, the woman sits there with her three kids—a blond girl of about six, a baby in a stroller, a toddler on one of those wooden high chairs, swinging his fat legs and absently eating something from his tray top. The woman flashes her a tentative grin. Ellen manages a push-button smile. She feels strangely annoyed, embarrassed by this woman's hopeful, pretty face.

Today the *Gazette*'s real estate pages are packed with grainy pictures and jazzy headlines for houses and condos: water view, single-family, move-in condition. Wait! Here's a downtown penthouse with a chef's kitchen and a rooftop balcony.

The woman is probably somebody's parent. It's a family who's driven from elsewhere in New England, or even halfway across country for yesterday's school graduation ceremonies at Coventry Academy, where Ellen Boisvert teaches French to grades 9 through 12. Or they're here to pick up their kid—he or she can't be more than a freshman or sophomore—for summer vacation. And now, the woman recognizes Ellen as one of her kid's teachers.

Yesterday, Academy graduation day, Ellen must have met a hundred parents, aunts, uncles, alumni of the quintessential New England prep school. As vice chair of the school's graduation committee, she exchanged a hundred handshakes and pleasantries. She knew that something about this petite, thirty-nine-year-old American disappoints them; they have been expecting somebody taller, more chic. But still they asked, "Now where in France are you from?"

"I'm not. I'm American. My parents were—*are*—French Canadian."

Most prep-school parents are too well schooled to show their disappointment. Or to say aloud that, for $42,000 per year, their kid should get a native-born language teacher.

Her lobster salad tastes bitter. Her hangover is settling in. Last night, she had too much red wine at the headmaster's end-of-year party where the faculty stood around nibbling on canapés and inquiring about each other's summer plans.

This school vacation, Ellen has only one plan: to find a new place to live, to move permanently up here from Boston to Coventry-by-the-Sea.

After her husband Fintan's death last year, she immediately sold their marital condominium in Boston. She knew from the realtor's doubtful look that it was priced too low, that Ellen had grabbed a premature and first offer.

In those weeks between the funeral service and her return for the school semester, she found some strange solace in packing up boxes. She wanted something in her life to feel controlled, achievable, complete.

The academy's faculty apartments were intended for the new-arrival teachers—gratis accommodation while they find their feet, adjust to a new school and this town along the Massachusetts seacoast. Now, as a second-year teacher, Ellen knows that her extended stay is the headmaster's concession to her state of young and sudden widowhood.

She looks up. Across these loud, chattery lunch tables, over the voices and the clatter of plates and the whoosh of the cappuccino machine, that woman is still watching.

Ellen takes a long drink of her sparkling water and returns to the *Gazette*.

The penthouse's bedroom has exposed beams and skylights for nighttime stargazing.

All this semester, when the snow piled up on the rickety wooden deck outside her faculty apartment, Ellen woke from a repeating dream of Fintan walking up the hill from work, just an ordinary day in which he expects to turn the key and loosen his tie and kick off his shoes, open their fridge for a drink of water or some dinner. In the dream he gets there and it's all gone—his couch, his bed, his suits and dress shirts in the bedroom closet. She's sold out and moved and forgotten to tell him.

Thwap-thwap-thwap! Something hard and plastic bangs against a table. Around the café tables, conversations stop, heads turning toward the racket. The blond woman's toddler squirms in his seat, screeching. "*No,* Mommy. I don't wan' it. Mommy, *noooo.*"

"Fiachra, d'you want to go home to Daddy? Is that what you want? Home again on the train, no walkies on the beach?"

Ellen knows that accent: Irish with inflections of Massachusetts.

This was Fintan's accent—a voice dithering between two countries.

She watches the woman shushing her son, then refilling her son's sippy cup from her own juice glass. They lock gazes. This time, the woman's look deepens, lingers.

Then here she is weaving among the Risen Planet tables, saying "excuse me" to the bicycling couple at the next table.

Her sense of dread deepens, clutches at Ellen's insides. Irish. Who? Who is this damn woman?

"Ellen? It is, isn't it?"

"Yes? Yes, I'm Ellen Boisvert."

"I knew it. I'm *Sheila*. Sheila McCormack. Well, *was.*" The woman waggles her left hand to show engagement and wedding rings. She gives a nervous laugh. "I'm Sheila Caputo now . . . I mean, since the old days in Dorchester, in that apartment."

Ellen's mind whips back over the years, more than fifteen years, back to those early days when she and Fintan were dating in Boston. It was the 1980s and there were Irish nannies, waitresses, builders, housepainters. A waitress? Yes, this girl must have worked with him in that ratty little bar, the Paul Revere Tavern, where Fintan was bartending when she first met him.

Now Sheila rolls her eyes at the memory of that single, party life. "You know, I was over there; we're just having a bit of lunch before going out to the beach, and I just *knew* you looked familiar."

Ellen sees that huge, triple-decker house with faded green siding—Springvale Avenue, Dorchester, where Fintan once shared a three-bedroom apartment with a bunch of other Irish guys—sometimes up to ten illegal tenants in that place. Someone was always crashing on the living room couch. It was a permanent party of beer and bravado stories about visas and bamboozling the airport immigration. To Ellen, a studious, twenty-year-old student at Catholic Saint Bonaventure College, it all seemed so unfettered, so cavalier and daring.

" . . . So I said, 'aw to hell with it,' I'm going to go over and ask anyways,' and Jesus, Ellen, it really is you!"

"Yes, yes," Ellen says with that stiff smile. Why does she feel such instant distrust for this woman? "I'm Fintan's wife."

Sheila McCormack glances down at the open real estate page, gives a knowing and sympathetic nod. "I was sorry, *really* sorry to hear about Fintan's . . ." She shakes her head. "Jeez, I mean . . . to just drown . . . a sailing accident. It must've been a terrible shock. Of course, all the Boston-Irish papers, all that praise and the obituaries. Actually, they could've written more about him, and it'd still have been true."

No it wouldn't, thinks Ellen, remembering those hyperbolic articles, the photos of her husband from assorted Irish fund-raisers around the city.

"Thank you. Yes. It *was* a shock." Ellen hears the widow-sad timbre in her own voice. After nine months, it has all become words, just blank words that have somehow lost their relationship to the actual event, to a man drowning on a stupid sailing trip that he should never have gone on in the first place.

But then, what *is* the poor-me-widow response after your husband dies when you had decided, finally, to leave him?

Lately, except in her night-dreams, she finds it impossible to picture Fintan—all of him, the entire assemblage. Instead, and at the oddest times, she conjures one feature at a time—his sharp nose, the pitch of his chin, his long jogger's legs.

Sheila says, "Katie—that's my baby—well, she's just nodded off in her stroller there; she'd sleep through a bomb, that one. So, ah, listen, we're here for a while." Ellen follows Sheila's gaze to the window table where Fiachra the toddler is staring over at his mother, obviously working up to another shrieking session. "So I was just going to get myself a coffee. Would you like to join us?"

Years later, in her replay of this day, this would be Ellen's crossroads of possibilities. She could have told Sheila McCormack's smiling, waiting face that she would absolutely love to have a coffee, but gee, she had to get back to campus. Or she had to meet a real estate person.

But the next half hour finds her sitting with the Caputo family inside the window, her newspaper stuffed into her shoulder bag. In that kiddie-loud voice, Sheila McCormack introduces her around the table: Fiachra, the toddler, Róisín, the six-year old girl studiously crayoning in the café's kiddie place mat, and Katie the baby asleep in her stroller.

Róisín sticks her pink little face beneath Ellen's. "Are you my mommy's friend?"

Sheila smoothes back her daughter's blond hair and says, "Yes, pet. This is Mommy's friend from a long, long time ago."

*

Ellen was right. Sheila McCormack-Caputo was one of those Irish girls who had turned up at those late-night Dorchester parties. "Jesus," Sheila says, "Weren't we daft back then, pure daft?"

Sheila says that she's living out in Westwood now, a development of reproduction Colonial houses with lots of room for the kids to play with their neighbors. They have a very active mother and toddlers' club. Oh! And every third Thursday of the month is dads' night babysitting and girls' night out, a potluck dinner and lashings of wine.

"Look, why don't you come some Thursday?" Sheila asks, delighted at her own ingenuity—at having something to offer the bereaved. "Or are you living up here now? I mean, since Fintan . . . ?"

"No. Well, yeah, sorta. I have a small faculty apartment where I teach . . ." Ellen inclines her head. "Coventry Academy. It's just a ways out of town, you'll pass it on the way to the beach . . . I've been there two years now."

"Oh, yeah. That's a prep school, right? Róisín here is starting kindergarten in September. Of course, we're sending her to a private *Catholic* school, not . . ."

Oh yes, Ellen remembers this about Fintan and his compatriots. When they met each other around Boston, the immediate questions and comparisons: what suburb, what job, what they had or had not achieved while living in America.

"So you came up here two years ago?" Sheila's voice is deliberately casual.

"Yes. Came up and interviewed in the summer, then started that September. September 2000."

"So you'd moved?" A tight, embarrassed laugh. "Of course, I'd lost touch really. Jesus, must've been a fair oul' commute for Fint—"

Why am I enjoying this? Why am I relishing the suspicions rippling across this Irish girl's pretty features? "No, Sheila. Not 'we.' Just me. *I* moved up here part time. I went back home to Boston on weekends, on all the school holidays."

*

Ellen's red-wine headache is a vise grip on her temples. Outside, she watches a man and woman wheeling their bicycles down the sidewalk, bump, bump, bump over the red-brick sidewalk, then stopping to read the menu in the café window. Bed pans, she thinks, studying their black bicycle helmets, the straps under their chins. The bike helmets are like inverted bed pans. Why have I never thought of this before?

"Listen, how did the mother, poor oul' Mrs. Dowd, take it all?"

Ellen draws her attention back to the Risen Planet Café and its empty tables littered with crumpled napkins, sandwich baskets, dribbled coffee cups. In the kitchen, someone has turned up the radio. Sheila's question is a mistake, of course. There *is* no "poor oul' Mrs. Dowd."

In 1985, when Ellen met Fintan, he said one of the reasons he came to America was to put his mother's recent death behind him. His father had died when Fintan was a child.

"Hmmm?"

"His *mother.* Fintan's. Back home. I mean, it must've been an awful shock."

Things are skidding, piling up inside Ellen's head. No, no. Mistaken identities. Sheila is misremembering some other old woman from back home.

"Fintan's—mother—was—dead," Ellen says, in the patient, steady voice she uses with her French students. *You must hand that paper in by Wednesday.* "When I met him. She had just died a few months before."

Sheila reaches across the table, sets one hand on Ellen's forearm. "Ellen, look . . . oh, this is bloody awful . . . oh, Christ. Look, Mrs. Dowd is not . . . Sure, doesn't my mother know her back home? I mean, they're not *friends* or anything, well, we're from the town, Ballinkeady, and the Dowds are . . . well, you know . . ."

"From out in the country. The village of Gowna, named for Lough Gowna, its nearby lake. And they once owned a hilltop farm, the house and land that Fintan had to sell after she died." Ellen stares at Sheila, waiting for verification. *Oh, hang on, I have the wrong Dowds.* But Sheila presses harder on Ellen's arm. That whispery, sympathy voice. "Look, maybe she died lately, in the last few weeks. Mam *did* mention that she hasn't seen her in town lately, in the shops."

In town. In the shops. But she was still alive when Fintan and I met, when we married, when we shared an apartment and later, our condo on Beacon Hill—the condo I cleared out and sold.

"Are you sure?" Ellen's voice comes high and pleading.

Sheila purses her lips and nods. "Yeah. Josephine Dowd. Jo, they call her. The husband is dead all right. Dead for years; he was a lot, lot older than her. Or that's what I used to hear Mam saying. But Jo, the mother? No. Mam and her used to have their little chats whenever they met in the supermarket"—Sheila makes quotation signs in the air—"the two mothers commiserating over their long-lost, emigrant kids and all that."

The kitchen radio is turned up louder. The tables are cleared, wiped down, though Ellen cannot remember the last lunch customers leaving, the two waitresses coming to clear the tables.

Katie, the baby, wakes up, stares at Ellen, a stranger's face, then starts to howl. Fiachra wakes, competes with his sister. Sheila lifts her baby from the stroller, sniffs at her lacy bottom. "Sorry, Ellen," Sheila shouts over her children's wails. "D'you know if they have a baby-changing table in the bathroom here?"

"Yes. It's . . . over there, down the hall to the left."

Sheila stands there, her baby bag over her shoulder. She's considering a good-bye hug, but decides on a handshake instead. She shouts over her children's screaming. "It was great to see you. And I never *realized*. I'm sorry. So sorry." She glances toward the bathroom door.

Ellen leaves, too quickly, taking her shoulder bag from the back of a chair. She leaves her newspaper behind on the table. The air stopped, trapped in her chest. She must get outside.

On the sidewalk, there's Fintan jogging down the street. It's the first time in weeks, months, when she's conjured all of him—his sweat-spiked hair, the patches of sweat up the back of his T-shirt, his long, pale legs flashing in the late-afternoon sun.

2

THE COVENTRY ACADEMY campus sits in that sudden, after-semester quiet. The white school vans sit parked outside the long, one-story janitor's shed. From the lawns behind the library, a lawnmower buzzes, grows louder, then fades again.

She takes the pedestrian shortcut between the Science and Humanities buildings, then crosses the trampled, foot-worn path across the lawn to the pine-needle parking lot and the faculty apartments. The apartments are six small studios in a converted carriage house, three upstairs, and three down.

Ellen thumps up the outside wooden stairs, then across the second-floor verandah, past her neighbor Viktor's front door. The blinds are drawn in his front window. Yesterday, just after graduation, he left for Manhattan and a gig teaching teenagers in a summer theater camp.

Her room is chilly. Even on the hottest day, the trees keep the place cool and smelling of dead pine needles. She snaps up her window blind; it thwacks against the upper window frame.

The clock tower chimes the hour. Three o'clock.

Her bed under the eaves is still unmade from this morning—when she woke late and decided to walk up to town for the newspaper and an early lunch. In the corner next to the bed is a tower of storage boxes, stacked on top of each other, labeled with black marker.

When she sold their condo, she had the movers deliver her furniture to her parents' basement in Patterson Falls, New Hampshire. But she stuffed her and Fintan's personal stuff into these boxes—his sports memorabilia, books, ornaments from their old living room, the birth and marriage certs and passports. Last September, she closed the door on their Boston condo for the last time and drove the last of their shared lives here, to this room.

Her leather school satchel sits abandoned on the faded red armchair. Behind her, the fridge clicks and hums.

At Coventry Academy, Ellen Boisvert's grades are turned in on time or early. At faculty meetings, she is attentive and silent unless she has something of substance to say. For those who don't bother to look any closer, colleagues assume a quiet, nerdy timidity. The more flamboyant teachers tease her for her adherence to set curricula, for her quiet, unassuming orderliness. They would never admit this—not even to themselves—but they assume and dismiss all this nerdy timidity as a by-product of Ellen's small-town, New Hampshire upbringing, the working-class kid's adherence to the established rules.

For the past two-and-a-half years, she has remained outside the staff lounge's avant-garde cynicism, the lunchtime exchanges on art or politics or pedagogy, the faculty friendships that are underpinned by a fierce and watchful rivalry.

If she has made any friends here, it has only been with Viktor Ortiz, her neighbor. There is an unspoken assumption that, as kids of tough, public-school families, they somehow belong together.

Her first overnight here was on a Monday at the end of September, two-and-a-half years ago. It was her first week on dorm duty. Climbing the wooden stairs, she felt a sudden release, a sudden lightness. She thought, When I open my rickety little door there will be nobody there, waiting, nobody sitting watching the TV, the air charged with some unnamed disapproval. She could drop her satchel where she wanted, place the milk on the wrong shelf in the fridge, walk away and leave a teabag stain on the trash can's swing-top cover.

All that week, she spent her evenings here reading in this red armchair, looking up from her book to savor this new thing, this new silence.

From her parents' TV-loud house in Patterson Falls, New Hampshire, to her college dorm rooms to her and Fintan's first shared apartment, she had never been truly alone. All that week, it was as if she could breathe all the air in the room.

On Friday, she drove impatiently south, over the Tobin Bridge and west along Congress Street, waiting at the traffic light to turn up their own narrow street on the most western edge of Beacon Hill. After a week away, she was ready to be home, to be a wife again. She envisioned a sweet homecoming. He might have dinner ready—a surprise. Or maybe they'd go out, somewhere warm and romantic in the North End.

Oh yes, she thought. Every marriage needed this—a little separation, then a sweet, sweet reunion.

"I'm ho-ome!" she sang, opening in the door to their tiny, 800-square foot condo.

Fintan was in the kitchen.

"Hey!" She tried again, walking down the short hallway.

The kitchen floor was covered in wet newspapers.

His backside jutted out from underneath the kitchen sink. She felt a familiar pinch of dread. He ducked back out, hitting his head. "*Fu*-uck, fuck, fuck!"

"What?" She started toward him.

"I got home and the shaggin' place was half-flooded!" You should have been here. That's what his poison look said.

He shook his head, narrowed his eyes at her, and went back to his task. She stood there with her joy deflated, the weekend suddenly gone sour. Fintan was good at that.

Later, it would be the same for a breakdown on the highway, a lost door key, his missed job promotion. They were all somehow her fault and, therefore, hers to fix or soothe.

After that, that first winter, it was easy to concoct reasons to stay overnight here, in this room at the academy where she could breathe all her own air.

*

Above the bookshelves, between the two front windows, she has hung three unframed posters—freebies from the foreign language textbook suppliers who send her samples of teachers' books and guides. There are two Paris street scenes in black and white. The third is of Rue Cartier in

Québec City. Though Roland Boisvert, her paternal grandfather, had never left their Quebecois farm, never set foot in a city or town until he traveled south over the border to Patterson Falls, New Hampshire. Just as, except for her college graduation, her wedding, and Fintan's funeral services, her parents, Donna and Thomas Boisvert, have rarely left their raised ranch in Patterson Falls.

For almost thirty years, Ellen's sister Louise, five years older than Ellen, has lived in St. Petersburg, Florida, with the leathery tan to show for it.

Now Ellen pours herself some ice water from the pitcher in her fridge, takes some Tylenol from the narrow kitchen cabinet. She takes the water out onto her second-floor verandah. Today, there's no music drifting from Viktor's apartment. Downstairs, Kierstin, the academy's new creative writing teacher's, car is parked under the trees. But there's no sign of Kierstin.

Ellen sits on a creaky rocking chair, sets her water on the ground. *Go away,* she chases the Irish voices in her head—Sheila's then Fintan's.

And what, just what do I care? What's it got to do with me? So I married a man who lied, who wished his own mother dead. Lying is the smallest of crimes. God knows he was guilty of plenty others. And she. Guilty, too. So stop. Go back in, take a nap to sleep off this headache. Or go get some boxes to start dismantling this room, get ready to live somewhere else.

Once, a year after their wedding, when his final green card came through, Ellen suggested a visit to Ireland. She wanted to see where he'd grown up. Wanted to visit the aunt he talked about so much, his Auntie Kitty.

His voice always softened when he spoke of her. Aunt Kitty used to come and visit from Dublin. As a boy, she brought him nice things. *A bit of a wild woman, me Aunt Kitty.*

But now that he was legal to live and work in America, Fintan had just started night college, a fast-track MBA. Money was tight. Always tight.

Ellen takes a sip of water, downs the two Tylenol.

The campus silence is unnerving. Ellen doesn't like Kierstin the writing teacher with the pale face and the long, sweeping hair. But now, she wills Kierstin to come walking across that lawn, to appear from between the pine trees.

One Monday afternoon, two weeks after the funeral, Ellen came back from class to a bunch of white roses and a bottle of wine on her coffee table. Viktor. Later, as the fall evening grew dark and chilly, they sat on this verandah with a bottle of cabernet. He listened to her grief-induced, disjointed ramblings, her unfinished thoughts, sentences that turned into out-loud questions to herself.

Relatives? Irish relatives. Shit. She hadn't thought of that. Until now. Yes, Fintan was an orphan, but surely there were cousins, uncles, aunts, great-aunts back there, back in County Mayo? How or when was she supposed to let them know?

"Simple," Viktor said. All over his town in Guatemala, you saw it all the time. An advertisement appeared in the local paper: "The family of . . . please contact." It was always an American phone number, a U.S. police department, a town where a hotel housekeeper, a landscaping worker or office cleaner had been found dead in a motel or a crowded apartment. False papers. No papers. A Spanish name long anglicized, simplified. So they put an advertisement in the local paper. *"Por Favor, Ponerse en contacto."*

Then, everybody in that town or village comes to visit and cry. Poor family. But they are the lucky ones. The ones who know. Because in that same town or village, there are mothers, fathers, families who spend years wondering, waiting.

"Ellenita," Viktor said. "I will look it up for you, find that newspaper and we will put an advertisement, in that small village, in that county in Ireland. This is something I can do for my sad little *Ellenita.*"

Later, when Ellen woke up to her darkened bedroom, she recalled the photos that Fintan had once shown her, the snapshots he'd brought with him from Ireland. Lying there and staring at the early-winter sky through her bedroom skylight, she saw those black-and-white snapshots of a younger Fintan, of the Dowd family. There was one outside a church, at Fintan's first communion. The father looked as if he should be the boy's grandfather. His mother was dressed in winter clothes and frowning at the camera.

No. Those dour faces told her. No newspaper advertisements. Not here, not in this chill, damp place.

For weeks she put it off. Then one afternoon, just before the Thanksgiving break, she forced herself to sit and write a short, one-page note on campus stationary, "To the family of Fintan Dowd, Gowna, County Mayo, Ireland." Inside: "I regret to inform you that your relative, Fintan John, passed away on August 22 last. Please contact me at above address or telephone if you require further information."

All last winter, she expected to see an Irish postage stamp among her office mail. Or sometimes, when the light was blinking on office voice mail, she fancied that she would hear an Irish voice, an Uncle John or an Aunt Brigid, or the Aunt Kitty from Dublin.

But there was nothing.

Through the trees the Academy clock tower chimes the half-hour: 4:30.

In her verandah rocking chair, Ellen tries to remember which storage box holds his family photos.

*

From the snapshots scattered across her coffee table, the young Fintan stares back at her from a black-and-white photo. Short trousers and knobby knees, hunkered down, his arm around a black-and-white collie dog. "Rosie," Ellen says aloud in her silent room. Yes, that was his dog's name.

She remembers herself and Fintan, all those years ago, sitting on his narrow bed in that bedroom in Dorchester, their legs stretched out in front of them, he setting out each snapshot along the cheap bedspread, like he was dealing playing cards.

I must've been only about eight in this one. That was my little Rosie. The voice softened, wavered as he spoke of his pet. Rosie who died of . . . And when? Had he ever said?

Here are official school portraits—a double row of children outside an old stone building. Little girls with severely cut bangs. Boys in cardigans and V-neck sweaters. Four teachers are seated front-row center. *That's Mrs. Galligan; "The Gallows Galligan," we used to call her. Oul' bitch. Get the back of that one's hand and you felt it for a week after. And that was the headmaster, Mr. McGrath. "The greyhound," we used to call him. Used to nod off asleep in his teacher's chair and then we'd all kick up holy hell . . .*

Pick me out there, Ellie, aw, go on, find me if you can. Ellen doesn't have to search for her husband. Second row, fourth from the left. He stands taller than his classmates.

Here's a faded Polaroid of eight first communion children outside a church. Three girls stand in front, their freckled, pious faces under white fluttery veils. Five boys, including Fintan, stand behind them, all dressed up in miniature suits and ties.

And then, here it is: that family photo. Fintan is flanked by his parents—his father stoop-shouldered, wearing the quintessential Irish tweed cap. The mother is taller than her husband, dressed in a mannish gabardine coat and stout winter shoes. Her lips are drawn together in sufferance.

Ellen says her name aloud, "Josephine. Jo." Jo Dowd who, if Sheila McCormack is right, lives in the house behind that farmyard gate where Fintan was hunkered down with his dog.

Ellen checks the red numbers on the digital bedside clock. Five hours' time difference. So it's almost ten o'clock at night over there. Yes, she should have done this earlier, but she was terrified, working up the nerve. Or she was hoping to find something in these snapshots to tell her that Sheila was just plain wrong.

3

"COULD YOU SPELL THAT, PLEASE?" says the man at international directory assistance. He types in the address as Ellen reads it off Fintan's birth certificate.

"K-n-o-c-k-d-u-f-f, G-o-w-n-a."

Breezily, as casually as if Ellen were calling for an Interflora florist, he says, "A listing for that name: Dowd, Mrs. J. Hold on for the number please." Then, the electronic voice: "The number you requested is . . . country code 353, 094 . . ."

For the second time today, Ellen feels the air trap in her chest. She hears Sheila McCormack's voice: *Look, maybe she died lately.*

Across the ocean, there's a double-barrel ring. Brrr-brrr. Brrr-brrr. Five rings. Six.

Good, nobody there. It's a telephone number that nobody bothered to disconnect. The man in International Directories made a mistake, too. There are two J. Dowds in Knockduff.

"Hello?" A woman's voice at last, very out of breath. "Hello?"

Ellen forgets how to speak. Then she forces out the words. "Mrs. Dowd?"

"Who *is* this?" Jo Dowd is still breathless. She has come to the phone from someplace far away.

Ellen stares at the first communion photo in her left hand. The aged voice, the Irish accent dubbed over this face, the unsmiling face above the gabardine coat. Now it's a voice down Ellen's phone, in her studio apartment.

"This is . . ."

The breaths come harder, raspier. Jo Dowd coughs into the phone. Then, "I know who you are. You're that Y—American. My son's . . .

You're that girl, his wife? The one that sent the letter? Ellen B—something or other."

"Yes."

Silence again. And that awful, labored breathing.

"What d'you want?"

"Pardon? Mrs. Dowd, I . . . I don't want anything."

"Your letter came. Is that what you're ringing for? Look, I don't know what ye do over there in America, but in this country, we tell a person about . . . about a death the right way, not making a public show."

Hack, hack, hack. Jo coughs again, then sets the phone down with a clunk. But Ellen can still hear her. Hack, hack, hack.

Christ. *Christ.*

Then Jo picks up again, the voice phlegmy. "There's nothing here for you, you know. If you think you can get anything, a red farthing out of me or this place, you've another bloody think coming."

With the phone, Ellen crosses to her front window. She watches the grey stone buildings beyond the pine trees, the swatch of summer sky above the campus rooftops. She'd like to scream back at this voice in her ear, this woman 3,000 miles away. *When I got up this morning, I never even knew you existed. Your son wished you, told you dead. So take that. And that.*

"Mrs. Dowd. I don't want anything. I just . . . I just wanted to make sure you really knew, that the letter made it to you. I'm sorry to have disturbed you. Good night."

She waits, expecting the old woman to apologize, to beg her for information on her dead son.

Loudly Jo Dowd hangs up.

*

In the house in Patterson Falls, New Hampshire, Ellen can hear the TV warbling from the living room. Her father, Thomas Boisvert, is watching *Wheel of Fortune.*

"I'm thinking of going to Ireland," Ellen says, the words just there, announced to her mother down the telephone before it's fully informed or decided inside her head.

Why has she called home? Why is she telling her mother this? She's thirty-nine years old, and they live almost a hundred miles apart. And, married or widowed, her parents knew or know little of her Boston life. Yet it has always been like this: Ellen sitting on a phone or visiting for summer or Thanksgiving and narrating, presenting her life to them. So here she is now: sitting in her studio apartment, with the detritus and snapshots of her husband's Irish life spread out on the coffee table while her mother-in-law's voice floats and echoes around this shadowy room, under the eaves, behind and under the bed.

Now, she'd like to say it again, as if repeating her intended trip might force her mother's permission or approval.

"Your father thinks he has a job at that new gas station out on Route 4. Early mornings, four days a week. Won't affect his social security. They said they'll let him know tomorrow."

"Mom, there are some things that Fintan left . . . unfinished." She hears the hollowness of her own words. She knows that Donna Boisvert has no truck with such vagaries, the lexicon of wellness magazines and new-age hogwash.

Dutifully, the Boisverts traveled south to Boston for a wedding and a funeral service. But during or after either event, Donna has made no comment, no commiseration to her widowed daughter. In Donna's mind, the drive south to a city said what it needed to say.

The wife of a laid-off paper mill worker, Donna Boisvert believes that keeping busy is the best approach to life's surprises or heartaches.

Now Donna says, "Your father's gonna be upset when he hears this, that you're flying over there after those terrorists last year, the plane and all those people and those buildings in New York."

Outside Ellen's window, the evening sun glitters, a golden-pink reflection off the west-facing windows of the Academy's dormitories. A Friday night. By now, Sheila McCormack is at home and tucking her kids in. Kissing them goodnight in fluffy, lamp-lit bedrooms, promising them that Mummy's always here. Or she's sitting in a living room telling her husband, "You'll never guess who I met today!"

Donna says, "Oh, did I tell you they put poor Ann Cote in a nursing home? Yeah, just two weeks ago. So there's another place with a sign outside it now; though beats me who'll buy a place like that. They done nothing with it since poor Jean passed."

"No," Ellen says. "No, you didn't tell me that." And then, "Look, I'll call you when I make a final decision. I mean about going to Ireland."

Silence. Silence is Donna's disapproval. "Mom? Tell Dad good luck with the job."

4

THE ENGINE GROWS LOUDER, a revved-up growl, then the fields disappear from underneath the Aer Lingus jet.

The plane bumps twice. The head flight attendant announces, "Ladies and gentlemen, welcome to Ireland. We ask you to remain seated until the plane comes to a complete stop. For those of you traveling on with us to Dublin . . ." Then she repeats the message in Irish. *A Cháirde, Failte romhaimh go hÉireann.*

I'm in Ireland, Ellen announces to herself, staring out the window at the approaching concrete, the low, grey clouds.

Just yesterday evening she took a bus to Boston's Logan Airport. In the departure lounge, she watched the sunlight deepening over the marshes and the town of Nahant across the harbor. While she was dozing in this tiny cramped seat, the world has fast-forwarded to daylight, to morning, morning in Fintan's country, where people are already standing out of their seats, the overhead luggage compartments snapping open.

On the car radio, the drive-time DJ is sending special birthday greetings out to Aisling McIlroy out there in Stillorgan, who, he's told, from a *very reliable* little birdie-source, is celebrating the big one today. "Twenty-one today! Wow, Aisling! An' listen girls, behave yourselves at that party tonight!"

Ellen turns the car heater up again. The headlights flash on. Shit. It's her second time doing that. A car coming in the opposite direction flashes back at her. Damn. She tries another car switch.

The night flight has left her feeling chilled and dry-eyed.

On the opposite side of the highway, the morning commuter traffic passes in a steady stream. In the cloudy May morning, there's something amusement-park silly about all of it: the cars, the roadside trees, the houses and passing fields. She's exhausted.

Then the highway gives way to a one-lane road and the woman on the car radio is inviting listeners out there to call in after the commercial break. Call with their opinions. About what? Ellen wonders as she speeds along, watching for the green road signs for Galway.

*

By Galway City she has been driving with the window rolled down all the way. She's still freezing, but she's got to stay awake. Everything stands at this strange, televised distance. Even the ocean, a sudden swatch of grey water sitting beyond a housing development. It seems unreal. She drives, shifts gears on automatic pilot. A man on the radio has called in to say yes, their family, his child was a victim of playground bullying. "Absolutely," the man is saying. "Nearly every day of the week, my son came home telling us about more name-calling, more playground insults."

"But surely you *complained* about all this to the principal or the board of management?" the radio-woman asks in an inflected, radio-empathy voice.

"Well, Marian, my wife and I did set up a meeting with the principal. And she basically told us . . ."

Today? Ellen wonders. Should I check into my Gowna hotel, the place I booked via phone two nights ago, just wash up, wake up, and then go find that farm in Knockduff? Find Jo Dowd's house?

" . . . Marian, we found the best and only approach for the parents of the bullied child, really, in this situation . . ."

No. I'll explore around the village first, get the lay of the land. Play tourist. Will Jo Dowd drive me away? Take a shotgun? A broom?

Suddenly, Ellen remembers Viktor's story. Nine months ago now, and there they were, Viktor and her sitting there on their verandah drinking wine on a warm, fall afternoon. She thinks of those parents and families in desiccated little towns and villages in Guatemala, left with nothing else to do but to beg, to concoct, fill in the blanks of their immigrant children's lives.

So will Jo fall weeping and contrite at my feet, begging for life details of a dead son?

So what, just what, will she tell Jo Dowd? Or what parts should she tell or leave out? Their fights, their silences, her own poisonous thoughts toward her husband?

*

She's stopped at a traffic circle. *A roundabout.* Here's Fintan's voice in her head, telling some story about his days at college in Dublin. *So there I was, on me bike coming up to the Stillorgan roundabout.*

She tries to read the green road signs at the Galway roundabout. *An Lár,* City Center. *Bothar na Trá.* Salthill. A car behind her toots the horn.

N-84. Yes, that's what she needs. The N-84 to County Mayo and Gowna.

Jo's voice: *There's nothing here for you, you know.*

Here's a Holiday Inn hotel, some housing developments, then a huge shopping mall. Another traffic circle. A roundabout.

The radio woman's voice: "Now, we'll be back after the break."

The road runs through a wide marsh. *Bog.* It's a bog. Across the brown scrubland, the wind buffets her tiny black Fiat.

Then the road suddenly narrows, the landscape turns green again—a checkerboard of tiny fields and stone walls. Now there's a hole in the sky, where a shaft of sunlight waits to break through.

On the car radio, a man is delivering a mid-morning news bulletin: A rail workers' strike is still looming, talks continuing. A Dublin raid on a house of illegal asylum seekers.

The road gets narrower still. There are ranch houses and gateways and a barking dog. Huge, black rolls appear in these fields. They remind her of gigantic pieces of licorice candy. It's hay. She's seen it in the States someplace, in the farms of New Hampshire.

She reaches a village with a Y junction and a stone church. The left road has a luminous green sign: "Gowna." *An Gabhna.* Five kilometers.

On the Gowna Road, she slows behind a farm tractor, the man's torso jiggling, keeping rhythm with the vehicle's motion. She downshifts to second gear. Now here's the sun at last, a pale clear light leaching across the meadows, turning everything to Technicolor green.

At a straight stretch of road, the tractor man looks behind at her, and waves her on and past him.

Overtaking him, she waves her "thanks," then catches his eye, studies the ruddy face. The man is about fifty. A Dowd cousin? A neighbor who's known the Dowds all his life? Then she pulls around and in front of him, just in the nick of time for an approaching car. Ridiculous. Sleeplessness has set her thoughts tumbling, racing.

The open fields give way to trim front gardens, a footpath where a woman in a white sweatshirt walks briskly with her black Labrador puppy.

Suddenly, Ellen wishes the road would go on and on. Or that she could turn around and drive back to Galway.

The sun has grown hot through the windshield. She rolls down the window to that smoky air. Turf. A turf fire.

We used to save turf in the bog; stripped to our waists and footing turf in the sun.

She takes this last curve in the road. Then there's Gowna: a street with its double row of houses, the sky tunneled between the slate roofs.

5

SHE'S BEEN STANDING in the carpeted lobby of Flanagan's Hotel for over ten minutes, studying the patchwork of yellow sticky notes along the flocked wallpaper above the reception desk, last year's wall calendar with its sepia photograph of one of the shops she's just driven past. "Season's Greetings from Gowna Meats."

At last a man, fiftyish, potbelly inside a red V-neck sweater, comes through the door marked "Bar." He's on his cell phone. "Right, right, well, sure, that's the six-marker, isn't it? Ha, ha, ha." Then he looks up and sees Ellen there, waiting.

"Look, I'll ring you back, Vinnie? Hah? Yeah. Five minutes. Right." He stuffs the phone in his jeans pocket.

"Oh. Hello! Sorry, are you . . . ? Are you there long?"

"I booked two nights ago. Boisvert?"

"Oh. Right." He looks around him, as if he's forgotten something, then takes his place behind the antique wooden desk and an open ledger book.

"Ah, you're Miss B—sorry, you'll have to give us a hand here with the name, I'm afraid . . ." He grins up at her. Except for the double chin, he looks like a hapless schoolboy.

"Boisvert."

"Right. French? But . . . aren't you the girl that rang and booked from America?"

"Massachusetts. My grandparents were French Canadian." The man gives her an impassive smile. He's obviously heard it a million times: American tourists rattling off their hyphenated heritages.

"Gerry." He reaches over the desk for a hurried handshake. "Gerry Flanagan."

So this is actually the hotel owner. Flanagan's hotel.

Gerry Flanagan pushes the Visa slip across at her, then opens a wide drawer to produce a room key. "Now. I put you down at this end, number 12, in the back. Most people want the back. No noise."

"Look, do you have anything in the front? I'd prefer the front."

Gerry frowns. "But . . . most people—"

"The front's fine, honest."

I want to watch for her. If she's out and about, buying milk and bread in that village store across the street, walking up to Sunday church.

He reopens the drawer to produce a new key, a new smile. He leans out over the desk. "Now. Just give us your lugg—"

He frowns at her carry-on suitcase with the Aer Lingus tags. "Ah, the rest of your bags, Miss Boisvert? In the car are they? I'll go out the back here and get them."

"No, this is it."

Then Gerry Flanagan takes her in, head to toe, not bothering to conceal his obvious sizing her up: this petite American woman in jeans, a white cotton shirt, shoulder-length curly hair clipped back each side. And just a carry-on bag for a week's stay.

"Right. You're third along the landing on the right." He tilts his head toward the beveled-glass door he's just come through. "We've finished breakfast a good while ago. But I could probably get the girls to do you up something. Bit of hot toast or a bowl of porridge. Or a coffee? You must be fuc— well, a bit on the tired side after the flight and the drive and everything." He's still eyeing her, that puzzled look, obviously failing to place her among his annual gallery of American hotel guests. "We'd a busy enough oul' weekend in the bar. Though the fishermen aren't in yet. Next week maybe, at the earliest. Great fly-fishing around these parts, you know. You're not after a bit of fishing, are you?"

A yawn escapes, making her eyes water. "Hmm? Oh, no. No fishing."

In room 13, the sheer curtains balloon in over her double bed with its white bedspread and starched pillows. The sun has made it all the way through, but it sits behind the slate roofs, leaving the village street in shadow. She sits on the edge of the bed, looking at someone's upstairs living room across the street. On the ground floor, under the window, the village store, "Gowna Foodmart."

Flanagan's room has a cheerful red carpet, two matching wall lamps and a wall phone with phone cord dangling above the headboard. On the opposite wall is a mirror with a long, white shelf underneath—her dressing table. She has already brushed her teeth, combed her hair, set her small brown barrettes on the sink in the small, white bathroom with the towels in mismatched shades of pink.

Cars pass, each one going clank-clank over a manhole. A delivery van stops outside Gowna Foodmart, and a man in a blue nylon coat hops out and walks around the side to a set of sliding doors.

Two farm tractors rattle past. Then another car, this one with a bad muffler.

The voices startle her, carrying up from the sidewalk. There's a whiff of cigarettes. She leans to see three teenage girls and two boys, almost directly underneath her windowsill. They're dressed in maroon sweaters and grey pants, striped school ties. Funny, it's the exact same uniform as Coventry Academy. It's as if the two places, the two countries are suddenly transposed.

One girl wears fishnet stockings and high-heeled, winklepicker shoes. One boy's trouser seams are ripped all the way to his knees; they flap-flap as he walks along.

Ellen is about to close the window, to draw the curtains and snuggle into bed, when the girl in the winklepicker shoes looks up, sees the woman leaning out and gawking from the hotel window. The girl nudges the others, points, then shouts up: "Hey! What the fuck are *you* looking at?"

6

BEHIND THE LINE of yew trees, a lawnmower drones, the sound growing closer, then fading again. Now there are just the crows cawing in the trees behind the church.

Ellen stands there in the pebbled churchyard to take in St. John's Church, Gowna—the stone Gothic steeple against the fading, evening sky. This is the church where someone took that snapshot of first communion Fintan with his mother and father.

An hour ago, she woke up in her little hotel room, hungry, shocked at the red numbers on her bedside clock: 5:10. Her first day in Ireland and she's slept all afternoon.

After a shower, she walked out into the hotel landing, up and down past the other room doors. She listened for sounds of other guests—a radio playing, someone on a phone, a bed creaking. But the hotel's upstairs was silent.

She went downstairs and past the bar door, where she could hear a television turned up extra loud. She thought to go in there but kept walking instead, craving a stroll and some fresh air.

In the church vestibule, the heavy wooden doors are fastened back to reveal a modern church with a central aisle and rows of pews in blond wood.

She has not been inside a church for years. Unless you count the hospital chapel where they held Fintan's memorial service.

In Boston, neither she nor Fintan belonged or attended, so Fintan's colleagues in the fund-raising department at Boston Central Hospital suggested the chapel for his service. She was grateful and relieved. In those days after his death, she wanted to be told where and when to show up, when to kneel, stand, when to shake hands, and when to eat an egg salad sandwich.

She dips her hand into one of the stone holy water fonts and crosses herself, "Nom du père et du fils et du Saint Esprit." The words, the remembered entreaties of her childhood.

The light is stained-glass bright over the pews. At the top, just beneath the altar, two older women kneel, heads bent, their whispery prayers echoing through the empty sanctuary. Someone has lit four candles. Along the side walls, the stations of the cross are little sculptures of polished brown wood. Jesus falls the first time.

Ellen Boisvert genuflects at a pew just inside the door. One of the women glances around at her, frowns, then goes back to her prayers.

Ellen bows her head, smells the soapy whiff from Flanagan's bathroom hand soap. Pray, she tells herself. God knows you need some prayers.

Kneeling here, her face buried in her joined hands, she could just as easily be back in St. Jean Baptiste in Patterson Falls, New Hampshire, amid that smell of damp Sunday coats and old women's perfume. She remembers that old man who always played the organ to accompany their school choir: *Sánctus, sánctus, dominus déus . . .*

At one end of Patterson Falls stood the French church. At the other end, the Immaculate Conception, the Irish church. When the archdiocese closed the French church down, crying insufficient funds, Thomas Boisvert and all his fellow mill workers took up a special collection to support their French church as their fathers had before them. They wrote, petitioned, opposed the Irish bishop. They lost. So for Ellen's last years in high school, the Boisverts and the other Franco-American families grudgingly attended the Immaculate Conception whose Irish American parishioners they found too blustery-loud, too pretentious, too damn smug.

She can't pray. So she buries her face deeper in her cupped palms and strikes a bargain with the gods or with universal karma or the kindness of the universe. For what? Deliverance. *Délivre-nous du mal.* Deliver us from evil.

She grabs onto the word. Yes, *Délivre.* Let me drive out there, out to that house in the country and meet a woman who weeps on my shoulder, makes me some tea, and then we both deliver up eulogy pieces of a son and a husband. And then, let her tell me something simple, as innocuous as a falling out in which a mother and son kept a transatlantic stalemate because each was too stubborn to make the first gesture.

Outside, the crows have grown louder in the yew trees. The lawnmower is silenced. At the end of the churchyard path, Ellen turns onto the village sidewalk and collides with a man wheeling a racing bicycle, the spokes going tick-tick-tick.

"Sorry. I didn't see you there."

"No. My fault." He's red-faced, fortyish, with an old-fashioned hair part to the side, a T-shirt over his black Lycra biking shorts. A whiff of sweat. She remembers that day, the day she saw Fintan—or conjured him—outside the Risen Planet Café. The day she found out that her mother-in-law was still alive.

He brushes his hands on his T-shirt. "Sorry again."

"I'm okay. Honest."

He flashes her a smile. "You're American."

"Yeah. Just arrived this morning. Nice village. Pretty church."

"Oh, thanks. Thanks. We do our best."

"Well, I must be . . ."

"Ah, are you staying around or just passing through?"

"No, I'm staying at the hotel."

"Aw, lovely. Yeah, sure, Gerry and Phyllis are grand people. They'll look after you all right."

"Well good-b—"

"So how long are you here for?" She catches it, his quick glance toward her ringless left hand, her marriage-ring finger.

"A week."

"Grand time of year for a holiday."

She looks beyond him to the little newsagent's shop with an ice cream and an *Irish Times* advertisement in the window. In the evening sun, Gowna looks pretty, colorful, like someplace from which you might send a postcard.

"What part?"

"Hmmm?"

"What part of the States are you in?"

"Boston. Well, no. I live there part time, I'm actually moving to the North Shore."

"Oh, lovely. I was living over there myself for three years. I was in Washington, actually. Catholic University, did you ever hear tell?"

The penny drops with her. Catholic University. So this is the pastor, the village's priest in his bicycle shorts and a sweat-stained T-shirt. "Yes, of course. I was supposed to go to college there—I mean in Washington—myself." She waves a hand. "But . . . that was years ago."

"Really? Where?"

"Georgetown. I had an academic scholarship." Does she sound boastful? She hadn't planned on blurting it out like this, to a stranger, but she can tell he's impressed.

As he should be.

The scholarship letter came to their house in Patterson Falls her senior year in high school. It brought the same tight-lipped silence as Louise's absconding to Florida to join her high school boyfriend at a motel job.

One night, when she was studying in their sisters' bedroom—no Louise now, just Ellen—Thomas Boisvert made a rare visit to his seventeen-year-old daughter's room. He sat on the very end of her bed. He wouldn't meet her eyes. "You're not going. Not to a place like that. There are colleges up here, in Manchester, Plymouth, even in Boston. Catholic colleges, for girls and families like—"

"—Like us?" Ellen finished for him, appalled at the surge of pure, white hatred for the small man perched on the end of her bed. Hatred for all that they were: factories, mills, years upon years of silent resentments.

But her parents wouldn't budge. She mailed back her refusal to Georgetown. By then, she had convinced herself that her parents were right. That September, she took the bus south two hours to Saint Bonaventure College outside Boston, where good Catholic girls got a good education.

The Gowna priest cuts across her thoughts. "So why didn't you go—to Georgetown, I mean?"

She shakes her head. "It's a long story. So you're the pastor here."

"Head bottle-washer. 'Jack of all trades and master of none' as they say." He sets the bicycle on its kickstand, then extends a handshake. "Noel Bradley."

"Oh, hi, Father. Ellen Boisvert."

He has the wide-open, hopeful smile of a lonely man. "So, is this your first time to Ireland?"

"Yes. Yes it is."

Another glance at her left hand. "So you're traveling with friends or . . ."

"No, no. I'm all alone. Just me." Then, before she can dither, she hears herself say it. "Actually, I was hoping to visit some relatives. The Dowds. You know them?"

He purses his lips. "Dowd. Dowd. *Dowd.* I'm only here two years myself." He clicks his fingers. "Oh, not Mrs. Dowd. Old Mrs. Dowd? Jo? Above in Knockduff?"

Her breath quickens. "Yeah, that's her. Well, I've never met her. Yet. Kind of a long-lost cousin and all that." She presses on. "Actually, I knew her . . . son. In Boston. Fintan, did you know him?"

Another furrow appears between the eyes. "Her son? No. No. I knew she was a widow, of course, but I never heard tell she had a son in America."

"So she'd be your parishioner then?"

Caution passes across his features. There's something he can't tell. Sanctity of the confessional? "Well, yes, Knockduff *is* part of Gowna Parish."

"Does she come to church on Sunday?"

He gives a purposeful laugh. It's an avoidance tactic. "Well, no. No. At least, not since I've been here, anyways. But, well, the elderly often don't, you know, especially traveling that distance. And, of course, she doesn't drive. She has no car up there."

Ellen remembers old Ann Cote, the neighbor who her mother said has finally gone into St. Francis's nursing home in Patterson Falls. Years ago, regular as the clock, the pastor from St. Jean Baptiste came on Fridays to bring her communion. It's part of a priest's weekly roster to visit the elderly, the shut-ins.

"But don't you go out there? For house calls?"

He gives her a pained look. "Look, I'd rather not say."

She flashes a tight smile. "It's okay, Father. I guess I shouldn't've asked."

He smiles back. Relieved. "Ach, no bother. So you're going out there yourself, are you, up to visit her?"

"Yes."

"So she's better? I heard she wasn't that well, a while back, there. The end of last summer. I only just heard it. This is a small place. But she was in the hospital anyways, I know that."

Ellen recalls that phlegmy, breathy voice down the phone. Two weeks ago now, the night she met Sheila McCormack. "She's ill?"

He shrugs. "Well, that's the funny thing. She came out of the hospital, then I made a few inquiries, you know. Well, the main thing is that I heard she's doing a lot better now. In fact, someone said they saw her one evening, out for a bit of walk for herself. So whatever it was, she must be grand now."

"Good. I'll give her your regards." She watches his guarded expression.

"Do. Yeah, do that. Give her my regards."

She begins to walk away at last, though she knows that he's still standing there and still watching her. "Oh, and . . . ah . . . Ellen?"

She turns. "Yes."

He seems to know something, read something in her features. "Look, if you need anything. Or maybe you'd like to come and sit in the back garden some evening and we'd have a beer." He shrugs. "I just thought you might need a bit of company, that's all. A bit of a chat."

Then he wheels his bicycle toward the church.

7

THE FIRST STONE plops through. She picks up another. This one plops, too.

No, this way, Ell. See, it's all in that flick of the wrist.

When he came to visit her at her Cape Cod summer job, or, later, when they drove to a lake in New Hampshire, Fintan always skipped stones over the water. He could stand there for hours just watching the stone skip, the plash-plash sound. He said that it reminded him of his youth. So once, he must have stood here on this pebbly lakeside beach, on the shores of Lough Gowna, doing what she's trying to do now.

She can hear music across the water. It's coming from someplace beyond those trees, the other side of a narrow, overgrown headland. It must be someone in a boat or a car.

He told her of a drowning here, out on this lake—a group of men from the opposite side in County Galway, out for a Sunday afternoon's fishing. Nobody ever figured out what happened, why a group of local men, experienced boaters, suddenly went down.

Ellen narrows her eyes to make out the town on the opposite side, the town where families, neighbors, lovers prepared Sunday supper, or woke from an afternoon doze and wondered why their husbands weren't home.

Just like she did.

When he drowned, he was attending a colleague's wedding on Martha's Vineyard—a girl named Abigail who worked with him in the fund-raiser and development department at the hospital.

The day before that Vineyard wedding, Ellen had driven north to the Academy for a late-summer, pre-semester faculty meeting.

The night before that, she and Fintan had fought. So they weren't speaking. Again. This time, it was all over a newspaper she'd thrown out in the recycle box, assuming that he'd read it, when he actually wanted an article in there. Or he said he did.

A newspaper. A forgotten pint of milk. His perpetual TV watching.

That summer, their last summer, it didn't take much to set either of them off.

That morning, she was gathering up her things and car keys for the drive north, when she saw that he'd left a sticky note on her briefcase: "Six o'clock. Joshua's Bistro."

The reminder nettled her. Of course she damn well remembered that a whole gang of his colleagues were meeting for pre-wedding drinks at a fancy bar in the South End.

She hated when he did that—in the midst of a huffy fight, he assumed that she could and would just put on an act, appear in a nice dress at whatever glittery fund-raiser he was attending for work or for one of his many Irish American organizations around Boston. She hated that she was supposed to pretend that they hadn't spent the evening before shouting at each other, dredging up their verbal ammunition.

As she drove north along Route 1, her fury seemed to stoke itself. Jesus, she had to do something. Something. Just tell him she was moving into the Coventry apartment. A temporary separation. Just for a while. She needed to get some real space, just to clear her damn head. And then, the doubts crept in: had she really caused this latest fight? Was she really as inconsiderate, forgetful, stupid as he told her she was?

Yes, she had to officially leave him. At least for a while. And she had to tell him. Now. This evening.

She stayed for the entire faculty meeting, telling herself that she had to, that it had nothing to do with her rage, her wanting to teach him a lesson. Then she got caught in evening commuter traffic on Storrow Drive.

When she got to Joshua's Bistro, their cocktail table was full of empty glasses, and Fintan and his friends had already paid the check. They were exchanging tipsy good-byes.

Across the table, she caught his tight-lipped fury.

Later, back in their Beacon Hill living room, he exploded. *You promised, fucking promised.*

Their words spat back and forth, back and forth under the ceiling fan in their living room. She accused him of sucking up, that all he damnwell cared about were outward appearances. Not her. Not them. Then, she stamped to their bedroom where she wanted to get out of her hot, sweaty work clothes. At the door, she turned with her final shot: "And I'm not going to that wedding tomorrow. You can tell your asshole friends whatever you goddamn want." Then she slammed the door.

Later, she watched him from the bedroom window, four floors down, in jogging shorts and sneakers, jogging up Beacon Hill. Even full of beer, even on a muggy August night, he never missed his evening run. While he was gone, she carried his pillow and one blanket to the living room couch.

Next morning, Saturday, she pretended to be asleep as he tiptoed in, took his pressed shirt and his summer suit from the closet. For that wedding on the Vineyard, a grand, outdoor extravaganza on the bride's parents' oceanfront estate, she'd spent more than she should have on a blue cocktail dress and silver strappy sandals. Now she wondered if the store would take them both back. Refund her money? Lying there listening to her husband getting ready in their bathroom, the picture of herself standing there pleading with a blank-faced store clerk made her cry. She'd bought the dress on sale anyway; marked down and then marked down again. But the loss of the dress, the sapphire blue dress that she'd never wear now, made her weep into her pillow.

Tomorrow night, she thought. When he drives home from that ferry. I'm going to tell him.

She listened for his car starting up in the street, then she got up and walked out to their living room, hoping, stupidly, for an apology, a note begging her to take a later ferry to Vineyard Haven, to come to the wedding after all.

She looked on the fridge, the TV screen, her briefcase, the usual spots where he left notes. Nothing. Nothing but that pillow and the indentation of his body from where he'd slept on the couch.

In their tiny galley kitchen, Ellen made coffee, all of her movements leaden, weighed down as the day grew hot outside. The ceiling fan went thup-thup-thup.

Sitting at their kitchen counter, she egged herself on. *Run some errands. Clean this place.* Fold up his blanket off the couch.

She pictured that ferry and its freight of stylish and educated thirty-somethings standing up on deck—the girls in their high-heeled sandals and dresses; the men in linen suits and bright, billowing ties.

Last year, Ellen and Fintan had been invited there for a Labor Day cook-out, to that old stone house over the sea, the sloping hydrangea gardens with their guest cottages and perennial beds. The porches with the solid old rockers, worn and shiny from a hundred family summers and croquet games on the lawn.

It was all a million miles, a universe away from those guzzling, boozy parties in Fintan's old apartment in Dorchester. And Fintan loved, courted, craved all that Brahmin, old-money style.

A man named Grant, cousin of the bride, befriended Fintan in one of the wedding tents set up on the lawn. After a long and boozy conversation, Fintan's newfound friend suggested a night sail, just up and around the headland and back. It was a chance to see the house and the family compound from a completely different and even more beautiful vantage point.

After the boat capsized, Grant made it to shore with a fractured elbow and bruised ribs. A doctor, also a wedding guest, made a call to have him medivac'd to a Boston hospital.

That night, Ellen woke to the bedside phone ringing. Fintan. Drunk, feeling contrite; calling to see how she was. Apology? No. He never apologized, but a call. Yes, she'd settle for that.

It was the Vineyard Haven police.

She rushed, half-dressed, through her darkened living room, past the couch where her husband had slept. At Woods Hole, she took the first ferry out.

The search took three days—three days in which the bride's family insisted she stay in that house over the sea. She dozed in a strange, ocean-front bedroom. She dreamed that Fintan was scrambling up the rocks under her window. She woke in the dark, certain she'd heard him calling her name.

A nude swimmer found a white dress shirt floating from a rock off Gay Head Beach. An hour later, they brought back the body of a young male. The police brought her to identify him—a blue, swollen face. His hair was set in a crazy, salt-spritzed frieze.

Every night for the ten months since, that face keeps appearing in her dreams.

*

She walks along the beach at Lough Gowna, the lake water lapping, knocking the pebbled stones together. The rhododendrons seem to be growing wild here, the blooms lush and purple, the leaves thick and waxy. In the spots where the rhododendrons block the path, she pulls the branches back to walk along the lakeshore. Of course, the lake and the houses on the hillside above are different, less vivid and exotic than the Bórd Fáilte pictures from the web sites she looked up before coming here.

I'm glad, she thinks—glad that it's not like those cutesy little photos. Except for the tinny sound of someone's radio, the sounds of Kenny Rogers singing, "Ruby, don't take your love to town."

She walks out into a clearing, onto another pebbled beach and a public boat launch. A black station wagon is parked up on the sloping path from the main road, its back to the lake, the front hood pitched upward. The two front doors are open so that someone can hear the car radio all the way down on the lake where there's a lone rowboat tied against a wooden dock.

"The shadow on the wall / Tells me the sun is going down," screams the song on the radio.

The man in the rowboat is bent over with his back to her, the crack of his ass showing above his pants as he yanks on an outboard motor. Even from here, even over the music, there is something unwieldy and enraged about his movements.

"Hello!" The voice startles her. Turning, there's a little girl, about seven years old, standing there in a pink sweatshirt and hot pink leggings. She has come from around the front of the black car.

"Hi," Ellen says. "Is that your car?"

The girl rocks on her heels. "My dad's. It's my dad's car." Then she points, "An' that's our boat."

"It's a very nice boat. That must be your dad." This little girl doesn't seem to have been warned not to talk to strangers—especially strangers who appear out of nowhere, at a lonely lakefront boat launch. Or perhaps she has, and that man is going to come now, yank his daughter away.

The girl sucks the end of the string on her sweatshirt hood. "My brother's here, too. We're sleeping at our granny's house. Mammy drove us here yesterday. Mammy has a different house. That's where we live. But then other times, we live at Granny's house, 'cos Daddy lives there, too."

"Right," Ellen says, glancing up toward the path behind them. Somehow, she feels she should leave. "It's great to have two houses."

"Deirdre," the man calls from his boat. "Deirdre, come over here!"

The little girl stares at Ellen. She senses she's in trouble. Then, she takes Ellen's hand and starts to walk down the slope to the water's edge.

"Howr'ya," the man says, straightening up and standing with his feet set apart in his boat. He has jet-black hair that falls over his forehead in greasy bangs. His hands and shirt are smeared with engine oil. "She's a bit of a chatterbox. Talk the hind leg off an ass if you let her."

"She's fine," Ellen says, feeling the little girl's hand in hers. "She was just telling me about your boat."

"You're here from America?" He nods past her shoulder, up past the main road and the matching white rental houses that dot the hillside above the lake. "Staying above in one of the holiday homes?"

"No, down at the hotel."

He wrinkles his nose. "Better off. I heard they're a pure rip-off. You'd nearly build a house for what that bastard's renting them for. Sure, he threw them up there one summer. Got the land for a song. JCB machinery there one day; houses the next. I heard some of the roofs are leaking already. Sure he sees them comin'—the poor tourists. Though Gerry Flanagan below gives nothing away either."

A bitter man, thinks Ellen. A man with something acerbic to say about everything and everyone. He pushes the black hair out his eyes, balancing effortlessly in his boat.

"Sure, enjoy yourself anyways," he says with a sardonic, twisted smile. "You staying long?" he shouts above the twangy song on the car radio.

"A week."

"That's long enough. Deirdre, let the nice lady go now. She has things for doin'. Here, come into the boat and help Daddy. We'll go for a spin later, the pair of us. Where's your brother anyways?"

"'Bye," Ellen says to the little girl, who's back sucking on her sweatshirt string. "It was very nice to meet you."

The man reaches a hand to tempt the little girl away across the pebbles, to help his daughter climb into the boat. Over his daughter's head, he says to Ellen, "Listen, we might see you down in Flanagan's some night if you're having a pint." Then he dips his head and winks at her.

8

WHEN THE SHOP DOOR pings open, the women stop their early morning chatter to stare at the woman in the bright yellow rain slicker. There are five of them gathered around the checkout counter at Gowna Foodmart. One is drinking tea from a paper cup. Ellen has the feeling that she's intruded on some private morning ritual.

The woman in a blue nylon shop coat leans past her friends. "Can I help you there?"

"I'm just looking," Ellen says, then ducks down one of the supermarket's aisles. Behind her, they start chatting again. One woman laughs, a loud, screechy laugh. Young, Ellen thinks. All of those women are too young to be Jo Dowd.

There's a morning radio show playing, the pop music loud and tinny through the store's intercom. Canned vegetables. Cleaning stuffs, toiletries, coffee, tea. As she turns each corner, she imagines an old woman there, an old woman hunched over her shopping cart who would look instantly familiar. But except for a young man stacking bottles of dish soap, the aisles are empty. This is ridiculous, she tells herself as she turns into another fluorescent-lit aisle.

Ellen finds what she came for—a roll-on deodorant, a bottle of apricot shower gel to replace Gerry Flanagan's little hotel soap bars.

At the checkout, the women part to let her through.

"Keeping showery," says the shop woman, nodding toward the village street and the hotel.

"Yes," Ellen says, puzzled. "I haven't used this brand before, but it looks really nice."

One of the women titters. It's the one with the paper cup of tea.

"The day," says the shop woman. "We're supposed to get showers nearly all day—heavy enough, too, they said there on the radio earlier."

"Oh!" Ellen says, feeling stupid. It's only her second morning here, and already, there's something about these Gowna people that can do that—make you feel foolish, an innocent. Not in the know.

*

The young Latvian girl with the long, dark hair is standing in the hotel dining room, polishing juice glasses. "Coffee today?" the girl asks, taking the pot and leading Ellen to the table inside the net-curtain window—the same table as yesterday.

The window gives onto the back of the hotel with its line of beer kegs against the kitchen wall. There's a wooden picnic table and benches. Today, the Heineken picnic umbrella drips with morning rain.

Yesterday, after her visit to Lough Gowna, Ellen drove back along the road that hugged the lake. The landscape was green and fresh and vivid. Lough Gowna and its islands glittered between the trees. Ireland of the postcards and the glossy coffee table books. But it was all tinged by her memory of that man in the boat—how he looked at her. She could still see his twisted, bitter smile, that lewd wink.

A week, she told herself. I'm just here a week—just long enough to visit my mother-in-law, to meet my husband's ghost. To put that ghost to rest.

Back in Gowna, she ate an early hotel supper and took another stroll up the main street, back up to the churchyard where, this time, there was no sign of the bicycle-racing priest, Father Bradley. She felt strangely disappointed. She wanted a friendly face, a glass of wine and the comforting oblivion of small talk, that stranger-on-the-plane conversation.

But the church doors were shut tight. The pigeons hoo-hoo'd at her from the trees behind St. John's.

Now the Latvian girl places a big plate of bacon, eggs, sausage, black blood pudding, fried mushrooms, and grilled tomatoes in front of her. It's enough for two people. "Enjoy your breakfast," says the girl, in her stilted English.

"Would you know where Knockduff is?" Ellen asks.

"It's a man?" asks the girl.

"No, a place."

The girl frowns at her. "I'm here. I live in Ireland, work for Mr. Flanagan"—she holds up three fingers—"three, three months." And then, "Martha. Martha knows."

Martha the cook is older, a hard-bitten little woman who stands there in a hairnet and a white chef's jacket. "There's nothing up in Knockduff," Martha says. "Only the one family."

"The Dowds?" Ellen says, watching the woman's interest pique.

"Yeah, and she'd be a fair age now, that one. But it's only about two-and-a-half miles, really. You go down through the village here, all the way along the lake. After the lake, start watching for an ould dance hall, nearly fallen in now. Once you pass that hall, watch for the turn, up to the right. Just turn up that road and keep going, up the hill, up into the sky!"

"Thank you."

"Are you looking at property up there?" Martha the cook asks.

"No."

Martha seems disappointed, as if Ellen is supposed to say, tell more.

"Is your breakfast all right for you?" The cook nods at the plate, gives a little sniff.

"Delicious," Ellen says. Then she spears a fried mushroom just to prove it.

*

Her wipers thwack-thwack against the rain. The same morning discussion program is on the car radio, the woman's smooth radio voice. "But Justin, surely that's exactly the point here! I mean, if a local housing authority is actually being asked to . . ."

A man interrupts: "Ah, yes, but Marian, it's crucial that we don't skew the two issues here."

Today, Lough Gowna sits down there as a mass of pewter grey. The road narrows, dips, and turns. She slows for three bicyclists, their rain capes floating behind them, their crumpled, drenched faces in her rearview mirror.

After the hillside vacation cottages, the chalets that the man said were a rip-off, she starts to watch for that dance hall, watching for a roadside honky-tonk sign.

There's a sudden clearing in the roadside trees. She turns in an overgrown parking lot where the weeds catch on the underside of her car. The dance hall is a long, low building with boarded-up windows. "Keep Out!" says the painted sign nailed to the padlocked double doors with flaking purple paint. Over the tops of the double doors and the boarded windows is a white plastic marquee sign with a huge slice of plastic missing to show the bare lightbulb sockets inside.

She leans over the steering wheel and angles her head to see it all—Gowna Dance Hall.

In Boston, a certain song on the radio would remind him of this place. Once, in that first apartment that they shared in Brookline, the first place where they lived as a couple, he suddenly jumped up from the breakfast table and took her hand and twirled her around that tiny kitchen in a sort of jitterbug two-step. *We loved this song. We couldn't wait for Saturday nights. Fancied ourselves as real John Travoltas.*

Now she thinks, Wait till I tell him that the dance hall is almost ready to fall in.

God. Shit. Her mind slipped again. No, Ellen, you won't tell him—about this or any part of Gowna.

She tries to picture this place thrumming with music, the twang of electric guitars. She pictures smoochy young couples sneaking out through that door, out into the marquee lights and around the back to those swampy fields.

She used to feel jealous of this place, of that entire secret life that he had before her, before America.

When did she stop feeling jealous? At least two, even three years before his death. In fact, she never felt jealous at a Boston party anymore, or at some Irish American fund-raiser dinner, where some businessman's wife cornered him at the open bar and cooed over his Irish brogue. Strange, Ellen thinks now. Funny how a derelict old dance hall can become only that, divested of its mystery, a borrowed memory. It's just an old place in the rain, as silent as the grave.

*

The chassis creaks, she shifts to second gear for Knockduff Hill. It feels like she's driving to the top of the world. She eases the car up into the ditch, sets the handbrake against the hill. She zips up her yellow raincoat, pulls up the hood. The stone pillars, the wide gate give onto an avenue that leads up between the paddocks to a two-story house in the distance, perched at the top of the hill. She could drive all way up there, but this is better, the quiet, stealth approach.

She reads the handwritten sign attached, wire-strung to the stone pillar: "No hill-walkers. No shooting."

She fiddles with the gate latch, holds the gate against the hill's gravity, then latches it shut behind her. In the rain, Jo Dowd's house stands grey and stolid against the leaden sky. In the distance, there's that second gate, the farmyard gate where Fintan posed for a photograph with his collie dog.

The sound stops her. What? She crosses the wet grass, steps around the pools of fresh cow dung to follow the coughing sound to an island of overgrown bushes and trees—a single outcropping in the middle of this otherwise pristine grazing.

Several sets of eyes peer at her from under the dripping trees. Of course, cattle. They're sheltering here, amidst that smell of rain and moss and wet rock.

A hazel rock. *I used to play in the hazel rock. Pluck and eat the hazelnuts, crack them with me teeth even though Mam said it'd crack every tooth in my head.*

As she steps closer to the house, the smell of a turf fire grows stronger. This was the first smell she got that day two days ago when she landed in Gowna village.

Just before the farmyard gate, Ellen stops on the avenue. She pushes back her rain hood to stare up at the house, watching for a face inside a window.

Jo

9

May 2002

JO DOWD reaches for her winter coat and a bobble knit hat from the back of the kitchen door. It's late May, summertime, but she's perished to the bone.

She buttons up the coat, pulls on the cap, and pulls the back door shut behind her. Then off with her, the walking cane tap-tapping across the lower farmyard to the orchard wall where her farmhand Ned's car sits parked, the car's roof dotted with white apple blossoms from the trees.

Go, go, go. She commands herself. Down as far as the hazel rock and back again.

She opens the yard gate and sets off down the avenue.

Every day she sets herself these tests of strength. Though for the past week, it's been harder. Yesterday, she made it a quarter of the way down when the hammering started in her chest. But she pushed herself onward. Jo Dowd was never *a peata,* a woman for mollycoddling.

Tap-tap-tap. Down the avenue between the stone walls, the fields where her cattle—best breeds of Fresian and Charolais—graze peacefully.

The pain is back. The summer air brought it back. And the pain means that the lump in her lung is back, too. Bad zest to all of it.

It comes at night, that dagger-pain in the lower back. It jolts her awake, then circles, snakes up to her shoulders. You can bear anything, she tells herself, then tries to go back to sleep. She reminds herself of all the pain, years and years of it, she has borne and borne well, without troubling a soul. Giving birth. And there were bee stings as a child. Or once, years ago, in one of the upper meadows, a hay fork went straight through her foot. The doctor—it was the older Fitzgerald then—came rushing up from the village in his old Morris Oxford car. He put her in the back seat and carted her away down the hill to a hospital in Castlebar, where the nurses said they couldn't fathom why the little girl wasn't screeching, howling with agony.

But she didn't. No, not Jo.

She stops, leans on the cane and fumbles in her coat pocket for the packet of Benson and Hedges and a white Bic lighter. She angles her head and chip-chip-chips at the lighter, then inhales deeply.

For the past two weeks, three o'clock in the morning and the pain sets her fumbling for the lamp and the brown jar of tablets that they gave her in the hospital. She spills one out in her hand and bites it in half, the taste bitter, poison. She always spits the other half back. Spare it, she promises herself. Spare it for again.

Then she shifts herself in the bed like an old cow in the manger, the bones scraping against each other. Waiting. She thinks of mad things, days long ago, things and people and songs and the dances they used to go to. Then at last, she dozes to the sound of the dawn birds outside her window.

The pain would go faster if she took the whole tablet. But she's afraid of what's ahead. So she rations them out, saves them up for that one night, the night when the pain will strike her blind.

But for now, today, she can still walk her own land, stand and smoke a fag in this summer stillness, listen to the pigeons hoo-hoo-hoo-ing.

It's almost a year since she first woke to the wind roiling in her chest, the pain creeping out her arm. She coughed up blood on the hankies beside her bedside. It was the height of hay season, the meadows cut, and Ned had the usual *meitheal* of men cutting, reaping, bailing. So it was only dust and hayseed that made her cough like that. She told herself this. She believed this.

Then, when the men were gone and the hay crop saved in its round, sealed bales, she rang the young Dr. Fitzgerald down in the village. Up the hill came that big station-wagon car of his. He stood in her kitchen wagging his finger at her like she was a bold child. Said she was sick longer than she was actually admitting. How she should have come down to the village to his surgery for tests. *Listen, Mrs. Dowd, would you not think, even now, about giving up th'oul fags? There are skin patches and chewing gum and herbs for your nerves.*

An operation, he says one day. *Maybe not,* he says another. *Mediastinoscopy* and *lobectomy.* He said those words, medical words, right there in her own house. And he said the cancer word. Cancer of the lung. Tom Fitzgerald is full of hot air and big talk, just like his father before him.

At night she dreams of things floating, swarming. She dreams of frog spawn, squishy, runny little bubbles that grow and spread like a rash.

The young Fitzgerald sent her to the hospital in Galway, where everything was white, all white, like a butcher shop. She hated the nurses with their trilling little voices and silly chat: *How are we this morning, Mrs. Dowd? You must tell us if you're feeling any pain?* Then here came those foreigners wheeling the tea trolleys, delivering her porridge and toast.

That first day there, she woke to a face over her bed: a pert little nun in a white blouse, a gold crucifix around her neck and the communion host in her hand. All that *seafóid* about her spiritual well-being. *Put your trust and faith in the Lord, missus.*

Jo cursed her from the bedside, told her she could keep all those old *pisreógs* for all those holy types in their beds with their rosaries. "The Lord has nothing to do with it," she said to the little nun's startled face. "The whole religion thing's nothing but a bloody hoodwink."

They marked her chest with a biro, then wheeled her into a machine like a giant toilet paper roll. They told her to talk into a microphone. *Are you all right there, Mrs. Dowd?*

Later, she woke to lights and noises and another woman patient who screeched into the night like the *bean sí.* They gave Jo tablets galore. Tablets that made her sleep so heavily that she dreamed of mad things.

She's eighty-two, you know. The nurses whispered across her bed. Little bitches.

When she came home, Dr. Fitzgerald wanted her in some kind of rehab place, a nursing home. "And what?" Jo demanded. "Just what would I do with my cattle and land and everything here?"

So he sent a visiting nurse up the hill who moved Jo downstairs to Mother's old bedroom off the parlor. The room Jo's mother had died in, over thirty years ago now. It hadn't been used since.

After the hospital, she slept nearly all day. When she woke, she saw Mother's face above her, an old woman staring down at her daughter lying there. Mother. Daughter. Musical beds.

You can give her soft, runny things, she heard the young Fitzgerald telling Ned. *They won't hurt her throat, won't scrape the radiation burns. And I'll give you extra tablets for the pain. Now, make sure she takes them. You know her form, how she is.* Poor Ned. He's a stock man, not a bloody nurse!

Now Jo stops on the avenue, leans on her cane to count the cattle: fifteen heifers, seven yearling bullocks. She stands there listening to that tearing sound as they graze the summer grass. She takes a last drag and stubs out the cigarette on the avenue.

The evenings, nights, she's spent out here in these fields, searching for straying heifers, their torchlights bobbing ahead of them, her and the boy's. Their voices echoing each other's *Bess, bess, bess, bess* as they tramped through the wet grass. Listening for hoofs crashing through the undergrowth. The boy always frantic—not for the missing beast, but mad for the homework he'd left behind on the kitchen table.

So here he is now. Again. God blast him. He comes whenever it suits him—stands here on the avenue or slips into her room, standing there at the bedside on those nights when she's awake with the pain. Or she wakens from a dream of him—not as a man, but as a *garsúin,* a young lad, himself and that bloody dog chasing through these fields.

The letter from America was waiting for her when she came home from the hospital, sitting there on her kitchen table where Ned had put all her post. A white envelope and an American stamp. She let herself hope. A letter at last. After sixteen years. So someone must have told him, told him about the sickness, the hospital.

To the Dowd family . . . I regret to inform you . . .

It was signed by a woman, claiming to be his American wife, but she had some foreign surname, not Dowd.

Once, there was a man who lived down the hill between here and the village of Gowna. He caught his arm in a threshing machine. For years afterward, they said he still felt it—the arm still throbbing, in an arm that they'd sawn away. A ghost pain.

And so it is with the boy's death—a son she hasn't seen since he left for America sixteen years ago. Never answered her letters. Never rang his own house. Never came home.

After the first few years, she cursed him to hell. Told herself she was a damn sight better off—a grown man to hold grudges, silences, just like his father before him. *Briseann an dúchas.* Nature, breeding follows on from one generation to the next.

The years went on: hay season, harvest, winter fodder, the men she hired to come and clear the land, excavate the rocks and the bushes. It all went on just dandy without the likes of him.

Then here came that letter. Her son's death is the man with the cut arm. It's someone squeezing her heart. And here he is now: a boy running across these fields, a ghost boy and his sheepdog, Rosie.

She feels the strength waning from her legs, her whole body. The wind feels trapped, guttered in her chest.

The hazel rock. You will. You must. She forces herself on, tap-tap-tap with the cane, her breaths coming hard and loud in the summer evening.

The hazel rock stands three-quarter way down the avenue—a single outcropping in her cleared fields. Even from here she can smell it—that whiff of damp moss, the musky bluebells between the limestone rocks.

*

Last winter she got better. The grass turned white and hoary with frost, and all that dry freezing air did a powerful job of cleaning out her lungs. For days and days, she hadn't a whit of pain. I'm good as new, she told herself. She believed this, too.

Christmas Day, she took her first walk out here again, out across the yard and out the gate, then down the silent avenue. So they were all wrong. The young Fitzgerald and the whole bloody lot of them.

*

Once she felt better, she decided to ring her, that American woman that wrote the letter. She read the phone number on the top of the writing paper—some sort of a university, an academy, the name in curly gold letters. Jo was going to give her a piece of her mind for sending a letter like that, cold as ice, sent to the Gowna post office instead of directly to a man's own house, making a holy show before the whole parish.

So many nights, she held that phone in her hand, listened to the taped voice: *You must first dial the country code . . .*

Then she'd drop the phone again. What to say? Oh, yes, what the dickens to say to a woman like that? The woman was probably already divorced from her son. Sure everyone knew they were all divorced—some of them two and three times—beyond in America. And money is their God. So she's looking for her money, this young one, her pound of marital flesh.

Jo hears a car engine behind her. Ned. Sure, who else? Here's the red Ford Fiesta with the dried mud and *cac bó* spattered along the doors. He's pretending he's knocking off early for once, just on his way home. But she knows that he's been watching her from the upper meadows beyond the house. He's sure she's going to fall and break something.

He pulls alongside her now, leans across the car to set the passenger's door open. *Ping-ping-ping.* That car noise that'd wake the bloody dead.

"They said on the radio there might be a drop of rain in it, ma'am." Those bushy eyebrows, those hooded eyes. Ned McHugh is a discreet and careful man. From discreet and careful people. "I'll turn the car 'round and drop you up and you can sit within at the telly and rest yourself."

That damn door still *ping-ping* as he comes around to the passenger's side. She elbows away his helping hand. Then she eases herself in there while Ned puts the cane in the back seat, sets it among the baler twine and boxes of cattle doses and animal feedstuffs.

He walks back around and he revs the engine. The pebbles ding off the wheels as they turn back uphill for the house.

10

SHE LIES THERE, watching the daylight through the flowery bedroom curtains.

She sets herself the usual mind test. Day: Monday. Date: The thirtieth of May. Year: 2002. And then, the final test: Pain? No, not so bad today.

Most mornings, she hears Ned's step in the back kitchen, then the kitchen presses opening and shutting. He comes, *mar dhea*, to look for cattle doses or a syringe for a weakling calf. He has started this pretense, this malarkey because he knows that she's sick again, that the cursed cancer's back.

She lies there waiting for him. Not a sound. Or has he come already? Has she slept through it all, his rattling around the kitchen?

One day last week—*was* it last week?—she woke to him standing there in the parlor doorway. First, she thought it was a dream, a vision. But there he was, in his stocking feet, the tweed cap scrunched in his hand, like a man tiptoeing into a church. Did he think that she was dead and that he'd have to ring someone?

She shut her eyes, pretending to be still asleep, but breathing extra loudly so he'd know, so he could tiptoe away again.

She must bring a clock in from the parlor. What the devil use is it out there on the parlor mantel where no one ever sees it? She never had a bedside clock before. A country woman wakes with the birds, the daylight. Up with the lark and gets on with the work. But these days, she's asleep when she should be awake. Asleep like a wino.

Up, up, up. She commands herself. Her clothes are looser now, her body thinner than ever before. But her body feels weighted, ballasted like a bag of drowning kittens.

Up, up.

Through the open bedroom door she watches the shaft of sunlight across the parlor, over the brocade couch and the glass-fronted china cabinet where her wedding china sat for years and years.

Up, up.

Her eyes flutter shut.

In this dream, Jo Burke is waiting for her turn at the mirror, waiting among all those chattery and giggly girls who stand on tippy toe to dab at their faces from a powder compact. Jo's sister, Kitty, stands next to her, spraying her hair. A girl called Rosaleen Dunphy is laughing and asking if there's any chance of a bit of that hair lacquer. The girls wear cinched dresses and high-heeled court shoes. Everyone knows everyone. They know each other's parents and sisters and brothers.

From the ladies' toilet they can hear the strains of Jack Power and his Sunshine Swing Band. "On a day like today / we'd pass the time away," the man croons, while another man plays the clarinet.

Among this group of Saturday-night girls, there is a kind of valiant desolation. These are the Gowna girls who have stayed, waited it out, stayed put in their own parish while their classmates and sisters have taken the boat to England to train to be clerk-typists or hospital cleaners or nurses.

When their faces are perfect, their hair scooped up into side combs, the girls leave together for the dance floor, some of them hanging back for the final check: Are the seams in my stockings straight?

When the fellas arrive, the band is in full swing and the girls are dancing with each other. The coy ones watch the door and wink at each other as the fellas parade past in a cloud of fags and a whiff of drink.

Kitty Burke, Jo's younger sister, is always among the first asked up to dance. Always swept off her feet. And there she is now, her face flushed under the lights, her eyes wild, her scarlet dress fluttering around her as she does a two-step with yet another handsome, Brylcreem young man.

Jo is tall and plain. She is only twenty-five years of age, yet she takes her place on a bench along the wall with the older women, the Gowna spinsters who, week after week, sit there with their hopeful smiles, their features set in valiant sufferance. Some are plain—big noses or too tall or mannish shoulders like Jo has. Another has poor eyesight. Four of them are passable in looks, but their families have no fortune or dowry. Or their families' land is already gone to an oldest brother or as dowry for another, older sister.

John Dowd never asks any girl up to dance. From the bench, Jo watches him standing there inside the dance-hall door, forty-five or fifty years of age if he's a day. He stands there with his bicycle clips still on, which makes him look ridiculous, like something that might come waddling across the big screen in the cinema in Ballinkeady. His small, pinched face is scrubbed pink above his stiff shirt collar.

And now, for the first time any girl can remember, John Dowd is crossing the dance floor, angling around the dancers and excusing himself until he's standing here. His face is cocked sideways like a begging dog. "Will you dance, miss?"

Your bicycle clips, she wants to say to him. But then, she looks into those petrified eyes and takes pity. She accepts his dance offer and tries not to look down past his waist.

They dance a two-step. He is an awkward dancer. He keeps stepping on her feet, her new suede court shoes that make her tower above him. Across the loud, smoky dance floor, she sees people smirking at them. And Kitty. Where's her sister Kitty?

After the first set, he asks her for a walk outside. Still she scans those laughing, sweating faces for her younger sister. As if she must get direction, permission. She has never been invited away from the dance hall before.

Josephine Burke and John Dowd leave the voices and the music and lights behind them to walk across the car park and then down along the lake road, down toward the village of Gowna, where he said he'd treat her to a mineral, a fizzy orange drink, from a late-open shop.

She listens to their footsteps in the silence, his and hers. Clack, clack, clack along the road. She watches fissures of reflected moonlight on Lough Gowna. She looks up at the moon's white, dispassionate face. Do something, Jo entreats it. Though she's not quite sure what she'd like the moon to do. Liven things up a bit, let her life up in Knockduff live up to her girlish hopes, the daydreams that bother her head while she's out in the byre helping Father to milk the cows.

His footsteps stop. The lake water laps in the distant as John Dowd steps nearer to her. He's trembling. When he kisses her, their chins collide.

I have been kissed, she thinks. At twenty-five, someone has finally kissed me, run his hands up over the bodice of my dress.

Later, when they are walking back to the dance hall, her mouth sugary and sticky from the fizzy orange drink, John Dowd stops to light a Sweet Afton cigarette.

He offers her one. She takes it, and he leans in closer, his face suddenly there in the light from his lit match. He looked better in the dark.

After that first night, the night when he brought her down to the village, he always asked her up to dance. It was assumed that she'd dance with nobody else. And twice more, Jo went walking out along the lake road with him. Now when he kissed her, she shut her eyes and imagined that it was someone else, one of the other men back up there in the Gowna Hall.

Each Saturday night a voice inside said, Tonight must be the last. I am a laughing stock. Yes, even to the wallflower girls, the girls who never get asked out to dance. So I will get rid of him.

The house at Knockduff turns secretive and whispery. Mother and Father have got wind of their courtship. At night, when Jo lies awake upstairs in the bed she shares with her sister, she listens to the mumble of voices through the kitchen ceiling.

A Thursday night, and Father is suddenly scrubbed and dressed in a suit and a starched shirt collar. He never wears a top coat except for Sunday Mass. But now, here he is checking his pocket watch and pacing the kitchen until the car lights arch against the front windows of the house. It's a hackney car, a car that Father has summoned.

Two nights later, Saturday, Jo has decided to break it off with John Dowd. When he crosses the dance floor to ask her to dance as usual, she's ready. All week in the fields and in the byre and while doing the household ironing, she has been practicing the words inside her head. But now the words won't come. She shakes her head. *No. No.* Then they lock gazes, his face full of injury. Silently, while the other girls sit there tapping their feet to the music and pretending not to wait and watch, Jo tries to tell him everything in their silent gaze: how she cannot let this man who is almost Father's age kiss her on the mouth, run his hands around her hips, over her breasts, his breaths coming faster, hotter, more desperate. How, honestly, she had hoped that life had something better for her.

At last he walks away, back across the dance floor, his shoulders hunched as he pushes through the dancing, twirling crowd, the young couples and their faces dappled in the dance-hall lights. He walks all the way out the dance hall door to his waiting bicycle, parked around the side of the hall.

Later, three o'clock in the morning and Jo and Kitty are cycling up Knockduff Hill. November, and the night is still warm. Kitty, her dress fluttering behind her, hums a song that the band had played twice that night.

The sisters stop to unlatch the first gate. They see the lights on in the house. "What? Oh, God, what? Bad news?"

They pedal the rest of the way up the hill, their heart thump-thump. Someone dead? A beast in distress?

"Up to bed, Kitty!" Mother commands. She's standing there under the kitchen light, her arms folded over her aproned bosom. "Up this minute to bed." Father sits hunched in over the hearth, swaddled in his scarf and knitted pullover.

Mother says, "There's sense in marrying a man like John Dowd. We know his people. And as a second son, he'll get no place of his own, no farm. But there's a place, a farm here. Your father's not getting any younger. And his bad chest. If there's nobody to work the land, the land commission will come; we'll lose it all. There are plenty watching this place with only two daughters, plenty with their eye on it, watching, waiting."

Father. Thursday night. So this is where he went, why he was dressed up and waiting for a hackney car. He was sent off to make a match for Jo. Jo feels her legs weaken. But it's a joke, a silly joke. No. No. No.

From his fireside armchair, Father will not look up to meet his twenty-five-year-old daughter's eyes. If he did, he would see something new there. He would see all that girlish youth, all her dreams waning.

Not Kitty of course. Kitty has just started her first job in town, the town of Ballinkeady, just three miles away. Every morning she cycles there to the drapery shop where she's serving her apprentice time. She's learning how to measure and cut dress material, how to measure a woman for her bust and waist size, how to say, "Good morning, ma'am" to the doctors' and solicitors' wives who come to buy their nylon twin sets and sheer stockings and skirts with box pleats. The very idea of an old man with sad eyes is out of the question for Kitty Burke of the rosebud lips and the high, trilling laugh.

*

Two months later, the 6th of January, the Feast of the Epiphany, Mother summons the hackney again. The weather has turned chilly at last.

The Ford Prefect car makes its way down the avenue, the headlights bright in the morning dark. They drive for a very long time.

In the back seat, Jo knows she is supposed to be excited. She is being brought to the city. She is being taken to buy her wedding dress and trousseau.

All week in the house, they have been scrubbing and painting. Mother has made her wedding cake, three tiers of a dense fruit cake that she has wrapped in the old flour bags to keep it fresh and ready for icing. There are two big hams hanging from the kitchen ceiling, and Mother has cycled down to the village shop to order grapefruits and bottles of sherry and shop bread.

In Galway City, the hackney drops them outside a church, a strange stone-fronted church on a city street. Mother and Jo go to Mass there, a holy day of obligation. Mother says that shopping without morning Mass would be flying in the eyes of God; it would bring bad luck on them, on her daughter, on the marital match.

Mass is over, and the sky is paling to a winter daylight over the city's slate roofs.

It thrills Jo—these buses and cars, house after house, shop after shop, lorries and vans. Everything is moving, moving, moving. Jo's heart skips. I love this. I love all of this, all these vehicles and people.

Mother and daughter turn down a side street to a shop where Mother tells the shop woman that they're here for a wedding dress—something sensible and serviceable.

"Nothing showy," says Mother. "Above all not showy."

From the woman's offerings, Mother selects a green dress—bottle green, the shop assistant calls it.

When Jo steps out of the fitting room, there's the shop woman with the pincushion ready. She stands on tiptoe to pull at the bride's shoulders, to settle the bottle green dress into place, saying that it will have to be let down, let out, made to fit a girl this size.

"She's such a fine strapping girl," the woman says to Mother. "God bless her. She must have a great appetite."

*

On the wedding morning, the hackney driver knocks on the back-kitchen door to ask for the kettle off the hob. The winter has turned cold at last, bitter cold, so just on the drive up Knockduff Hill, the hackney car windows have frozen over again.

Then they are all ready at last—the Burke family walking out across the yard, bride and bridesmaid, mother and father. Father wears a trilby hat and a wool topcoat and an extra scarf for his bad chest.

Then the man drives them down the avenue, down through the fields that are white and hoary with frost.

After the church, there they are again, driving up the avenue. But this time, there are five cars. In the first one sit Mister and Missus John Dowd.

The temperature has dropped lower. The hackney man keeps rubbing, rubbing at the windscreen.

In the car's back seat, John's hand has grown sweaty in hers. Jo looks out the back window to see the other cars behind. It's his people and hers, all of the car wheels spinning, engines revving, the avenue shiny with ice.

In the end, their driver turns into the front paddock, the tires crunching over the frozen grass. The other cars follow, one after the other, bumping across the field where they have traction at last.

The car doors bang shut. The women pick their way in high heels. The men pull their topcoats tighter.

Up the hill they trudge, their footsteps slipping. Jo, who is leading, reaches behind her for her husband's hand, and he reaches behind him for his mother's, who reaches for her husband. Now they are a chain of people, a wedding waltz, step, step, stepping up the hill. Then sliding, falling again.

11

THE TRAIN CONDUCTOR calls out the station stops: “Athlone! Clara! Tullamore!”

These are places and towns that John and Jo Dowd, the honeymoon couple, have only heard of on the wireless or in the newspaper. At each country station, people stand waiting with their coat collars pulled up, their breaths fogging on the freezing afternoon. From the train windows, the Dowds watch the pools of frozen water in the fields, the bare trees against the January sky.

Then at last the train is nudging into Westland Row Station, Dublin. Train doors are suddenly slapping open. On the platform, people push ahead of them toward a waiting bus. They all have a purpose, but not Jo and John. It feels ridiculous, going off on holiday when they should really be at home.

She stands there waiting for him, watching his slow gait along the city footpath.

From the train, they walk up along the River Liffey with its smell like stale coffee. Then there’s the porridgy smell of the brewery.

“That’s the Guinness brewery,” John points, stopping to stare at the street-side gates. “St. James’ Gates. Now fancy that.”

She hobbles along in her wedding shoes. She wears a winter coat over her going-away suit, which is blue wool, a cream blouse, leather gloves with a little button at the cuff. In her suitcase is her wedding-night trousseau.

A week ago, in their bedroom, she and Kitty rehearsed that word, whispered to each other and screeched and tittered at its implications. Now, a week, a wedding and a train journey later, the word has turned heavy, sour.

They walk on, watching the red brake lights from the cars. Across the river, there's a building with a domed roof: the Four Courts. She recognizes it from a school history book. Then at last, they're approaching the bridge, O'Connell Bridge, where men and women keep rushing past, their shoulders hunched into the wind from the river.

"Nelson's Pillar," John is pointing out to her. "God, that must be it, there. Look at it, Jo." All day, except for their wedding vows, it's the first time he has actually said her name.

"Oh, is that a fact?" she asks, feeling suddenly contrite. It's not his fault: this bitter cold, her high heels, the terror in her belly.

"It is," he says. "It is that a fact."

They walk on down O'Connell Street. When they reach the GPO, the General Post Office, she waits for him to announce this, too. And she will muster some surprise, even pleasure. But he does not. And then she tells herself again. It's not his fault.

They turn into a narrower street, then another, where the houses are much smaller than their own house at home in Knockduff. "Guests & Teas," says the sign in the window.

In the doorway, the Dublin woman takes them in, looks them up and down: first Jo, then John. There is something about this County Mayo couple that amuses her. She smirks as she leads them into a doilied little living room, where she inquires about the weather way down the country. She brings biscuits on a plate. She congratulates them on this morning's nuptials. She smirks again as she says it—nuptials—as if savoring a joke to tell someone later. "God," the little woman says, "I remember well the morning myself and my poor Jim got married. Above in Whitefriar Street. But Jim is long dead now, God rest him."

The tea curdles in Jo's stomach. Her eyes drift to the ceiling above them, the room upstairs.

Kitty said that there was a girl who worked with her in the drapery shop who had a friend who had emigrated to England to train as a nurse. The friend had promised to post them back French letters, straight to the shop, so Mother would never know. In England, the girl said, you could just buy French letters in the corner shop, without a bit of shame. Same as you'd buy a lipstick or a packet of fags. From the shop, Kitty sometimes brought home English books and magazines, sneaked them in the house to the sisters' upstairs bedroom. At night, Kitty would put on an English accent as she read from the magazines' advice columns: *Dear Maggie, I am six years married and we have four children, but I don't want to have any more in family. Yet every Sunday night, my husband still wants . . .*

Kitty would keep on reading as Jo stuffed the corners of her blanket in her mouth to stop herself laughing and waking Mother and Father.

On those nights, Kitty declared she would, yes, she really *would* do it if a fella asked her nicely. But only a fella that was gorgeous and that she was in love with. God, it might be fabulous. And she wouldn't get in trouble either. Once they arrived in the post, the French letters wouldn't let her get in trouble.

The landlady is stacking the tea cups on a tray, saying that in honor of the occasion, she has given them the best room in the house. So off they go now; she wouldn't *dream* of delaying them.

The room is lit by the Dublin streetlight outside their window. Jo had, in fact, been hoping for darkness. The bed sheets are cold. It's the coldest that Jo has ever been in her life, lying here against the wall in her wedding trousseau. She peers over the blankets at him, where he's standing there with his back to her, next to the dressing table, stepping out of his wedding trousers. In the streetlights, his legs are waxy white. He looks like a patient in a hospital.

There is no blood at all. And there's no giggling or panting, nothing like what Kitty and her English magazines had promised. First there's the shock, a stab of pain between her legs. But it's bearable. Much, much worse is the embarrassment, the ridiculousness of a man lying there on top of her grunting, snuffling like a pig.

12

JO HOOKS HER CANE on the edge of the kitchen sink and plugs in the electric kettle for tea. This morning she's going to entice Ned back inside. She's going to set a place for him at the kitchen table, where they'll have their breakfast together. Just like old times. Just like when Ned and the seasonal hired men used to come from the hay and the plough field for huge meals of new potatoes and saucepans of cabbage, boiled carrots, pans of roasted mutton from the oven. She can see them now: those men, sunburned and flecked with hayseed sitting around the table, the caps crooked on the chair rails, salt and butter and meat bones sucked dry.

The morning sky is overcast. In the orchard, the crows are loud and busy. For once, despite the pain tablets, she's up at a normal time. She checks the electric clock on the wall. Eight o'clock. Where is he? Ned McHugh is never late.

Last night—*was* it last night?—Yes, yes, she's sure of it. There she was, awake as usual, pitch dark outside, and here the pain came creeping through her, her legs, arms trembling. Like someone had plugged her in. So bad she had to switch the lamp on again, rattle the pills in their brown bottle. Christ, Jo thought. Two. Only two of the hospital's pain tablets left. This time, the pain was so bad that she downed a whole tablet, then lay there, waiting for the trembling to stop, waiting for sleep.

She must have dozed off. For here she is now, the kettle on the boil and up with the lark and waiting. She has a brilliant plan. God, yes. She should've thought of it before.

Her cheeks feel hot, burning. But the pain hasn't returned. And her mind is seething sharp. The tablets are great for that.

She takes the packet of fags from her cardigan pocket. She lights one, then sets it in an empty saucer next to the sink, next to where she crooked her walking stick.

Wait! Is that the gate, the yard gate clanking shut? Yes. And a car, his old Ford Fiesta bumping across the yard, parking in his usual spot along the orchard wall.

She watches Ned slip from the car—the small, tidy man, grey moustache and a tweed cap. He looks to the sky, grimaces at the cloudy morning, the thick, cotton-wool clouds.

Here he is now, the stooped gait, heading for the back door. He doesn't look at the house, at the kitchen window. She wills him to look, to see her here waiting. She doesn't want him to get the shock of his life when he finds ma'am up and dressed and the kettle in and her cheeks scalding hot.

She watches the doorknob turn. It's like something in a film.

He lets out a little yelp at the sight of her standing there, up and about and leaning against the sink.

He pulls off the cap. "Jesus, what's . . . what's wrong, ma'am?"

"Nothing's wrong, Ned. Nothing." Already she feels some of the excitement wane, and she wonders if the tea, their breakfast together, is a daft idea. Unsuitable. "I'm fine," she says. "Never better." The cigarette hand shakes, so she sets the fag back in the saucer. But now she has too many hands. What should she do with them all? She shoves the right hand into her cardigan pocket where she feels the €100 note folded there.

She cocks her chin at him. "Ned, I need a message from the town. That's if you wouldn't *mind*."

His face relaxes, relief flooding.

"I'll pay you for your time, your petrol."

"Ah . . . no ma'am sure whatever you w—"

"—I want you to drop into Vet O'Laughlin in the town, in Ballinkeady. Tell them we've a beast with a limp in the back leg, one of the black-and-white Fresians that went down, her foot caught in the hazel rock below."

His eyebrows furrow, puzzled. "Not a bit of bother, ma'am. But when did you find her? We should bring him out."

The electric kettle boils, the water gurgling. The tea. They were going to have lovely hot tea and a bit of a chat. But she's shaking too much, her body is plugged in again, plugged in and trembling. The kettle boils on, the noise loud between them.

Her voice comes high, rushed. "No. Arrah, why would we want to draw him on us, that fella? Thinks he's the cock of the walk. Sure it's a young heifer, she'll recover soon." She laughs, madly, at her own joke—a cackling laugh that makes Ned flinch, the eyes furrowed deeper with worry, then suspicion.

She picks up the fag again. Takes a puff, blows the smoke out her nose. Better. Yes. Calmer. "Tell him the beast is in pain, and we're waiting a while before deciding whether to put her down or not. That she might be better if she had relief. So get a few injections or them patch things—d'ya remember them patch things he gave us for that Charolais there, last year?"

She gives another cackling laugh. "Lord, I used to think the bullock looked like a bloody child with a nappy on it. Ha, ha, ha."

From her cardigan pocket she shoves the €100 at him. She meets his frightened gaze. Look, we both know our little game here, her look says. But just do it. The vet will be a lot easier than the bloody doctor, that young Fitzgerald barging in here and sending me off to some stupid nursing home that's full of piss and old women. Get me these animal pain things and I'll never ask again. Never ask for another thing.

Ned swallows. Then she watches it fully dawn on him, what ma'am is really asking—to drive the three miles into town, a place he rarely goes, never needs to go. But he'll visit the vet and make up stories about a beast in pain, a beast ready, possibly ready for the place in Ballyhaunis where they slaughter and make pet food out of dead agricultural beasts. A dose, a box of patches—Fentanyl, yes, that's the name for them—that he'll bring her, faithfully, leave them with the other cattle doses in the kitchen cupboard as if they don't both know what they really know.

"Here," she whispers, shoving the money toward him. The kettle keeps boiling. It's supposed to click off. Why won't the bloody thing switch itself off today? Her cheeks are two hot coals. She's ready to jump out of her own skin.

Above all else, Ned McHugh has never once let an animal suffer; never let it bellow in pain. Surely he can do the same for his mistress, the woman he's worked for for thirty-two years?

She unhooks her cane from the sink edge. Tap, tap, tap across the scullery tiles, until she's standing next to him. Now Jo leans on the cane, stoops to tuck the €100 note into the top pocket of his jacket. "Please. I'll not ask again."

He nods slowly. "I'll do that, ma'am." Then he puts the cap back on his head and turns for the door.

13

MOTHER SENDS A CAR to the bus stop in the village. It's waiting for them when they arrive, the same man and driver who, a week ago, drove them down through the frozen landscape to their wedding at St. John's Church.

Today the thaw is setting in, Gowna's houses and shops drip-dripping with melted frost. As they drive away from the village toward the lake, the man is asking John questions: "Tell us, had yez a brilliant time above in the big smoke?" In the front passenger seat, John is keeping small talk, describing it all, the colossal size of everything: the buildings, the houses, the train station where they waited for the train back home.

From the back seat, Jo watches the distant lights across Lough Gowna, that town in County Galway where people are already sitting around their nighttime supper tables, eating toast or rashers or banana sandwiches. She loved the city. But she hated the burden of pretending to enjoy herself. Who thought it up anyway, the very idea? Whoever it was was a stupid person, the idea of a holiday away with a stranger, a holiday straight after your wedding. She's been counting the days to be home, to the house and the fields where she can hide again, where she can lose herself in the crevices of her old life.

They drive past the Gowna Dance Hall, empty and closed until Saturday night. She watches the back of her husband's head and sees him back there, once, a whole lifetime ago, crossing the dance floor in his bicycle clips to ask her up to dance. If he hadn't? If he'd decided to stay on the men's side, smoking his Sweet Aftons and making small talk with the other men? She wouldn't be here now. Things happen that easily, she thinks, watching the dark landscape float past the car's back window. One small thing, a decision like that. But a small thing sets off something else. Like a marriage. So if the accident that makes it happen is so small, then maybe the thing itself, the result, is just as small. One man or another. Maybe it doesn't even matter.

The tea table is set in the kitchen, where Mother flutters around, passing a plate of scones and treating the new couple like visitors. Father tells John how many ewes have dropped already. Mother asks if they were frozen stiff above in the city.

Kitty arrives from work, her eyes bright and her cheeks red from pedaling home in the January night. She regales them with the usual stories of the town and how the shopgirls pass the change from counter to counter, down along the shop in a shuttle contraption that flies above their heads like a bird. She mimics the women who come to select blouses and cardigans, who send their housemaids to collect a bolt of dress material, spending a guinea or a half-crown like it's only tuppence. She starts to tell about a fat woman, a bank manager's wife, who's so fat that it takes two shop girls just to measure her for a girdle.

Jo screeches laughing at her sister's story. It's so delightful to be home again, to chat and laugh with her sister. Sitting here, she realizes that for the entire honeymoon, as she sat with John in a Dublin café or cinema, she was prenarrating the city already, its lights and houses and shops, saving it all up to tell her sister.

A cough from the top of the table stops them. Father. He frowns at his daughters. Mother looks at Kitty, and says, "Now, that's enough. You know your father doesn't like that kind of talk."

After tea, Mother ushers Jo and John upstairs to their new room. There's a surprise waiting for them in the big room at the front of the house. Mother and Father have ordered them a new double bed from a hardware shop in Ballinkeady.

On the bed are two white pillowcases that Kitty has embroidered with a rose in each bottom corner.

"I emptied out the wardrobe," Mother is saying, pulling the doors open to the empty insides. Standing in her new marital room, Jo wants to run across the landing, pitter-patter like a child to her and Kitty's old room.

Next morning, she wakes to a pale winter sunlight outside the window. Eyes still shut, she listens for him, the familiar little snores next to her. She feels that now-familiar ache, that wet between her legs. The shame! Oh, Christ, the shame! And here in her own house, with her mother and father asleep across the landing.

When she reaches for him the bed is empty. He is already up and gone.

She lies there listening to the sounds from downstairs: Mother rattling the poker in the fireplace. Then Mother's footsteps across the kitchen. The clanking sound as she sets the pot of animal swill on its hook. Jo listens for men's voices. Nothing. So John and Father, their bellies full of boiled eggs and hot toast and scalding tea, have already left for the yard and the fields.

14

MOTHER'S EYES STRAY to her older daughter's waist. Jo catches her mother's knowing smirk. There is a woman's justice here. On a farm all things spawn themselves into the new season, into the next generation. It has happened in the very room where Mother, as a new bride to this house, conceived Jo.

Down in the village, Dr. Fitzgerald examines Jo in his surgery. She hates lying there, hates that this grey-haired man who smells of aftershave and always wears a good waistcoat and pin-striped trousers has the power to do this. Has the power to tell her "yes" or "no."

"Great my dear," he says, in that false, staged way of his. "You're expecting."

Kitty, she thinks. I must tell Kitty.

Father is sick again, always sickly in the spring with his bad chest, the coughing, coughing from his bed, the old newspapers crafted into birds' nest shapes, makeshift spittoons. Every morning when Jo brings him his breakfast, she collects the night's paper spittoons, carries them to the kitchen fireplace, where the phlegm sizzles in the flame.

John and Mother and Jo hold the fort, keep everything going. It's the end of lambing season, so they're out half the night, the flashlight shining under bushes looking for birthing ewes.

Now that she's fully trained as a drapery assistant, Kitty has got herself a job in a much bigger drapery shop in Galway City, where she lives with other girls in a rooming house. Half of the county is jobless or gone to England, but for Kitty Burke it's been no bother to get a new and better job. On her days off, she and her new friends walk on the promenade at Salthill. At night they go dancing at a grand, beachside dance hall.

Mother let her younger daughter move away on one condition: Kitty is supposed to come home on Sundays, for Sunday dinner. But for the past few weeks, Kitty has sent a letter saying that she's not feeling well; she has a little chill. Mother reads these letters and clicks her teeth about the dirt and filth and germs of the city's back streets.

Jo knows the letter is just another of Kitty's fibs. After each of Kitty's excuse letters, the week stretches ahead as a disappointment.

Without her sister, without Kitty's stories and chatter and rushing through the house in her high heels, the days at Knockduff are identical. With Kitty gone, the four of them have settled into their own, deep silence, a silence that seems to have a life of its own.

The first Sunday in March, Kitty is finally coming for Sunday dinner. This will be the day to tell her Jo's news. While Mother peels the potatoes for roasting, Jo practices before her dressing table mirror. *Kitty, I'm expecting. Kitty, I'm expect—Kitty, you're going to be an auntie. Auntie Kitty.*

An hour before Sunday dinner, a shiny black car appears at the end of the avenue. A man gets out to unlatch the first gate, he shuts it behind him, then the car comes bumping up the last stretch of avenue to the yard.

From the bedroom window, Jo watches as the man parks just beyond the yard gate. But nobody gets out. Then Jo watches the heads together, the arms, the bodies clasped. At last, Kitty steps out, blows a last kiss back at him.

The man reverses and turns while Kitty stands there straightening her skirt. Then, in her high heels, Kitty picks her way across the muddy farmyard.

At the dinner table, Kitty asks for a linen dishcloth to spread over her new blouse. Jo watches how her sister eats in this new, compact way—the delicate little forks of potato, little slices of roast beef. Her plate is still half full when Kitty announces that she couldn't possibly eat another bite, while Jo, whose waist is already thickening, gobbles down the slathers of meat and spud and carrot. She's already craving the trifle and custard and tea that will follow. These days, she could eat the house.

Jo catches her sister studying John, a perplexed look, as if Kitty can't quite recall how John Dowd got here, in this house, at their family table. Jo sees herself through her sister's eyes. Nowadays, she smells of the yard and the stables, her legs have the permanent mark of her black Wellingtons. She keeps her thick hair clipped back with hair clips because it's easier that way.

Across the table, Jo watches her sister's animated face, the red-lacquered nails fluttering like bright butterflies. She shuts her eyes and wills it to last, wills the man in the black car to run his motor into a ditch, to break an axle or burst a tire.

After dessert and tea, the men go back to the fields while Mother sits by the range and dozes. Jo shoots her sister their old, secret look and darts her eyes toward the kitchen and the yard. The sisters tiptoe out across the scullery, close the back door softly behind them.

Out in this blustery March day, the apple trees creak above their heads.

"Kit, I'm expecting. A baby."

Kitty shrieks. "How long? What day? It's going to be a girl. I just know it's a girl!"

Then Kitty takes her sister's hands and twirls her around. In the yard, the sisters skip and dance, ring-around-the-roses. "Brilliant!" Kitty shrieks. "Such fantastic news!"

So Jo supposes that it is.

Jo and Ellen

15

THE SMELL OF TURF SMOKE is stronger here, just inside the farmyard gate, so close to the Dowds' house. Ellen watches a small man walking across the yard. It's a smaller, second farmyard that sits just beyond the house. His shoulders are hunched into the rain. He wears an old tweed cap and a thick moustache.

The man uncurls a green water hose from over his shoulder, bends to set the end over the edge of a water trough. He hasn't seen Ellen yet. Hasn't seen the American girl who has walked up here in the rain.

The name comes to her. Fintan's voice: *We had a man who used to work for us in the busy season, a farmhand. Ned. Then, after my father's death, he came every day.*

Ellen wonders if she should cough, announce herself. No. Too late. He's straightened up and now he's standing there staring at her.

"Hi. Um . . . Hello. Hi there." She takes a few steps closer, as if approaching a cross dog. "I'm here to see Mrs. Dowd."

She watches him flinch at her voice, her American accent. Then realization dawns across his face. He stubs out the cigarette with his boot. He looks down the yard past her, obviously wondering how she has suddenly materialized like this. He fumbles in his pants pocket. He takes out another cigarette but doesn't light it.

"Is she in?" Her voice is gentle, tentative. He knows, she thinks. He somehow knows who I am.

"Yeah, she's *in* but she's . . . ah . . ." She follows his gaze toward the grey stone house. From here, it looks huge—a big, stolid farmhouse with a slate roof and double chimneys. The curtains on the gable window are drawn. It's Jo's room. She can tell.

"She's still sleeping?"

Ned has the same guarded look as the village priest. "Well, when the day is wet like this, she's not that . . ."

"Right."

"She was asleep this morning anyways, when I went in. It's th'oul damp. Plays hell with us all."

"Look, could I just go in? See for myself?"

He meets her eyes at last. Something about her drenched state softens him. "If you don't knock or make noise, she probably won't even waken. So no differ."

Inside the back door is a line of hanging rain coats, winter coats, woolen hats, rubber gum boots standing toes to the wall. An electric clock ticks loudly from the patch of wall above the window. There's an electric kettle next to the sink. The house smells of boiled cabbage.

In a second, inner kitchen, someone has set a fire in the ceramic range. On each side of the range sits a high-backed wooden armchair, the arms worn shiny with age. The chair opposite the television has a stack of white bed pillows.

On the table is an upturned teacup on its saucer, a Yoplait strawberry yogurt, an unopened packet of wheat bread. Someone has set a bunch of fat green grapes in a white bowl.

*

Jo starts awake. There's a noise, a noise that woke her. She was dreaming again, some daft dream about John and Kitty and Mother. The noise now. It's in the kitchen. Clank-clank. Is it the range door? And there are footsteps back and forth. No, not Ned. The footsteps too light for Ned. And it's not a dream. Not now. Someone's in the house. Was someone supposed to come? She forces her mind to remember, forces it awake and all the way out of the murk, the clouded murk of sleep and tablets. No. Ned has already been here. Earlier, she heard him tiptoe in, half-opened her eyes to see him standing at the parlor door again. This morning? Yes, this morning. Not yesterday.

Tick-tick-tick. She listens to the rain in the yard, drip-dripping onto the window-sill.

Another noise. Down in the kitchen, there's someone pacing. Jesus. She lies still as a corpse. It's someone who has come to rob her, to kill her in her own bed. Ned. Jesus, Ned where are you?

On the telly, on the news, all those stories about old people tied to their own kitchen chairs and left there for days, their life savings robbed, their bodies beaten black and blue.

No. No. By hell, it's not going to happen to her. She levers herself up on her elbows. Yes. Good. Her walking stick is there, crooked on the bottom bed rail. If she's careful, she can walk out there quiet as a ghost. *She'll* surprise them, whoever they are, not the other way around. She'll beat their bloody brains out.

*

Ellen is turning to leave, to tiptoe back up through the scullery when she hears the sound. Turning, she sees the old woman standing there, a walking cane held high, a murderous face under wild, grey hair.

They stand there. Jo has Fintan's deep-set eyes. Jo's mouth falls open, a puppet unhinged. She's fully dressed in crumpled pants and a stained, beige cardigan. The old woman has obviously been asleep. At last Jo lowers the cane. "I heard someone. I heard someone in the house."

"Hi. Mrs. Dowd? I'm . . . I'm Ellen. I'm sorry to just come like this, but Ned said it might be okay." Ellen hears how stupid, how whiny-childlike her voice sounds. She pushes on. "We talked on the phone. Last week." Jo is older, so much older than the first communion photo in the church. And across the sweltering kitchen, Ellen gets a body smell, a sour, sulfuric whiff.

Jo Dowd sniffs at her. "You . . . you better sit down a minute."

*

Ellen listens to the scullery cupboards being opened and slapped shut, then a kettle on the boil. Then at last, Jo crosses the kitchen with a metal teapot. She walks slowly, painfully. She sets the tea on the table, then produces an empty mug from the big cardigan pocket. She sets the mug in front of Ellen. "I've no milk. I don't take milk myself."

From her chair, Jo reaches into the windowsill, which is crowded with old magazines and letters. Jo produces a tin ashtray that is already overflowing with ash and cigarette butts. She sets it next to the upturned cup, then pushes away all the other breakfast things—the yogurt, the bowl of grapes. She produces a gold packet of cigarettes and a disposable lighter from her cardigan pocket, then offers the packet across the table. "Take a fag?"

Ellen shakes her head. "No thanks."

Jo pours the tea. Then she lights up and takes a long, deep draw. Ellen watches the cigarette trapped between the brown-stained fingers.

Jo reaches back into the windowsill again. This time she produces a white envelope, which she tosses onto the table between them. Ellen stares at the three postal stamps with the American stars and stripes, the faded post-office mark, "Essex County, Massachusetts." It's Ellen's own handwriting: "To the family of Fintan Dowd, Gowna, County Mayo."

To the family. This family, here. Now. This old woman in her dirty cardigan and her fierce, sunken eyes. This old woman who keeps puffing on her cigarette and won't meet Ellen's eyes.

Ned saw this letter. That's how he recognized her just now, outside in the yard.

Loudly, Jo sets her teacup down. "Last week . . . or whenever it was . . . on the phone. You must've thought I was coddin' or something. I told you on the phone that there's nothing here for you. And I'm telling you the same thing now." For the first time at the kitchen table, Jo fully meets Ellen's eyes. "You shouldn't have come."

What? Ellen asks Fintan inside her head. What was it about this decrepit old woman that you wanted to keep from your own wife, to lie about her very existence?

Jo looks a little demented. She jabs a cigarette hand at the letter. "That's a quare way to inform a mother of her son's death."

These are Fintan's eyes—the day when their kitchen sink had leaked and he was spitting, raging mad. Or once, when he ran out of gas on a rush-hour highway. There he is standing on the shoulder of the highway seething, screaming, blaming.

Jo says, "August. Last August. Nine months—nine months and you could've written to me, lifted the bloody phone. To his own mother. When a person passes like that, you let the family know straight away."

Jo takes another slug of her tea, another drag of the cigarette. "Look, I believe in calling a spade a spade. I'm not one for any of this soft talk or *plamás*. We weren't on speaking terms, myself and my son. Well you'd know that, wouldn't you? But of course you know that." The voice trails. "Years ago, before he left for . . ." Jo looks back to the crowded window, the swatch of dripping sky.

"An' I suppose a wife does what her husband tells her. He wouldn't contact, wouldn't come home to visit his own mother, so neither would you. Right? Take his side." She turns back to the table, meets Ellen's eyes. Jo's pupils are huge dark pools. The woman is someone's mad cartoon, a caricature gone wild. "Everyone says the Yank women are only little *peatas*. Not much good for anything but fashion and cars and skite-ing around the place—that and all that oul' yap. Sure, don't I see it all there on the Oprah program?"

Jo doesn't know that her son lied, said his mother was dead. She thinks he was just stubborn, vindictive, silent. Bad blood. Across the table, Ellen watches the face, those mad eyes.

Ellen feels relief. She's glad that Jo doesn't know. How would an old woman across the sea know a thing like that? And now, Ellen is not going to lambaste a sick woman with the truth, the story of her own erasure.

Suddenly, Jo's face turns red. She coughs and coughs, just like on the phone—that deep phlegmy cough. Hack-hack-hack, her eyes bulging, watering.

Ellen rounds the table to stand behind Jo's chair, watching the nubs of Jo's spine through the cardigan. I don't want to touch her, Ellen thinks. I can't be so intimate with this decrepit, smelly flesh, this woman who hates me.

Another cough, this one deeper, the air gurgling in Jo's chest.

Ellen grabs Jo under the arms, to help her to stand up, to catch her breath, but Jo jabs her elbow back, catches Ellen's right breast. "The phone?" Ellen asks. "Where's your phone?"

Jo shakes her head. No. No bloody phone calls.

Ellen runs to the back kitchen for a glass of water. Ned. Will he be there, magically, suddenly appear from the yard? When she returns, Jo has stopped coughing at last. She's sitting there masticating, swallowing phlegm.

"Here. Drink it." Ellen sets the water on the table. She hears the village priest's voice: *I heard she wasn't that well, a while back, there. The end of last summer. I don't know what it was. Maybe nothing. But she was in the hospital anyways.*

Jo reaches back into the cluttered window and produces what looks like a wad of newspapers. It's a paper spittoon, a hunk of newspapers crafted like a bird's nest. Into it, Jo spits something deep and thick.

The rain has grown heavier and loud against the kitchen window.

Jo has lit another cigarette. The color is coming back in her cheeks. Her voice comes quavery. "You said he drowned . . . ?"

"Yes. Out on a boat, a sailboat off Martha's Vineyard. It's an island."

"Isn't that where Teddy Kennedy was?"

"Yes. We were at a wedd—"

"—Were ye still married? When he . . . ?"

Ellen starts. What does the old woman know? "Yes. Yes, we were still married."

"Sure, what business had he in a boat? When that boy left here he couldn't swim."

"No. And he never learned. Actually, I used to tease . . ." Ellen stops herself.

Jo squishes out the second cigarette, sits upright in the kitchen chair, holding her breath, blinking, as if waiting for some pain to pass.

"Mrs. Dowd, are . . . are you all right?"

"It's just a bit of arthritis. In my back. At my age, it's hardly disco dancing I'd be."

Now Jo reaches for the teapot again, though the tea has to be cold. This time, the voice turns sly. "There's nothing here for you, you know. I told you that."

"Mrs. Dowd, I—"

"—Well, if you're thinking you're the widow of the only child and all that. Well, faith an' I've news for you. There's nothing to be got." Jo waves a bony hand to take in the window, the dripping gardens outside. "I've it taken care of with my solicitor in the town. Where it's all going. When I'm gone." She leans toward Ellen. Taunting eyes. "When I'm dead."

You're already supposed to be. Dead. "I . . . assure you, Mrs. Dowd. I haven't come for anything like that. I have a perfectly good job."

Jo jabs toward the letter. "Yes. I see. Looks like you're some class of a lecturer or something."

"A teacher."

"Then what brought you here?"

"I guess I thought . . ." They lock gazes. "My husband spent his youth here. So I thought I'd just see the place where he left, once lived. He talked a lot about it, about Gowna. And he talked a lot about you."

"Did he?" Jo's expression is doubtful. But there's a glimmer of hope. His mother wants to believe this.

"So I had my summer vacation and thought I'd just take a jaunt over. I'm staying at Flanagan's. Flanagan's Hotel."

Jo sniffs. "So you're like them all so, all the Yanks that come. Except you came to look up *his* roots, not your own?"

16

ELLEN. Jo recites the name in her head, rolls it around among her racing thoughts. *Ellen.* Funny how that name is changed now, all changed. Even though it's the same signature on that letter Jo got late last November. But now, in just one day, it's all changed.

She can't go walking the land today—not with this jittering in her back and legs. And she's tired, dead tired.

The telly warbles from its shelf. There's a fella sitting on a high stool with a guitar, a studio audience full of women in frilly blouses and fixed smiles, all singing and clapping along to his song. It's an afternoon program for old people. "Oh dear / what can the matter be? / Seven old maids they were locked in the lavatory." The audience women laugh and pretend not to watch the panning camera.

No walking today. Not with the rain dancing off the yard. Jo's high fireside armchair and its stacked-up pillows can't trap the pain, the pain that snakes and circles up her back. And it can't contain this awful jitter, this rat-tat-tat through her bones.

" . . . and nobody knew they were there," sings the eegit on the telly. The audience laughs obligingly.

Jo picks up the remote. Her hand trembles as she clicks onto another channel. This time it's a children's program, though there's not much difference between the two. Now it's more nursery rhymes and *isn't that right, boys and girls?*

Children. Jesus, she never thought to ask the girl, Ellen, the Yank if there are children, Jo's own grandchildren, little American kids with high-pitched voices.

It's a shock to think of it, this hour of her life. A strange thought, to imagine some young lives that would keep going on, long after her own life is over.

Is that why that girl came here? To claim some sort of Irish life or money for her kids? Jo glances toward the kitchen table, the two dirty teacups, the teapot, the grapes that nobody has touched. She stares at the empty chair where, just over an hour ago, her boy's wife sat, the American accent, voice here, still here in this kitchen. She sees the small hands, the pretty little face, the sad, secretive eyes. Oh, yes, the Yank girl is telling lies about something. Jo Dowd would bet her life on it.

Ellen. She's a hundred miles from how Jo imagined her.

Jo has never told anyone this, and certainly not that Fionnuala McCormack, that chattery little woman she used to meet in the supermarket in Ballinkeady—the one who had that daughter in America. What was her name, the daughter? Siobhán? Sarah? No. Sheila. Yes, Sheila McCormack. The mother thought the sun shone out of the daughter's backside. She loved delivering news from Boston. *My daughter knows your son over there. Isn't it grand for them, neighbors' children you might say, in a foreign country. Sure, there's nobody like your own people . . .*

It was Fionnuala McCormack who told Jo where her son was, where he worked. And Fionnuala told Jo about the marriage to that Yank. The little woman is like one of those talking dolls. You just pull the string and she blathers on and you just have to nod your head and say, "right" and "oh, is that so?"

There she is now, leaning over the supermarket trolley in a red winter coat, that little lipsticked face. *Tell us, Mrs. Dowd, had you a great time at the wedding beyond? Was that your first time in America, Mrs. Dowd? It was? Oh, well next month now'll be our third. Sure you never feel it really, on the plane, the dinner and the film and a bit of a sleep and sure, before you know it, aren't you landed beyond? So your Fintan met you at the airport I suppose? Oh, yeah, our Sheila's always there waiting when we get off the plane. So, tell us, ye'd a great time so. Ah, it's sad really when they get married, isn't it? Like, you're happy they met someone but still there's an oul' twinge of sadness, too . . .*

Jo remembers that day, the day that silly woman told her about the boy's marriage. The two women were standing under the terrible white lights and with the supermarket smell of roasting chickens. She watched the little mouth still moving—yap, yap, yap—and she imagined her own big hands above that red coat collar, her own fingers squeezing around the little neck, throttling that woman like a chicken.

Afterward, all the way out home to Gowna in the hackney car, the words thudded through Jo's head: *He's married. My boy married.* And then, here came that stupid hope: Maybe this Yank will soften him, make him ring or write to his own mother.

For years, Jo used to finish her jobs early on St. Patrick's night. She came in from the yard to watch the St. Patrick's Day parades on the telly. She sat right here watching all those bands and dancers and the American police marching between tall grey buildings. She watched the people leaning and waving from balconies. It was stupid, she knew that, and she used to mock herself as she sat scanning the faces for him. But she imagined that he had just appeared, on the screen. That he'd come walking around a corner, just there from beyond the police barriers.

After that day in the supermarket, Jo used to picture the girl he married. Sitting here by the range, darning a sock or patching a trouser, one eye on those American television comedies with the gust of laughter after every line. That one with the wispy blond hair? No, that one, the short brunette? Or what about that one with the pointed bust and the glittering teeth? Was Jo's American daughter-in-law just like her?

Now they have a dog on the children's program. It's one of those pet dogs with a red collar and floppy ears. "No, no, no. Now, remember what we said, boys and girls? You have to *guess* his name," says the presenter, a fella that looks more like a woman than a man—more like a woman than an actual woman.

Now Jo's daughter-in-law has come. To this house. And she's not a bit like those television girls. Jesus, why hadn't Jo asked? Surely a woman should know if there are children, young Dowds, her own flesh and blood, sitting in an American house in Boston?

The racket from the telly makes the pain worse. Jo clicks the mute button, then watches the man with his studio smile. Now the television dog is sitting in a round-backed chair, its paws set on the desk, its head turned as if waiting for the interviewer's next question.

Jo used to have a dream, a repeating dream of a little blond girl with her hand clasped in a man's hand, both of them walking down a footpath in a busy city, amid cars and buses and noise.

Always in that dream, Jo would be looking straight at the child, face to face, the little girl staring at her, a chubby little hand pawing at her grandmother's face. Jo would open her mouth to talk to her, to say "hello," but her own voice would suddenly turn mute. The words, the endearments just there—*Mo leana, mo leana bán*—but Jo's voice wouldn't come. In her upstairs bedroom, Jo would wake up and lie there. Flitters of the dream stayed. She could still see the little girl's face. That dream always left her sad.

Maybe the girl in the dream was an American grandchild.

*

The telly glows blue and bright in the dark kitchen. It's the nine o'clock news already. What? Impossible. She must have fallen asleep here in her chair, her head lolling back against the kitchen wall. The house is freezing; the fire in the range gone out.

Now the pain has leaked, crawled up and down her spine to the rest of her. And the shakes! Jesus, the shakes!

Jo eases herself out of the armchair, gropes for the walking cane looped on the kitchen chair. Tap-tap-tap across the kitchen floor to the light switch, then across the front hall to the parlor. Fifteen more steps. Fourteen. Twelve.

She can see it from here, the pain patch, one of the pain patches that Ned got her at the vet's. She can taste it now, already, the tiny dab of white powder that she puts on her tongue. It's worse than a broken tablet it's so bitter, poison-bitter. But it always stops this pain and shaking.

17

ELLEN IS STANDING in the shadows, watching a crowd in a town square. The people stand in the sunshine whispering, watching, waiting. There, under a lamppost, stands Louise, Ellen's sister. And there's Viktor Ortiz, her colleague and next-door neighbor at Coventry Academy, standing there in his ponytail, holding his leather satchel. Viktor calls to her: "*Ellenita! Ellenita!*"

Brrring! Brring! A girl on a bicycle comes weaving among the lawns and pathways. The crowds part for her, laughing. The voices and excitement grow. "Brrring, brrring!" The girl rings her bicycle bell again.

From her shadowy place, Ellen knows she's supposed to join them, join them all, supposed to be there in their midst, the welcome party for the bicycle girl.

"*Ellenita! Ellenita!*" Viktor calls again, beckoning frantically. "You gotta come here."

The bicycle bell is louder, more insistent. Brrr-ring! Brrr-ring!

Ellen starts awake, the dream-voices and faces still there in the bedroom. A stripe of streetlight shines between the flowered drapes. I'm in Ireland, in Gowna. It was just a dream.

The ringing persists. It's the phone on the wall above her bed.

"Hello?" Ellen says. The bedside clock radio says 4:40. Someone is heavy-breathing down the phone. "Hello? *Hello?* Who *is* this?"

It's Thursday night. Friday morning.

The telephone breaths come heavier. Some weirdo. Just hang up. Then Jo Dowd's voice: "Are there children?" Jo's voice is slurred, a vinyl record set at the wrong speed. "I never asked you. But then, here I was dreaming of a girl, a lovely *girlín,* and I never asked you. When you were up here. Have I grandchildren?"

The quilt has slithered from Ellen's shoulders. A cold, damp breeze comes through the hotel bedroom window. "Mrs. Dowd? Where are you?"

"I *have* to know, you see. A person should know if there are grandchildren. If I'm leaving anyone after me."

"Mrs. D—"

"A woman wrote to me. Wrote to me that he'd died. She sent a letter. Then another woman came, up here to the house . . ." The voice stalls.

Ellen grips the receiver tighter. She listens to the deep, syrupy breaths. "Mrs. Dowd?"

There's a loud thump. The telephone line buzzes. "Mrs. *Dowd?* Where are you?"

Ellen hangs up. She sits and waits for the phone to ring again. Then she crosses to her dressing table for her purse, the Dowds' phone number. When she dials Jo's house, there's a busy tone. Shit. Jo hasn't hung up.

*

The heavy dawn mist shrouds the house, its grey contours. This time, Ellen drives all the way up the avenue and parks outside the farmyard gate. At last, there's the light in the gable window.

Ellen pushes in the back door to a man's voice booming through the downstairs of the house. Relief. Someone is here. She follows the voice into the kitchen, where it's dark except for the blue glow of the television. The voice is a newscaster's homogenized accent delivering an early-morning news program.

Through a shadowy sitting room, the lumpy silhouettes of couches, armchairs, Ellen sees the strip of light under a second door, the gable room. "Hello?" she calls.

Jo's bedroom stinks of old cigarettes. Someone has bumped into the bedside lamp; the shade is cockeyed. Jo is slumped and snoring in a chair between the dressing table and window, still in the same cardigan and trousers, sitting there facing her own empty bed. Her head is lolled forward on her chest.

The buzz from the dangling black telephone receiver rivals Jo's snores. Ellen creaks across the linoleum floor to hang it up. Then she touches her mother-in-law's shoulder. "Mrs. Dowd?"

Nothing. Ellen taps, cartoon-like, on the shoulder. "Jo. Jo. You've got to wake up!"

"Oh!" Jo starts awake. The eyes are wild. There's no recognition. The pupils are tiny.

"I'm Ellen, Fintan's wife. Your son. You called me. At my hotel."

Jo stares blankly. A lock of greasy grey hair droops forward, escaped from its hair clip.

The bed has a long dent under the blankets, like an animal's burrow. On the nightstand, there's an ashtray, a glass of curdled milk, empty pill bottles, and what looks like a small, miniature diaper. "Mrs. Dowd, you should get into bed now."

Jo blinks back at Ellen. Then she looks to the bedroom window where it's still dark out. The mist has delayed the summer dawn.

At last, the words come slow and slurred. "Father hasn't been feeling that well, you know. The chest. His bad chest. Did you know that? And Kitty's gone. Kitty's gone off and away to Dublin again. I'd only just come in from the fields. So I woke up. He drowned, the doctor said. Father, my poor father, drowned." Then the chin lolls forward again.

"Look, Mrs. Dowd, I'm going to help you back to bed, then I'm calling 9-1-1."

Jo stares at her. "Ach, it's time to get up now anyway. They'll all be up here, from the church, the funeral. Father. Father's dead. Nobody knows. Ned can do the herding. Though they printed it in the paper, *The Independent*."

Jo starts to get up, her right hand rising, scrabbling at the air. She leans on the edge of the dressing table, sets it rocking on its legs. Jo levers herself up further. Then she stands there, frozen, her eyes popping with pain.

Ellen grabs her around the waist, a drowning grip. Then the two women limp across the room, where Ellen lowers her slowly onto the bed. "Jo? Jo? Are you awake? Answer me!"

Her arm still supporting the older woman, Ellen eases her further into bed, sets her like a mannequin against the pillows. The loud snoring starts again.

Ellen crosses to retrieve the black phone from the floor. She dials zero. Zero for the operator.

*

"*Fin*tan?" says Dr. Tom Fitzgerald. He's standing in Jo's kitchen, taking Ellen in, head to toe. "You're Fintan's *wife?*" The red-haired doctor is smiling, a staged smile. But there's something in his expression that is edgy, terrified.

Ellen nods. "Yes."

"Well . . ." The doctor swallows. Then he looks past Ellen's shoulders toward the hallway, Jo Dowd's narrow staircase. "Is he . . . ?"

Christ, Ellen thinks. He doesn't know. Jo got my letter and never even told her own doctor that her son, her only son, was dead.

"He's not here, Doctor. He died. Almost a year ago. So it's just me. I'm here." She gives a tight laugh. "Well, as you can see."

The doctor blinks at her. "Died? You're not serious?" He runs a hand through his red hair. Ellen studies the little gingery hairs along the back of his freckled hands.

"I'm Ellen." She feels stupid. Tom Fitzgerald is still staring down at her, his head cocked to the side. Waiting for her to add something else. "Boisvert," she says. "Ellen Boisvert."

"I'm sorry for your trouble." He extends a handshake. He seems slightly relieved.

The doctor is the caricature Irishman. His freckled face under red hair that is thinning at the temples. He wears a rumpled shirt under a beige corduroy jacket. "I'm sorry. I'm . . . God. And she never bloody told me. Never! Heart?"

"What?" Did Fintan have one? Yes. No.

"Was it a heart attack?" the doctor prompts. "That young, it's usually . . ."

"No. He drowned. In a sailing accident." She says those words again, so easy, so practiced, like a prayer. Her husband's death has become a story, almost a party piece. "It happened last August."

He is calculating dates. "August. Yeah. That was when she got sick first. Didn't ring me of course until it was all gone too far. Coughing up blood; hardly able to get out of bed." He stares at her, bewildered.

"So you knew him?" It comes in a whisper.

"Knew him? Yeah, of course. He was a class behind me at school, down in the village, you know. Then we were in college in Dublin together—though he was commerce—business studies, and I was premed. Neighbors' children away together, up in the big smoke, you know. The college students' code of secrecy." He mimics that zipping-the-mouth-shut motion. Then he flashes her a smile. Dr. Tom Fitzgerald likes to be liked.

On the kitchen table is a box with a pharmaceutical company's name, a box of animal pain patches, a veterinarian's typed label: Mr. Edward McHugh.

Fentanyl patches, Dr. Fitzgerald called them. It's what Ellen thought was a diaper on the bedside table. Jo, it seems, has been ripping them open, measuring, gauging, and ingesting tiny amounts of the animal powder for her pain.

Earlier, Dr. Fitzgerald went searching for other secret supplies. He yanked open the cupboards in the scullery, even looked under her bed while she slept. But so far, he has only found this one box.

He opens his doctor's bag, takes out a gadget and starts to punch buttons, typing something in there. Parp-parp-parp.

"What's going to happen with her?" Ellen asks, gesturing her head toward the parlor.

The doctor levels his eyes on her. "She's not in a fully fledged overdose—respiratory distress—I mean, not from the fentanyl anyway, but of course, she knew what she was doing; knew to take just enough. But then there's her normal distress from the cancer."

He goes back to his gadget and deletes something.

Cancer. The word is just here, pronounced aloud in the freezing kitchen. Suddenly, Ellen knows she's been expecting it, that she has known this, ever since that day she came here. Jo Dowd has cancer. All that coughing and those lies about arthritic pain.

Dr. Fitzgerald drops his gadget back into the bag. "Sorry. I have to log that immediately or else it's no good."

They are sitting at the kitchen table, Jo's metal teapot set between them, a mug of scalding tea each. Dr. Fitzgerald says, "You know, I did wonder why Fintan never came home when she was in the hospital. When we admitted her, I asked her if there was anyone she wanted me to ring, to contact—meaning, of course, her son. But then, you learn as a local doctor not to 'go there,' as they say. Even in a family you've been treating for years—actually, my father treated her and her sister, years ago—but you never know what happens in families. Especially with someone like . . ." He grimaces. "Well, sick or well, Jo can be a little . . ."

"Impossible?"

He laughs. "Yeah. But tough as nails, too. After the hospital, I got her the usual homecare. But she ran her day nurse out of here. Did she tell you that? Oh, no, of course she didn't. I got a phone call one day from the community health clinic in Ballinkeady saying there was nothing they could do. Nothing. In fact, the poor nurse—young, you know, and new to this end of the country—was ready to pack in the nursing gig altogether. Find a new career for herself."

"And you, Doctor?"

"Oh, call me Tom, please."

"Tom. You must've known she was in relapse? All this pain? The coughing?"

"No. No. I tried visiting a few times. I'd drive up the hill with the big lie that I was 'on my way someplace' though that's a tough one to swallow when you're the only house up here. But anyways, I came to visit and she'd meet me at the back door with the coat and hat on and the walking stick. She said I might have time for wandering the countryside bothering people and gossiping, but she had her land and cattle to check on."

He shrugs. "You can't force someone to call you out to their house. Or even come and see you." He studies Ellen. He's obviously deliberating whether to go on, how much more to tell. "I mean, we even tried the priest tactic—you know, parish priest—"

"Father Bradley?"

"Oh, you met him? Yeah, Noel's a grand fella. Did he tell you he's a champion bicycle racer? He's won nearly every race in Connaught. Well, anyways, myself and Noel met for a few pints down in Flanagan's one night, and, breaking my healthcare code of privacy of course, I tell him the story, see if *he* can give it a go, do the visiting priest on his rounds, visiting the elderly, part of the priestly 'job description,' you might say."

"And?"

Over his tea mug, Tom Fitzgerald pulls an "ouch" face. "Bad. Very bad. Noel comes up on his bicycle, *mar dheá* just out for a run, and there she is out with the stick, walking the avenue, mistress of all she surveyed."

"She gave him what for?"

"Yup. That's one way of putting it. Noel tried the caring priest routine—gives her the standard speech about the role of spirituality in healing and wellness. And she jabs the walking stick at him and says, "Isn't it time you got yourself a bloody job like the rest of the countryside? A job and a wife and kids? Then you mightn't have time to be out on your tricycle, bothering busy people with your oul' *pisreógs.*"

Tom Fitzgerald pours himself another cup of tea. He asks cautiously, "You *did* know she had cancer?"

She shakes her head. "No. This is my first visit. Ever. I only arrived Monday. I'm at the hotel, Flanagan's. That's where she called me earlier. Tonight."

He narrows his eyes to study her sitting there, her nightgown bunched inside her jeans, the blue sweatshirt she pulled on in her hotel room. Yes, ever since he came from Jo's bedroom, there's something he's been trying to figure out; something that doesn't add up for him.

"So you never came to visit?"

"There was no love lost—some sort of falling out between my late husband and his mother."

"Do you know what 'twas about?" He's studying her face. There is something guarded, hooded in his look.

She shakes her head. "No. They didn't speak."

Silence stretches between them. "Doctor, what's going to happen now? Happen to her?"

He spreads his hands. "We'll have to get her back into the hospital to run more tests. Re-stage her cancer. I mean, I'm presuming that's what's wrong, what"—he glances toward his leather bag—"why she went ordering Ned to get her illegal pain stuff. But the tests'll tell us everything. Then she'll have to have some kind of around-the-clock care, no matter what she says this time. Under the circumstances, a nursing home is the only choice." He looks around the chill, darkened kitchen—the clothesline strung above the range with two tattered dishcloths draped there. "She can't stay here. That's for sure."

They both stop, startled at the sound of the back door, then the footsteps, light, slow. Here's Ned in the kitchen doorway, the cap scrunched in his hand; the downcast look.

"Ned," Dr. Fitzgerald says in that expansive voice. "Musha, how'rya Ned? Come in!"

"Doctor? I saw your car and I got a bit of a fright."

"She's fine, Ned. She'd a bit of a turn, gave us all a bit of a fright, but she's asleep now."

Ned stares at the veterinarian's box on the table. He looks to the floor, a reprimanded child.

Dr. Fitzgerald says, "You could go in if you like, Ned. Just to see her."

"Ach, no, Doctor. No, 'long as I know she's all right. Anyways, I've jobs for doing abroad."

*

Tom Fitzgerald stands there in the yard, between the house and his Volvo station wagon. Turning, he lifts one hand to shade his eyes from the morning's pale sun over the house. He calls to Ellen in the back doorway. "You have my mobile number. Ring me *immediately* if there's anything unusual. Anything at all. I've to make a few calls, but then I'm back for the afternoon. So I'll be in my surgery—my examining room. I'll come back out here around fiveish. We'll just let her sleep."

We'll let her sleep. He assumes that Ellen is part of Jo's care, or at least, she's part of today's emergency team. Ellen's voice comes exhausted, scratchy. "Sounds fine. I'll stay here."

Tom heads to the car. Then, "Oh, and Ellen?"

"Yeah."

"I'm sorry. Again. I . . . I still can't really believe . . . I mean about Fintan."

18

"NO. THESE *ARE* THE ONLY OPTIONS," says Tom Fitzgerald.

They are sitting in a triangle at Jo's kitchen table—Jo in her usual spot inside the window, Ellen and Dr. Tom Fitzgerald along the side, their backs to the kitchen range. The doctor rocks backward on the kitchen chair.

Jo's face is flaccid. Still dressed in her stained old cardigan and the crumpled brown pants, but she's surprisingly chipper and rested. Ellen watches the old woman's eyes stray toward the windowsill, toward the ashtray and the cigarettes, where they're stashed under a newspaper.

Tom brings the chair legs down, a loud thwack on the linoleum floor. "Mrs. Dowd, we can't know what's going on, what the prognosis or treatments are until we get you admitted. Sorry. No other choice."

Jo sniffs. "Yes. Yes, I'm not an *óinseach*." Then she coughs, that haunting, gurgly cough. But now Jo gets her breath sooner, faster, as if to defy the young doctor.

With a dry little laugh Tom says, "No, you're certainly not a fool, any woman who can swindle a poor man like Ned into getting you un-prescribed medicines."

Jo's eyes snap. "That's my business. Not yours." Then she turns away to the window again. Her grey hair is pillow-flat. It badly needs a wash.

Tom shoots Ellen a defeated look.

Since he left this morning, Ellen has wandered around Jo's house and yard, then napped on the parlor couch, listening for sounds from the bedroom. Once, she woke with a stiff neck and lay there listening for the sounds of breathing from beyond the door. I could just leave, she thought.

Tiptoe out through that back door and into my rental car and keep driving to Shannon Airport. She may never remember my being here. From across the sea and my newly found apartment or condo in Coventry-by-the-Sea, I need never inquire for her, never call the hospital in Galway where they plan to take her for another round of tests. And afterward? I will never know whether my husband's secret mother is alive or dead.

Now Jo says, "What if I make up my mind to just stay here, here in my own house? No more of them bloody machines and the wakening you up in the middle of the night for nothing; bloody nurses talking to you like you're gone *seafóid* in the head."

Tom Fitzgerald sighs, then rocks the chair backward again. "You *could* stay here. For a while. Maybe even three days until I get you a bed in the hospital. Sooner, not later. But we can't plan your next treatment until we know more. Look, as it is, it's a miracle you didn't kill yourself with them pain—"

Jo interrupts. "Couldn't I just get some sort of a n—"

"—A nurse? You *had* a nurse and you sent her crying out of here."

Jo abandons caution and reaches into the window for the packet of cigarettes. She lights up, then inhales defiantly, blows the smoke toward the doctor. Tom rolls his eyes toward Ellen, shakes his head. I don't believe this, the look says.

The cigarette relaxes Jo. "I didn't like that woman. She was stupid. So once you"—a mimicking voice—"'decide my treatment'—what'll ye do with me then?"

"Depending on the results, they might discharge you. But then you'll need home nursing care. Twenty-four hours. We'll get a day nurse from the health board, no problem. And for the nights, we can just put in an advertisement for a caretaker, someone—"

We. We. We. Again. He keeps saying "we," Ellen thinks.

"—Someone that'd rob and murder me in my bed?"

Tom flinches from another gust of cigarette smoke. "Mrs. Dowd, it's standard care for someone in your situation."

Jo jabs her cigarette hand at him. "An ad? Sure there's nobody in this country'd take a job like that nowadays. Only foreigners. An' I won't have one of them here, won't have some latchigo from Latvia or some godforsaken place sleeping above stairs in my house."

A phone rings. Tom reaches into his inside-jacket pocket, looks at the small screen, snaps the phone open. "Hel-*lo,* there?! Okay, love. I'll be parked out front when you're finished, all right? And does Trina need a lift, too? Uh, huh. Right. See you. Bye-bye." He snaps it shut.

"My daughter, Riona. Goes to ballet lessons after school."

Tom raises his voice down the table. "Now, Mrs. Dowd, I'm going to get onto the hospital first thing tomorrow morning, and then I'll give you a ring here, or call out, so you can tell me when you're packed and ready."

"Keep your bloody voice down; I'm not deaf."

"Right, well. Tomorrow. Until then, you should get more sleep. And for God's sake, eat something."

Then for the second time that day, Dr. Tom Fitzgerald walks across Jo's kitchen to her back door.

*

Ellen and Jo stay at the kitchen table, the silence stretching between them. Jo has another coughing fit.

Ellen starts, "Can I get you?—"

"—I'm fine." She coughs up into the paper spittoon from the window. Jo winces when she shifts in the chair. She's obviously been holding off, waiting out this latest lower-back pain.

Earlier, Tom Fitzgerald left some pain pills—real, prescribed pills, to be taken at bedtime or as needed. One should last twelve hours. They work on a slow release.

Jo's voice is defensive. "I'm sorry I rang you last night. Sorry you had to come out here, interrupt your holiday."

Ellen takes her in—all of her, the cardigan, with the cuff edges burned and scorched from the kitchen range. The long grey hair filthy. I have already touched her, thinks Ellen. Could I actually stay and help the old woman get undressed again, offer to help her into a hot bath, a clean nightgown, pack a hospital bag for tomorrow? "I can stay tonight," Ellen says, almost a whisper.

Silence. She watches Jo's mouth moving, how the lips twitch, disappear.

At last, Jo says, "It's been a quare few hours, a quare night. I'd like to be left alone a while, in my own kitchen, my own telly to think things out about all this hospital rigmarole."

Down the table, Jo's eyes are mournful and defeated. "There's three rooms upstairs—two of them with beds in them. Pick which one you want. There's sheets up there someplace in the hot press. That fella"—she tilts her grey head—"he'll be back here tomorrow bothering me. If I stay alone all night he'll be even worse, I suppose."

Ellen looks down at herself, her crumpled jeans, the nightgown still stuffed inside the sweatshirt. "I need to go down to the village anyway; get some overnight things, grab something to eat. Then I'll come back. Will I bring you back something?"

"Take your time. I might even be gone to bed when you come back."

Outside, the early-evening sunlight is a surprise—the birds scrabbling and twittering in the apple orchard. There's Ned's car along the orchard wall, and Ellen's own black Fiat is there, just outside the yard gate. How strange that this summery day has gone on brightly, loudly.

Ellen doubles back into the house, across the scullery to the kitchen door. Jo has moved from the table to the chair by the range. The television is on; she's lit a new cigarette. The television burbles—a police program in which they enlist the public's support: "If you were in this area of Limerick and remember any suspicious activities . . ."

Ellen leans against the door jamb until Jo looks up and sees her. "I thought you were gone," says Jo.

"There weren't—aren't—any," Ellen says.

Jo looks annoyed. "What? Aren't any what?"

"Children. Mine and Fintan's. That's what you asked me, what you wanted to know when you called my hotel last night."

"Oh. Right." Jo is letting the words, the facts sink in.

"You wanted to know."

"Yes. I'm sorry."

"Don't be. It's a reasonable enough question."

"No. I mean I'm sorry you didn't . . . *don't*."

Now Jo stops watching the TV to meet her daughter-in-law's gaze. "Like, if that's what you wanted."

No, Ellen says silently to the old face across the kitchen. No, I didn't want your son's children.

She thinks this, says it aloud in her mind. Then, Ellen Boisvert knows that this has always been true.

19

SHE'S GOING TO SLEEP in Jo's old upstairs room, where she can hear the old woman knocking through the parlor ceiling. When Ellen got back from the village, Jo was asleep in her bed again, still in her clothes, snoring lightly.

Now Ellen sets her overnight bag against the upstairs landing wall. The door at the back of the house on the left of the landing beckons her. It was his room. She knows this.

The ceiling light is yellow-dull inside its green tasseled shade. The bedroom smells of old wood and dust. The small window onto the backyard is rimed with dirt and weather. Behind the door is a twin bed with a brown headboard, a blue candlewick bedspread pulled up over the pillows. Taped to the wall above the bed is a child's collage of blue and red satin ribbons. They're the prize ribbons you win at a horse or agricultural show.

Ellen yanks back the bedspread to a bare mattress, a faded striped print, two uncovered pillows with a mildew smell. She kneels on the bed to read the prize ribbons' white satin centers, the gold lettering: "Rosie Dowd, Second Prize, Cloonmount Sheepdog Trials, 1978." "Rosie Dowd. Two-year-olds. Best of Show." "Mayo Regional Sheepdog Trials."

Elsewhere along the bedroom walls, the green paint is stippled white from where someone once hung posters.

In the closet, two long-sleeved, checked shirts hang from the wire hangers. There's a pair of corduroy jeans, worn at the knees. She leans into this old, wooden armoire to bury her face and sniff his clothes. She searches in each pocket. In one, she finds a torn-off ticket like you get for readmission to a movie theater or a concert.

The bottom of the armoire is stacked with piles of hardcover books. They're business management and accounting textbooks. In each flyleaf is Fintan's erect, pointed handwriting: "Fintan J. Dowd, 23 Oak Grove Avenue, Whitehall, Dublin. If found lost, return to 01-564899."

She turns the books around to read the margin notes in faded pencil. Inserted between the pages are torn-off sheets from a spiral notebook with numbered lists, diagrams.

Shoved between the last two heavy volumes are some newspapers: *The Connaught People, The Western Farmer's Journal.* The newssheet has turned brittle and yellow. The photos are grainy. April 19, 1977. June 12, 1975. September 25, 1972.

Ellen carries the news pages across to the bed, where she sits and spreads the papers out across the blue bedspread.

"Fintan Dowd of Gowna, and his dog, Rosie, who won 'best-of-show' at the Annual Kiltubber Agricultural Show." "Fintan Dowd, Gowna, and his sheepdog, Rosie, who took first prize at the Rathloe Sheepdog Trials." "Mr. Vincent Thornton, manager and sponsor, Bank of Ireland, Ballinkeady, presents a savings bond for twenty pounds to young Fintan Dowd of Gowna, whose dog, Rosie, won first overall prize at last Sunday's sheepdog trials."

More clippings: a gallery of his young life: at age thirteen, fifteen. A halo of curls, those huge, framed spectacles, a triumphant, beaming grin. In one, he is on his hunkers, his arm around Rosie, just like in the Polaroid photo he brought to America. In another, he's wearing a Bay City Roller T-shirt, freckled arms; he's wearing the corduroy trousers in the wardrobe. A paisley-pattern shirt, a huge, butterfly collar, more bellbottom trousers. And here, in the last one, he's sporting an upper lip fuzz, the shadow of a schoolboy moustache.

She looks up from the news clippings, looks cautiously around his old room. The house and the night outside the window are silent, dead silent.

She carries the news clippings back to the wardrobe, replaces them where she found them, then piles the other textbooks on top.

A yellow envelope drops from a book. It's addressed to him, that same Dublin address from the books' flyleaves. She tilts the envelope into the light to read the return address: *Miss Carmel Cawley, 10, The Lane, Gowna,*

County Mayo. There's a greeting card inside, yellow roses in a vase. "Thinking of You." Folded into the card is another small news clipping.

"F, Aren't we just *gorgeous???* Love always, C."

On the card's left, inside flap: "P.S.: Don't worry. I might have something sorted already. Surprise!!! More at the weekend. C."

She studies this news photo. It's a close-up of Fintan in a tuxedo and bow tie. The girl comes to just above his chest, she's slightly turned toward him, her chin pitched toward the camera. Her dark hair is in a chignon, her bony shoulders under a gown with spaghetti straps. Just at the photo's bottom edge, they're holding hands.

Ellen crosses the room to bring the photo and its caption under the ceiling light. "Fintan Dowd, B.Comm, First-class hons., and Carmel Cawley, attending the University College Dublin Annual Ball at the Burlington Hotel, Dublin."

A university dance. And he took along this girl, a girl called Carmel Cawley who lives—or lived—in Gowna.

She's very pretty. With her dark eyes, she looks more Spanish than Irish. And she's older than Fintan. There's something world-worn, almost cynical in her features. Ellen brings the picture closer. A typesetter's smudge? No. On Carmel Cawley's left hand, her marriage finger, is a sparkly little ring.

*

Next morning Jo's eyes are bright and fierce as she sits there, propped against her pillows. She flutters a hand toward the chair next to the dressing table. "Sit."

Ellen obeys.

Jo's eyes are fixed straight ahead at the open parlor doorway. She has been preparing something, a speech. "I'm going to die soon." The voice is flat and expressionless.

"Mrs. Dowd, you don't actually know that."

"—So I've thought about it like I said I would, like I told that fella. No. No hospital for me. Once is enough. Enough of those bloody lies that nobody believes—not even the doctors themselves, except they make a few euro off it all. Sure don't I know I'm finished? So I'm staying. In my own house."

"But you'll—"

"It's not easy what I'm going to ask you. But you can't spend your life working with stock like I have, without knowing exactly the length that's left. So I know it won't be long. Young Fitzgerald below says I have to have someone. My husband has three grand-nephews. Thick as double-ditches all three of them. I wouldn't have one of them past that threshold." Jo raises her right hand, rubs her thumb and forefinger together—the international sign for money. "They'd be here for the one reason only. You can bet your life on that. Watching the land, what they can get. So I'd rather pay someone fair and square, a stranger." At last, Jo turns her gaze from the parlor door. She fixes her hollow eyes on Ellen. "You."

"I'm not exactly a stranger."

"It'll be two months. No longer. You said you're a teacher, so you're on holidays anyways."

Two months. Sitting here, Ellen and Fintan's lives come rushing through her head like a vintage comedy where everyone keeps rushing about, doors opening and closing, each looking for but just missing the other—while, all along, the audience knows and laughs. New jobs, a new apartment, night school, promotions, both of them studying for their master's degrees. Doors banging, yesterday's clothes in the laundry hamper, a succession of notes left on the fridge, on the kitchen table: *Back at eight. Gone for a run. Chicken in fridge. Gone to library.* Married for thirteen years, but it could just as easily have been thirteen weeks, or thirteen days.

Or a few hours or days can be longer than forever. Like those days on Martha's Vineyard, the days when Ellen waited and slept in a stranger's house until they found his body. She can still feel the heft of that time, hour by long, endless hour.

Jo's grey hair is splayed against the discolored pillow. Fintan's eyes. Fintan after they had pulled him from the sea off Martha's Vineyard—swollen, blue-faced, his hair in a salty starfish.

Last night, when Ellen dozed upstairs in Jo's old bed, she saw that drowned face in her dreams. This morning she woke up from her fitful sleep. She felt a terrible, wailing sorrow.

"All right," Ellen says. "Yes. I'll stay. And no, no pay."

20

"WE'LL PAY FOR THIS YET," the woman from Gowna Foodmart says, hands on hips and looking up at the pink evening sky over Flanagan's Hotel. The woman has followed Ellen out onto the sidewalk to take her sandwich-board sign—"Fresh sandwiches. Take-away Coffee & Tea"—in for the night. "We'll get rain sometime. Bound to."

"Goodnight," Ellen calls over her shoulder, hitching the cardboard box of groceries higher into her arms.

"Right," the woman calls, carrying in her sign.

Ellen's little black Fiat is parked just up past the hotel's parking lot, and her one suitcase is packed up and sitting on the back seat, ready to move into Jo Dowd's house.

Her steps are loud going up the sidewalk. There's Gerry Flanagan's domed head watching her over the café curtain in the hotel's lounge window.

Earlier, when she checked out of the hotel a day earlier than scheduled, she stood at the hotel desk, pan-faced at his sly little questions: *You going off touring around someplace else for yourself? Or back to the States? The husband couldn't survive without you?*

In the hotel parking lot, four cars and two farm tractors are parked carelessly, at angles to the high, cement wall. Four men sit around the wooden picnic table, pints of beer under the Heineken umbrella. There's one extra big tractor parked against the wall, the machinery hitched up high behind it like a set of giant brown teeth. The men eye her as she walks past.

She sets her box of groceries on the car's passenger seat. She locks the car again to walk up past the houses with their front windows set open to the summer evening, a radio or TV warbling from a curtained living room.

The window boxes are bright with pink and red geraniums. Someone is barbecuing in a backyard.

She studies the sidewalk, the cracks in the cement, the green, scummy triangles where a drain pipe has spit out onto the sidewalk.

Ellen turns down Church Street, past the churchyard with its yew trees and the cooing pigeons. It would actually be nice to bump into Father Noel Bradley again. It would be nice to sit in his garden and have that beer he promised. And ask him, please, to open up the church records and check . . . what? Marriage records? Fintan Dowd and this girl called Carmel Cawley? A young marriage? Married in that era of no Irish divorces?

No. Stop. She shushes her racing thoughts. But in her mind's eye is that newspaper photo in Fintan's old room. An engagement ring. Or it could just as easily have been a dressy cocktail ring, a family heirloom, something to match her sparkly earrings and evening gown.

After the church and the newsagents, she turns down another street and then, here she is at the top of the lane that circles around the back of the village. There is no signpost. But this is it: the lane where Carmel Cawley once lived. Perhaps she still lives here.

Some of the one-story cottages are tourist-pretty with their tiny windows and natural stone walls. Others sag onto the sidewalk, their paintwork flaking. The neighbors on opposite sides could probably shake hands across the lane with each other, door to door.

In one house, through an open window, someone is sanding wood. In another, a baby is crying.

Number 10 stands halfway down; its dark grey paint is faded and flaked. The house's white trim has turned green with rain. Even in this warm evening, the front windows and doors are shut tight.

What if this Carmel girl really lives here? One of those women who never left town?

In Patterson Falls, New Hampshire, Ellen sees those girls in the supermarket or wheeling children along one of the town's side streets. Or once, on a summer weekend home, when Ellen's parents took her along to the potluck supper in the backyard of the town's firehouse, she met over half of her old classmates there—each of them fussing over dishes covered with tinfoil. Across the picnic tables, these girls she once knew introduced their husbands, screamed at their kids, then asked her about life in Boston. All of it tinged with resentful sarcasm, an assumption that she, Ellen condescended to or pitied them.

Have Carmel and her family already heard about me? Has someone in Gowna already said something about the American woman way out there on the farm in Knockduff? And now Carmel Cawley is watching me from a secret window.

The Cawleys' door opens. A man steps out, pulling a sweatshirt down over his head, over a stained T-shirt. From the sidewalk, he turns back into the doorway, calls something to someone just inside the house. Then he turns back to the lane and sees Ellen, his puzzlement giving way to recognition.

It's the man she saw at the lake, at Lough Gowna, the man with the little girl, the one who was fixing his rowboat.

"How'ya! I didn't expect to see you still around these parts!" He tilts his head toward the back gardens and fences behind him, and the backs of the Main Street houses. "Still staying below at Flanagan's?"

"No. Yes. Hi." Why has she lied to him?

He closes the distance between them on the sidewalk. "I left my tractor parked down there—in the car park. Listen, would you fancy a pint? Or a gin or something?"

She forces a smile. "No. Thanks, but I have to be somewhere. See someone."

He arches his eyebrows at her. He doesn't believe her. He shoves his hands in his jeans pockets. "So when are you off back to the States?"

"Not for a while yet."

"Right. Sure, maybe another time. He gets in a band on Saturday nights. And the fishermen should be down at the weekend—the mayfly lads. We could have the chat, the pair of us, maybe an oul' dance, too. I'll ask for you below at the hotel."

Then the man saunters past her on down the lane, turns into the street.

Something wet and cold brushes Ellen's leg. It's a small dog, black face with a white smudge between the eyes. She can smell its filthy coat, its bad breath. It sniffs her feet.

"Go home." Ellen tells the dog—and herself. The smelly dog obeys and trots on down the lane. Then it stops to lift its leg against a drain pipe.

Is this Carmel Cawley's husband? If so, why is he asking her for drinks? Yes. She remembers his little girl, the little girl said that she and her brother lived part time with her mummy, then sometimes with her granny.

Cat

21

TERRENCE RESTS HIS ELBOW on the ledge of the open car window. He taps on the steering wheel as they wait for a group of tourists to cross at the traffic light, all dawdley and slow, the leader guy glancing up from his London A-Z street map, pointing up the street. Japanese, all of them, with their backpacks and cameras and tight jeans. They're looking for Willington Market. Tourists always are.

From the passenger's seat, Cat Cawley sneaks a look at Terrence, who is her mother Carmel's latest boyfriend. They've moved into his flat, her and Mum, and now Cat Cawley has her own bedroom in the basement that smells a little bit. But still, it's a nice big room with lots of drawers and a full built-in wardrobe for her stuff.

Terrence always wears the same thing—these stupid dress shirts with the wide collars, white or pink or bright blue, and those really awful jeans, and a pinkie ring. He looks like he's going off to play piano in an old people's pub or a nursing home.

The traffic light turns green, and Terrence puts the car in gear again. But now an old woman in a green coat toddles across, pulling her wheelie plaid shopping bag behind her.

Usually Cat takes the tube. But this morning when she got up, there was Terrence sitting at the kitchen table smoking a fag and reading his *Daily Mail* and offering to drive Cat to her weekly dance lesson at Miss Jarkowski's Dance Studio in Kentish Town. Of course, when Terrence is being nice to his girlfriend's sixteen-year-old daughter, that only means one thing. It means they've had another fight last night, him and Mum, another fight as they staggered up the hill from the Rose and Crown. And now, Saturday morning, and Terrence is giving her a lift to dance class 'cos he's sucking up.

They're driving again—past the shops with silver security shutters locked over the front windows, past an Internet café, a pub, an Indian takeaway, a bus stop, a corner shop with bright pink signs for special offers on Bacardi. There are spindly trees in a small town park, a children's playground outside a row of council flats. In the car, Terrence always plays a really bad radio station, and sometimes he even sings along—stupid songs that nobody's ever heard of except him.

When he changes gears he brushes her leg. Always. Always does that. Pervey sod.

He turns and smiles at her. "All right then, Catherine?" he asks.

Cat. Stupid wanker. She's told him ten million times that's what she wants to be called. "Yeah. Fine." She starts picking some black nail varnish off the nails on her left hand.

Just what's Mum see in him anyway? Not her type, Terrence, and he's totally not like her other boyfriends, who actually were kind of fun. Like that bloke—what was his name?—Fawad or Fur—something? Cat quite liked him, actually. Except that Fawad didn't have a nice big flat where they could live for free, her and Mum, and this huge big car that still smells all new inside.

They turn down a side street, then another, a shortcut that Terrence always takes to avoid the Saturday market crowds—the vendors with their vans and shopping trolleys, the tourists just walking and gawking.

In her basement bedroom, Cat always goes to sleep with her earphones on, falls asleep to one of her new CDs, 'cos anything's better than listening to him and Mum through the ceiling above her bed, usually screeching at each other like two cats. Or sometimes, she listens to them shagging, and their bed going creak-creak-creak.

Once, a long time ago, back when she was just a kid, she used to play this mind game. Like, Cat used to imagine that one of the boyfriends would actually turn out to be her real dad. It used to go like this: They'd be in their flat, her and Mum, or in one of the boyfriend's flats, and suddenly, Mum would call up to the living room or the kitchen to where Cat was watching the telly and Mum would say, "Catherine, babes, can you come in here a sec? We've got something to tell you."

And there they'd be, Mum and this guy, sitting there on the bed, sitting straight up, feet on the floor and arms folded, just dying to tell her their secret: "Catherine, Frank (or Trevor or Fawad or Richie or . . . well, whatever) is actually your father, your real father. We wanted to keep it a surprise."

Once, at a party in someone's flat, a party down in Earls Court, one of Mum's Irish friends told Cat that once, years and years ago, Mum had this boyfriend in Ireland. A boy she was in love with. Like, long before Mum ever moved here.

Then last year, when Cat was fifteen, they actually went there, to Ireland, to that village called Gowna and her gran's grotty little house in a tiny lane. And on the way there, they stayed at another house, a house with a really, really old woman named Kitty, which Mum said was really Cat's name, the woman that Cat was named after and, therefore, was sort of her grand auntie. The old woman Kitty started crying when she saw Cat.

Dublin was cool. For three nights, they stayed in that house in Dublin, and the woman Kitty made them hot chocolate and stuff. Each night, Cat fell asleep listening to Mum and her talking downstairs.

After Dublin, they had to take a train then a bus to that awful little Gowna place, the place her mum grew up.

Mum called it their summer holiday. Which was a laugh, when all the girls at Cat's comprehensive were gone off to Spain or Lanzarotte, and here were Cat and Carmel Cawley stuck in that village where, when Cat went walking down to the corner shop, the woman kept gawking at her and saying, "Oh, you're Carmel's daughter? Home from England are ye? *Really?*"

Mum's brother, Cat's uncle Tony, took them out on the lake in his rowing boat and Cat refused to wear sun cream and Mum got pissed off with her and anyway, the lake and the boat were boring. At night Mum and her brother went down the village to this little hotel, where they brought Cat along, 'cos Gran always went to bed early. Every night Mum and Uncle Tony got really rat-arsed trashed.

Now Terrence turns the car into Charlemont Street. She steals another look across at him. Ugly sod. Oh, and there's a little spot of blood where he must've nicked himself shaving. Good. Serve him bloody right.

Then at last, he turns into Smith Street, the street with the Red Dragon Chinese restaurant and Miss Jarkowski's dance studio, though the studio never has any sign outside, unless you count the handwritten one at the top of the stairs.

"Um . . . this is fine," Cat says. "Honest. I can walk the rest." Because even though it's a nice big car and everything, she can't let the other girls, the other girls in the Saturday dance lessons, actually *see* Terrence.

But he drives on like he hasn't heard.

And then, they're parked outside the Red Dragon with the silver security shutters over the window that the Chinese man will come and pull up soon, rat-tat-tat, and they'll start cooking their food that you can smell all the way upstairs in the dance studio.

"Thanks. See you," Cat says, clutching her backpack and one hand already on the car door handle.

"Hey!" Terrence says, laughing. "Hey!" Then he clutches her shoulder, that big stupid hand on her new Hilfiger T-shirt. "Hey, you're in a right hurry this morning, aren't you?"

"Miss Jarkowski's dead pissed off when we're late."

Then he lifts himself off the driver's seat, like he's going to scratch his arse or fart or something. Terrence takes a wallet from his back pocket and takes out twenty quid and hands it to her, just like that. "Just like your mother, aren't you? You and Carmel?" Terrence winks at her. "Should've been twins. Love your nice gear and your makeup and all that. Go on, then. Buy yourself something after your class."

Oh, yeah. Must've been an extra big fight with Mum last night.

"Oh, thanks," Cat says, taking the twenty quid. And then she gives him a little smile. "Oh, when my Mum gets up, tell her I'll ring her on my mobile. Bye!"

She opens the car door and hurries across to the red door next to the Red Dragon and up the dark, narrow stairs to her Saturday morning lesson.

*

Except for Miss Jarkowski herself, Cat Cawley is always the first one here on Saturdays mornings, the first girl to push in the door to the shadowy studio, no lights on yet, just the daylight from the front windows and the reflected light from the mirrored wall.

This morning, Cat can hear Miss J is talking to someone on the office phone, and there's the usual whiff of cigarettes through the shut office door. Some of the other girls said that Miss J actually lives there, that she sleeps on her office couch and the Chinese guys let her use their downstairs shower.

Cat thumps across the dance floor to the two bamboo screens set in the corner where she sets her backpack on the chair, unzips it for her purple leggings and her tank top.

Now Cat crosses the floor again. It's still so cool, this big, silent room, watching her own reflection, her short, Goth-black hair with the fringe cut at an angle over her eyes. Miss Jarkowski never lets them switch on the laptop and the music. So Cat hums a song to herself and practices her dance moves in the mirror. It's actually worth setting her alarm for and even having to listen to Terrence's shit. Yeah, there's absolutely nothing better than practicing her moves, all alone in the red mirrored room.

Here, Cat can forget about the girls at school—how one day they sit beside her at lunchtime, then, on another day, they suddenly decide they hate her again. This year, it's another new school 'cos her and Mum have moved into Terrence's. Dancing, she never even thinks about those stupid cows. And she even forgets about Mum back home asleep in Terrence's big bed. Mum who has quit her job again and been really kind of weird lately.

22

DANCE CLASS IS OVER and Cat is just crossing the floor to the studio door when Miss J shouts over all the girls' chattering voices. "Um . . . Catherine," Miss Jarkowski says. "Yes, you. Could you come into the office please?"

Crap. So Mum's Visa didn't go through again. And now Miss J's going to kick Cat Cawley out of class.

Miss J's office desk is always packed with papers and DVDs and stuff.

"Catherine," Miss Jarkowski says. Cat braces for the usual speech: like, how the dance studio's not a charity, blah, blah.

"Sit," Miss J says, nodding at the blue office chair across the desk from where the teacher is standing and smoking. "Move all that stuff." Cat takes a stack of printed flyers from the chair, sets them on the desk and sits. Then Miss J just stands there inside the window, her black bushy hair and her bony shoulders silhouetted by the open window. She points to this printed e-mail in front of her. "Catherine, there's this show. I'd like you to audition for it; they've got two teenage girl parts open, and you know, I think you could get in. You're really quite good. Though of course, you absolutely have to practice more."

Then Miss J goes on about other stuff. Cat watches her mouth moving, but the truth is that Cat can't actually hear anymore, can't hear the actual words. Because inside her head she's repeating her dance teacher's words to herself. A show. An audition. Miss J says I'm good.

Then Miss J's gawking straight at Cat, and Cat knows that she's just asked her some question that Cat is supposed to answer. Miss J raises her dark eyebrows and goes, "The audition's on Wednesday night, and I'll go with you, of course. But if you got in, *if* you got one of the spots, then you'd have to actually be there, twice each week for practice." Miss J taps the sheet of paper with a pen. "You must commit. No saying 'yes' when you actually don't turn up. You'd—have—to—commit."

Still Cat just sits there letting the words go plop-plop-plop through her head. *She's asking me to audition for a show, a real show. Good. She says I'm good.*

Miss J gets tired of waiting for Cat to say something. She hands Cat the piece of printed paper. "Look, have your mother take a look at this and then tell her to let me know, yes? Have her ring me by Monday morning, all right? Here. At the office. Or no, I'll give you my mobile number."

*

Cat is on the tube, the Piccadilly line and standing just inside the door, her backpack over one shoulder. The guy next to her smells of fried onions.

Mum hasn't texted her back. Weird. Since Cat left the dance studio, since she ran out of Miss J's office and down the stairs, Cat has rung Mum three times already. But Mum's phone just keeps going to voice mail. She's just got to tell Mum her news.

Cat checks her mobile again. Come on Mum. Answer back.

Terrence's car is gone from outside the house. Fab. So now they'll have the afternoon together, just her and Mum.

Cat turns her key in the front door. "Mum! Mu-*um*! Hey, guess what? You'll never guess!"

Cat goes to their bedroom. There's a radio playing. It's Mum's clock radio next to the bed. But there's no Mum, just the duvet pulled back and Mum's nightie there on the floor. Cat checks the en suite, then goes back up the corridor to the kitchen. "Hey! Mum! You here?"

Terrence's overflowing ashtray is still there on the kitchen table, his dirty coffee cup from this morning, the *Daily Mail* left open at the sports pages. There's a smell of toast, fresh toast, so at least Mum's had breakfast already.

Wait. There's someone downstairs, in Cat's basement bedroom. Mum? No, Mum knows it really pisses her off if Mum just goes down there. Or Terrence? What if Terrence's parked his car 'round the corner and he's down there just nosing about in Cat's stuff?

Cat is halfway down the wrought-iron stairs to the basement. "Hel-lo?" She's afraid now. What if it's not Mum or Terrence, but someone who broke in through those street-level windows? "Mum, is that you?"

Two more steps down, then she leans over the banister and there's Mum standing there. Yeah, well, there's a relief.

Then Cat sees that Mum's actually dragging things from her built-in, Cat's tops, jackets, jeans, the empty hangers jangling.

Cat rushes down the rest of the steps and across the room. "Mum! That's my stuff! What are you doing with my stuff?"

"Packing, Catherine," Mum calls over her shoulder, as she pulls out more stuff. "Packing. What's it look like I'm doing? We've only got about an hour 'til that wanker gets back here."

Then Mum turns around and she pushes the bundle of clothes at Cat. "Here, get these into a bag. I already rang my friend Sasha. We can stay with her for now."

It's a bruise. There's a big red bruise under Mum's right eye.

The words trudge through Cat's mind: My mum's got a big bruise on her face. So she fell downstairs or bumped into a door. Again.

No, says the other voice inside Cat's head. No. You silly twit. Someone hit her, someone hit my mum.

Now Mum crosses to Cat's dressing table, yanks open the top drawer and starts pulling out Cat's knickers and thongs.

"Mu-um!" Cat pleads, dumping her clothes on the bed to walk over and catch Mum's elbow, to stop her pulling all her knicks out of the drawer. "Mum. We *can't* move. Not again. 'Cos Miss Jarkowski said I might be able to get into a show, a real dance show. She says she's got to talk to you."

Turning, Mum aims Cat's knicks toward the bed but she misses, so they land, one by one, fluttering onto the brown carpet. "Catherine, just for once, just this once, you have to get a bloody move on. Or I'm gonna leave this stuff behind. Now just put all these in a bag."

Then, Carmel Cawley yanks open the second drawer and everything from the dressing table top—Cat's eye pencils and lip gloss and CDs—go crashing.

"Mu-um," Cat pleads, feeling the tears in her throat, hard stinging tears and hearing how blubbery her voice sounds. "Aw, for Chrissake, Mum!"

Then Carmel turns on her daughter. "What? What part of 'getting a sodding move on' don't you understand?"

"But Miss Jark—"

Mum moves closer to Cat, her eyes really crazy now, until their noses are almost touching, mother and daughter. Mum's been crying. Cat can tell. Mum touches the bruise. "And this, Catherine! What part of this do you not understand?"

It blurts out before Cat can stop herself. "But . . . but Mum, Miss Jarkowski's got this show and she actually wants me to audition!"

"Christ, Catherine, I wish I never let you enroll in that dance place. I should never have let you talk me into those bloody dance lessons of yours."

23

CAT STUDIES the back of the van driver's head, his black, greasy hair over his shirt collar, his head barely topping the back of his driver's seat.

He was waiting at the train station for them, just standing there waving them over and pronouncing their name—Cawley—in his foreign accent and getting it all wrong. Her and Mum followed him to a white van with "Cripton Academy" written in curly letters along the side, beneath the van's side windows.

He put Mum and Cat's suitcases in the back, and then he drove them along this road with all these trees and a roadside sign for a garden center. After the garden center, there were just more trees and then these really big houses like you'd see on telly or in a school history book.

Now here they're actually in the town—Cripton. Hey, here's a High Street, which doesn't seem that bad, really. The usual shops, lots of shops, a Tesco and a Sainbury's and two pubs with black window shutters and flower boxes on the windowsills.

Cat's starving. Except for a Mars bar, which she bought while Mum was buying their train tickets at Victoria, she's had nothing since this morning.

All the way down here on the train from Victoria they haven't spoken, her and Mum. And now they're still not speaking as they're being driven in this van to this boarding school called Cripton Academy, where they get a free flat 'cos Mum's got this new job working in the school kitchen.

The truth is that Cat's gotten used to not talking. Actually, it's been like this ever since they left Terrence's place that Saturday, when they moved into Mum's friend Sasha's flat and slept on her living room couch. Cat hasn't spoken to Mum since Mum made her ring and tell Miss Jarkowski that "thanks but no thanks," that she can't, after all, make that audition. No chance of an audition when your things are all stuffed in two suitcases—first in Mum's friend Sasha's flat, and now in the back of a school van. Not when your Mum's all mopey and dead pissed off.

The only good part has been that, when Cat came home early afternoon, arrived up the stairs to Sasha's flat without her school backpack and without even pretending to have been at school that day, Mum didn't even ask why Cat's skipped school again. It was like Mum was suddenly blind, like, couldn't even look across Sasha's little kitchen and see her, a sixteen-year-old daughter standing there, all smelling of fags and with no homework and no backpack and her nose all runny from just taking the tube and then getting off at a random station, any station at all, and then just walking around that place, a different place every day, just walking around and looking in the cafés and shops or nicking a CD and then sitting in the park with her headphones on.

On the train, Cat ate the rest of her Mars bar and kept her headphones on and just watched the backs of other people's houses and offices. Actually, she'd stopped caring where they were going; didn't care what this new place and Mum's new job were going to be like.

An hour and a half, the train journey was, which could've been worse. So now, for her dance class on Saturdays, Cat's going to have to get up at about six o'clock, and she's going to have to figure how to get from this academy place to the train station. Unless this poor sod driving this van can drive her there. Maybe he's got to drive everybody everywhere.

The Cripton High Street shops and buildings are gone. Now there's two lanes of traffic and then a roundabout with signs for all these other towns and a big green sign for a shopping center.

After the roundabout, the man takes this road with more big houses, some with ivy growing on their garden walls.

Cat sneaks a look across at Mum, who has her elbow resting on the van's window ledge, her chin set in her upturned hand.

It's been three weeks since they left Terrence's place. Sasha's place was cool, and Cat liked Sasha and Sasha's partner, Joel. But the pullout couch in their living room was really wobbly. More than once, Cat overheard Sasha saying, "You should just go to the police, Carmel. You really should. Look, I'll go with you. He can't just get away with it, babes. He just *can't*."

Did she? Mum, like, did she go to the police and tell them all about Terrence? Ugly wanker! Mum's never said. Often, lying awake at night on that wobbly couch with the street lights all reflected and shiny on the ceiling above their couch, Cat imagined Terrence's face on the telly news. She pictured him being taken away in a van, except that van was black and Terrence was handcuffed—big handcuffs with spiky edges. And there was a big Alsatian dog sniffing at Terrence's arse.

Mum's bruise turned purple first, then yellow. Now, in the Cripton Academy van, you can still just see it, even though Mum's started wearing lots and lots of makeup.

The van driver changes gears, then slows to turn in between a set of stone pillars, one with a white sign with black letters, "Cripton Academy."

They drive down this avenue with speed bumps and lots of trees on each side. Cat ducks her head to see the buildings beyond the trees, at the end of these huge lawns.

The van driver slows for the girls walking along the road, just up ahead. One girl has shiny black hair swinging behind her. Another has a red sweater draped over her shoulders. They're wearing matching white blouses and grey skirts. The middle blond girl glances behind, laughing at what one of her friends had just said. The girls walk single file then, trooping along beneath the van's small windows.

Out the van window, Cat studies them: blond hair, black hair, and then the third, farthest away, has short hair and Paki skin. They don't look up or wave. Are these her new classmates?

"There," the driver points toward a one-story building with a line of metal windows. It reminds Cat of a clinic where Mum used to bring her once, a long time ago, a place where they gave kids injections and tested them for stuff.

After the van drives away, Mum and Cat start to wheel their two suitcases behind them down the pebbly path. In the distance, just past those trees, someone is playing tennis, a ball going thock-thock.

The building's door opens onto a tiled, fluorescent-lit corridor with a double row of doors all the way down. There's a smell of food, lovely food, something, like, tomato and spicy. Cat's tummy rumbles again.

Cat almost collides with Mum's suitcase when Mum stops at one of the doors, Number 13, where someone has written the "3" in with black marker. "Right," Mum says. "This is us. They said they'd just leave it open."

There's something about Mum's voice that softens Cat, makes her feel guilty for being such a bitch on the train. Stop, she tells herself. Maybe it's not all Mum's fault, really.

The living room has the same tiles as the corridor outside. There's a big brown couch, a coffee table, an empty corner shelf for a telly. There's a fridge in the corner with its plug curled across the floor. Under the metal windows sits a small kitchen table and two fold-out chairs.

Cat follows Mum into the second room where the two single beds have no blankets or sheets on them. On the bed nearest the door, the striped mattress has a round stain.

Mum crosses to open the bedroom window, and Cat hears that tennis ball again: thock-thock. Then, Mum crosses to the built-in, where she pulls a string for the light.

"See?" Mum says, turning to Cat. "See? Lots of room for both of us, both of our stuff."

"Yeah," Cat says, plopping onto the bed without the stain.

It's the first time Cat's actually spoken since this morning, since they said good-bye to Sasha and hugged her and said they'd text the minute they got here.

"And the beds look comfy," Carmel says, crossing to the other bed with the mattress stain. "'Course, you *would* hog the good one, the one that nobody's pissed on." She grins at Cat. Then Mum bounces on her mattress. "Here, Catherine!" Mum pats the mattress. "Come on over here."

So Cat goes and sits next to Mum, though she's not sure why she should. Has Mum suddenly forgotten that they're really supposed to be fighting?

Again Mum bounces her bum on the bed and Cat bounces back. Mum laughs. Though there's nothing really funny. But Cat laughs, too. Laughs 'cos it's nice to hear Mum laugh again. It's been weeks.

Then, Mum reaches over and brushes Cat's black fringe out of her eyes and goes, "It's not so bad, is it, babes? Go on, say it's not so bad. We can go down the market and get nice rugs and some wall hangings and once we've got my bedspreads unpacked, the place will actually look quite nice. Right? I mean, where else are we going to get a free flat? And all to ourselves, no bloody men?"

So Cat manages a small smile. Just to make Mum happy she says, "You know, Mum. I quite *like* this place. Honest. I think we could make it cool. Dead cool."

Jo and Ellen

24

TAP, TAP, TAP. Ellen starts awake in Jo's old, abandoned upstairs bedroom. The tapping sound is coming from under her bed.

Then nothing.

She snuggles further under the heavy blankets to go back to sleep.

Tap-*tap-tap*. She checks the bedside clock. Shit. 8:37. She's overslept again.

Downstairs she listens outside Jo's door for that raspy breathing. She wishes there were a window in this door, a spy-hole through which to check from the parlor.

She pushes in the door to a wide-awake Jo, the raccoon eyes above the bed cover, and the walking cane—Jo's tap-tap Morse code—set alongside her, right there in the bed. Amid all these sick-room accoutrements, the cane is the last vestige of the old spitfire Jo.

Ellen presses the large button on the bed's side until the toothless face, torso, and pillows elevate. Jo has the expression of someone strapped into a dentist's chair.

"There? Is that good?"

"More." The toothless voice is whispery, pitiful.

The bed rises a few more inches, until Jo is sitting upright, eye to eye. Ellen clanks down the bed rails.

Then she crosses to open the drapes to this summer morning, the last Thursday in June. She lingers at the window long enough to let Jo put in her teeth. Then she turns back to the bed where Jo, dressed in a clean white nightgown, sits blinking into the daylight.

Everything in this room has been washed, scrubbed, sanitized. There's no more sour body or hair smell—just the whiff of protein drinks and antiseptic.

Her teeth in, Jo looks better and more like her old defiant self.

"Ready for breakfast? Tea?"

In a month, Ellen and Jo's lives have shrunk to fit this room. There is no space for other, outside things. Neither is there any space for abstract notions: death, life, a life before, a life ever after. Their only reality is this daily routine of doctor and nurse visits, temperatures, blood pressure, protein drinks, dosages.

Ellen has read this about nurses, psychotherapists, doctors. Even the largest or most life-saving job boils down to its component parts, a roster of daily tasks. Anything deeper would mean freefall to a place where you wreak havoc, not good.

Jo makes a face. "I don't want anything this morning. But that bloody nurse *tells me* I'm supposed to. They tell me everything—when to get up, lie down, when to breathe." This amount of talk brings on a coughing bout. Ellen waits it out. She is no longer frightened by it. Wordlessly, she hands Jo the stainless steel, health-board-issue spittoon.

When Jo has caught her breath, Ellen asks, "But will you eat some breakfast if I bring it?"

"I'll try something, sure. Just to keep you happy; off my back."

*

The tray sits lengthways along Jo's legs. The tea, half-drunk, smells strong and tannic. Jo has drunk half a glass of NutraFruit, a chalky protein that the nurse leaves in the scullery fridge—different fruit flavors and loaded with vitamins, minerals, electrolytes. Though inside her new, department-store nightgown, Jo keeps getting thinner.

Now, the last ice cubes clink against the white-smeared glass. Ellen gathers up the tray, pours the last of the NutraFruit into a yellow plastic sippy cup on the nightstand.

"My fags are in the drawer there, the top drawer."

"You know Dr. Fitzgerald said—"

"—There's an ashtray there, too. And matches."

They lock gazes. Ellen is supposed to be on the doctor's side. But truthfully, Ellen is pleased.

For the past week, there were days when Jo was either too listless or too fast asleep to smoke. Or even to argue. This sparring, demanding mood is the sign of a good day, a good day ahead.

"Lookit, if you're going to live in my house you'll do as I bloody tell you."

Oh, no. Not again. Ellen knows this speech. So let's hear it. Jo has made it before: the day before yesterday, and two days before that. But Jo forgets. Jo forgets a lot.

And each time, because she knows she's expected to, Ellen parrots the same defense. "I—am—not—'living in your house.' I *have* a house, a place. In Boston. I'm staying here because—"

"—Because the young Fitzgerald thinks I'm going to burn down the house at night."

"Yes. He does. And with reason. You've—"

"—And because nobody else wants to mind an old woman."

"That's not true."

"Foreigners. Refugees. In this country, that's all that'll do a job like that now."

"*I'm* a foreigner."

"Yes. You are. But . . ." Jo's voice turns wheedling. "Aw, go on. Lookit, if you give me a fag, I'll try and eat something later on. A bit of scrambled egg or a drop of soup. Or maybe you're not into cooking today. I could never stand it, to tell you the truth, all those years of peeling and mashing and standing over a hot range. But in our day . . ." Jo shakes her head. Then she cocks her head at Ellen, a begging puppy. "Get us a fag. Go on."

"If I get you a cigarette you have to keep your promise to eat some lunch later."

"I'm a woman of my word."

Ellen brings Jo the pack of Benson and Hedges. Jo takes one, gleeful, triumphant. Ellen holds the Bic lighter for her. They have an hour and a half before the nurse comes.

Ellen crosses to the window again, this time to pull it all the way open for the smoke.

Her sister Louise used to do this. January nights and six feet of snow outside their bedroom window, but there was fifteen-year-old Louise Boisvert kneeling on her bed, her backside cocked backward as she puffed her Marlboro smoke into the subzero New Hampshire night.

The air outside Jo's room feels sweet and pollen-laden. The chaffinches cluck under the house eaves. Ned's car is parked in its usual spot under the orchard wall. This week, he's having some men in to cut the top meadows. The next two weeks, they'll be baling hay. Turning back to the bed, Ellen says, "It's going to be another beautiful day. A scorcher, the TV said last night."

Jo has relaxed with her cigarette. "Tell me, are you still all right up there? Did you sleep last night?"

The question surprises Ellen. Then she recognizes it as a veiled apology for the taunt about being a foreigner. "I'm fine. The room's fine. I . . . thought I might dust again, vacuum a little. Later. I promise not to disturb you."

When Ellen was driving up the avenue from the village yesterday afternoon, she met Nurse Ryan, the visiting nurse from the health board. The two women pulled over to chat, compare notes. Ellen asked about the coughing. Did Elaine Ryan think it was getting deeper, worse? The nurse said the doctor has Jo on antibiotics—trying to keep it to an oral dose until they think it needs something heavier. But everything considered, Jo Dowd is doing far better than expected. Just keep getting her to eat, drink lots of water, keep her breathing and fluids up.

Nurse Ryan gave Ellen an impish grin. "I know she's still smoking."

"Yeah, I figured there's no harm now. And they're a good bribe—something to make her eat or behave."

"Ach, no harm now. The cigarettes have done what they've done."

On the kitchen table sits the health-board-issue log book of times, doses, initials. 15/6/2002, 3:00 p.m. 300 mg. ER (Elaine Ryan). 14/6/02, 8:00 p.m. 300 mg (Ellen has learned the Irish way of date, month, year). 14/6/02 2:00 p.m. TF (Tom Fitzgerald).

Now Jo cuts across Ellen's thoughts. "Do whatever you want up there. I'll never be up there again; we all know that." A last puff and then Jo squishes out the cigarette in the tin ashtray, glances mischievously at the bedside clock. "Here, empty this in the range. And give it a good scrub or *that one'll* find it. Listen, you haven't told anyone below in the village about being . . . about us being related? About my son's death?"

"Who would I tell? Nobody except the doctor. And Nurse Ryan."

"You know, I think that young Fitzgerald has an eye on you. Oh, I know he's married to yer one there, and he's the two kids, spoiled *maistíns*. You'd think nobody ever had a child but himself. But they never lose the eye, you know. Men. Oh, I see him looking, gawking at you. Probably thinks you're going to get this place. Did I tell you he came in here beating around the bush the other day? Th'oul red head on him all cocked to the side like a priest hearing confession. 'Now, have you settled your affairs, Mrs. Dowd?' says he to me. 'It's important, better for your health and peace of mind that you settle your affairs, your assets, especially with a place, a big farm like this.'"

Ellen says, "Hmm . . . Right. Jo, why don't you just lie back now and I'll let the bed d—"

"—'Settled my affairs?' says I to him. 'Well now, maybe I have and maybe I haven't.'"

"Will you drink some of this w—" Ellen has heard the "settle the affairs" speech before. Almost every day for almost a month.

"—Well, that put the wind up him, didn't it? Just like the rest of this parish, with their wondering and whispering. Where'll it go? One hundred acres up on the hill. Where'll she leave it? That young Fitzgerald probably thinks he'll get a bit of it himself. I wouldn't put it past—"

"Right. Do you want to come to the toilet with me, or do you want to take a nap and then Nurse Ryan will take you?"

Jo gives a vindictive tilt to the chin. "So like I say, there's nothing here for anyone. *For anyone*. Let them all wonder, wonder all they want. But except for a little nest egg for Ned, this damn place, every perch and acre of it, is going back to the land commission. They can build a bloody skating rink or a massage parlor or whatever the dickens they want up here for all I care. I've it all settled with my solicitor in Ballinkeady. And *that* should set them all writing letters up to the government and them all fighting like tinkers to get—"

"The toilet? The doctor said it's good to get up, walk a bit. Every day. So will it be me or Nurse Ryan?"

Jo gives Ellen a pouty look. "You, I suppose."

Jo's nightgown floats in a tent behind her, her long, grey hair down her back. In the parlor, she searches, grabs at the edges of couches, armchairs. Now and again the hand leans on Ellen's shoulder. They stop, wait for Jo to steady herself and catch her breath. Then they're off again.

In the downstairs toilet off the front hall, Ellen stands in front, the two women chest to chest. Ellen lowers Jo onto the raised, orthopedic toilet seat. Once, the day she first came here, Ellen cringed at the thought of touching this flesh, at such intimacy with this old woman. Ellen shuts the door and stands guard outside until Jo calls or knocks.

The trip to the toilet always exhausts Jo. When she eases her back into bed, Ellen goes to draw the curtain again. As she tiptoes away, Jo is already asleep, the old woman's lips moving, the room loud with her whispering.

25

THE SOUND BRINGS JO RUNNING to the back door. There's the boy, aged five now, standing there in the yard, pitching pebbles against the gable wall. Thwap, thwap, thwap.

The curtains are drawn in Mother's room, the room in the gable of the house. It's been a week since Father's funeral. After their Sunday lunch, Mother went to bed to sleep, to keen her rosaries into the shadowy, silent room. Kitty is upstairs packing her suitcase, packing up her black funeral dress and her black patent shoes.

"Stop that," Jo calls to the boy in a loud whisper. "You'll waken your grandmother."

Here's a car coming up the avenue. It's the car that came, that dropped Kitty off when she was summoned for Father's last hours, his death at three o'clock in the morning. "Stop that," Jo whispers to the boy again, just as the black car parks outside the yard gate.

Kitty comes downstairs and out to the back door. She smells of perfume. She's wearing a grey swing-back coat and wet-look high boots to her knees. Kitty works in Dublin now. She's shop floor manager in a large department store on Talbot Street.

Tears are trapped in Jo's throat. She could not swear that the tears are all for Father—or not specifically for his death. No, this awful sadness is for all of this, for her sister leaving, for the impending silence of the house.

The boy abandons his little pile of pebbles to walk to the gate, where he stands there, tall for his age, staring through the slats of the gate at the motor car. The man, who is Kitty's latest Dublin boyfriend, waves through the windscreen at the ragged little boy, then he mimics turning the steering wheel round and round. He beckons to the little boy to open the farmyard gate and come and try it out, to play a game of car. But the boy stands there, frozen and unsmiling. He's perplexed by the man's smiling, waving presence.

At last, Kitty kisses Jo's cheeks and walks with her brown leather suitcase to the gate and the waiting car. Jo follows a few steps and then stops. It's not her place to go out there. If Kitty had wanted to, she would have invited Jo out there to make introductions. So Jo stands there, a lone, foolish figure in the middle of the yard.

She watches Kitty hoist the suitcase into the back seat. The man comes around to hold the passenger's door open for her. Kitty kisses the man—right there, in full view of the house and Jo. Then, with a last wave they drive away, the red brake lights going down the avenue.

Inside the house there are a million things to get done before Mother gets up again. There's bread to be made. The boy's school clothes have to be ironed and set out for tomorrow, Monday morning. The calves' buckets need scalding before John comes in from the fields.

These days, since Father's death, Mother winces, considers any movement or noise or work in the house as a blasphemy, as disrespect for the dead. So Jo should hurry, tiptoe back into the silent house and finish her jobs.

But still she stands there in the yard, transfixed by her own sadness, by this stodgy, leaden grief.

Thwap. Thwap. Thwap. The boy is back pelting his stones against the gable of the house. He pelts and then walks to the gable wall to collect them from the ground, then returns to his spot to start again.

"Stop that," Jo calls to him. "I told you to stop it."

He stares at her, his eyes wide beneath the curly hair. He should be out helping his father, she thinks. Up in the cow byre and not here just wasting time.

His five-year-old's stare turns sly. Then, he walks toward the gable again, slow and measured, the occasional glance back at his mother. He bends to collect the pebbles again. Then he walks slowly back to his pitching place.

Thwack.

Jo feels the fury rising. The fury and wailing grief become one.

She watches his slow motion, the little hand, the eye on her as he takes a swing, then pelts another pebble. *Thwap.*

She crosses the yard to him. *Thwack.* This time it's the sound of her hand across his face. "Cursed little devil. When I say to stop, you'll stop." She slaps his face again. She watches his chin quiver, his frightened eyes. Then he wails. "Noooo!"

His screeches make her more furious. Slap, slap, slap. She can't stop herself. There is a high, cathartic joy to it, the sound of her own hand, the track of her hand there, on his freckled cheeks. "Ah, no, Mammy, *noooo.* Noo, noo."

Thwack. Thwack. "Do what you're told. Do-what-you're-told."

The boy keeps up the wailing, his face red and swollen, his little legs skirting the ground as she yanks him back into the house.

26

THEIR PASTA AND SALAD DINNERS FINISHED, the Fitzgerald children have grown fidgety. Eyes start to shift and elbows are straying across the patio table for brother-and-sister jabs.

Riona and Lorcan Fitzgerald are hybrids of their mother and father, the doctor and his wife. Riona has Ruth's blue eyes. Lorcan has his mother's dark hair but his father's pale, freckled complexion. Riona is thirteen. Lorcan is eleven.

Across the candlelit table, Ruth Fitzgerald says, "You know our friend Ellen here is a teacher in America. She teaches French. Riona's taking French this year, aren't you, pet?"

Ruth is obviously a little younger than her husband. Thirty-five, Ellen calculates, across their candlelit dinner table. Thirty-five, slim, and very pretty with her thick, dark hair clipped into a high, bobbing ponytail.

Lorcan says, "*I'm* not going to like French. Not next year, when I move up to the community school on the hill. I mean, at the *moment,* I absolutely *hate* Irish, and like, that can't be that much different, can it? All that grammar and stuff?"

"Lorcan," Tom scolds. "That's not very polite."

"So what *is* your favorite?" Ellen asks Lorcan. "Your most favorite?"

"Maths. I love maths. I'm the best in my class."

"Lorca-an," Tom Fitzgerald pleads again. "It's not nice to boast."

"Are you?" Ellen laughs. "You know, I bet you are. The very first day in my class, I can always tell which of my students will be good at things. Teachers can just tell."

Lorcan sets his chin in his upturned hand, fixes his gaze on his parents' American dinner guest.

Ellen knows this young boy's dreamy look. At Coventry Academy, there's always some young freshman, some sophomore boy who falls slightly in love with Mademoiselle Boisvert.

Riona elbows her brother again. Ruth says, "All right, you two, upstairs. I rented you that DVD. You can have an hour before bed, then watch the rest tomorrow night."

The kids cross the slate patio to the French doors. Lorcan opens the door, then peers back out across the candlelit patio at Ellen.

"Lorca-an! You'll let the midges into the house!" Tom commands. The boy slaps the glassy door behind him, then thumps across the kitchen, giggling.

Tom Fitzgerald shakes his head, crosses himself. "Jesus deliver us all from now on. The awkward age and all that. Sex 'n' drugs 'n' rock 'n' roll."

It's a Sunday evening. Two days ago, Friday, Tom came up the hill to Knockduff on his usual check. In Jo's kitchen, he insisted that Ellen come for some dinner, wine, some company besides the nurse and Ned and Jo. He wanted her to meet his family.

Now, with the kids gone, Tom's and Ruth's and Ellen's forks and pasta spoons clink too loudly; the candles and the table and wine are too cozy, too pent up and intimate.

Ruth says, "Well, speaking of drugs, we might as well finish this bottle. Ellen?" She offers the bottle of California cabernet.

Earlier, when the per-diem nurse arrived at the house in Knockduff, Ellen drove down the avenue, following Tom's directions to turn left on the Gowna road, then past the old dance hall and on toward the village, watching for the Fitzgeralds' stone pillars and their sloping blacktop driveway to this newish, peach-colored house with its attached, one-story building with the sign on the door, "Doctor's Surgery."

Now, twirling a nest of spaghetti around and around, Ellen wonders if she shouldn't have made some excuse, politely refused his invitation. Because there's definitely something edgy about the Fitzgeralds. In the kitchen there was all this staged business with food, wine glasses, appetizers. Around the patio dinner table there has been all this deliberate prompting of their son and daughter toward more and more kid-speak, more precocious questions about America and Boston; more exchanges about the kids' school and music lessons and summer vacations.

But now it's just the three of them—Tom at Ellen's left; Ruth sitting opposite Ellen, her back to the house. The patio smells of freshly mown grass, of the sloping fields all around the house, stretching from here to the village.

A shaft of sudden light from the children's upstairs window falls across the patio. Ruth's pretty face is half in and half out of this light.

"Ruth, did you say that you grew up here, too? In Gowna?"

"Hmm? Oh, yeah. Yes. Well, outside. We were—*are*—ha, ha, ha. Well, my folks are still alive, and thriving, actually. Fit as fiddles. My Dad's still farming away, but just a small place, thirty acres. You've driven past it out on the Galway road."

"So you knew Fintan, too? I mean, at school, around town?"

Tom Fitzgerald stops eating, his knife and fork suddenly silent. Ruth keeps a determined smile. "I was actually two classes behind him at school. And I was one class behind this fella." She nods playfully at her red-haired husband.

In her mind's eye, Ellen thinks of that school photo of Fintan's, the rows of girls and boys outside an old school. The girls in their white kneesocks and severely cut bangs and pigtails. Ruth Fitzgerald was one of them.

And Tom was probably at that university dance, the dance where Fintan and Carmel Cawley had their picture taken.

"Of course she knew him," Tom interrupts gustily. "Ellen, as you've probably gathered by now, everyone knows nearly everyone around here, except for the odd new blow-in. And much more so back then than now."

"Right." Ellen starts on her cold spaghetti again. Round and around.

Then tell me why a man like that lies about his parents. And tell me about that girl, the girl named Carmel Cawley who very obviously adored him. What happened? Who ditched whom?

Tom leans backward, rocks on the chair's back legs. It's his most maddening habit. Ruth's smile has grown hesitant.

Tom says, "Oh, Fintan Dowd was the brains of the school. But then, my father, God rest him, used to say that she, Jo, was, too. By far the brightest girl in her class. Though of course, in her day, it didn't matter whether a girl was brainy or not. 'Twas all the same. Nothing for them but to marry into a farm of land or emigrate to England to train as nurses or work as office cleaners. But look, I'm sure I'm not telling you anything you don't already know, that Fintan didn't tell you."

"Yes. He told me lots. And he was bright," Ellen says. "Did you know he graduated first in his MBA class in Boston; studied for his degree while he worked full-time, got two job promotions in the process?"

Tom clanks the chair down. When the conversation turns to the near present, he's visibly more relaxed. "No. But I'm not surprised. The teachers above at the school loved him; apple of their eye. Needed no teaching, Fintan Dowd. In primary school, he even got to skip a class—common in those days, for the brainy ones, just push them onward. He was actually *two* years younger than me, but he got put ahead, and that's how we ended up only a class apart. Of course, fellas like Fintan and myself were only counting the hours until we'd finish school and get out of here. I mean, except for th'oul Gowna Dance Hall on a Saturday night, there was absolutely nothing to do."

And who was he dancing with there? With that girl, Carmel, with the dark eyes?

"Tom, you said you knew him in college, too. In Dublin?"

Here's another husband-and-wife glance across the table. Ruth reaches for the water pitcher, gestures it toward Ellen. Ellen shakes her head. "No, thanks."

"Yeah. I used to see him around campus. Of course, he was in comm, or business, and I was in premed. Though Fintan didn't really come to many of the college parties—mad parties, out in these packed student flats in Ranelagh or Rathmines. Jeez, when I think of them. We wouldn't put Ginger our cat in one of them now."

"Fintan didn't? Live on campus?"

"No. He was in digs, a rented room, someplace way out across the city, on the north side. I never went there. Sometimes my father'd be in Dublin on business and Dad'd give us both a lift home to Gowna. But we always collected Fintan in Bellfield, on campus. Fintan'd be there with his bags packed and ready." He turns to Ellen. "We probably saw more of each other in Dublin than if we'd stayed here in Gowna."

Ellen cocks her head in a question.

Ruth sets down her water glass. "As one of the local peasants myself, let me fill you in. Our Tom here was the village doctor's son. The Dowds were—are—certainly one of the bigger farmers around. But they were still from Knockduff, out the country, outside the village itself, metropolis that it is. So the Dowds would've looked up to the Fitzgeralds. And, being from a small farm myself, we looked up to the Dowds and their huge, thriving place out there on the hill." Ruth sits back, spreads her hands. "That was small Irish villages for you. And it still is, despite whatever 'we're all so egalitarian and modern' Celtic-Tiger bullshit you might have heard." Ruth shoots her husband an impish look.

Tom pulls a mock-contrite look. Then he leans, rocks, back on his chair again. "We-*ell,* so I got told. But still, some of us came home to roost, didn't we? Ha, ha, ha. Sowed the wild oats but then came home an' took over the father's practice and got the house and the cat"—he slaps his forehead—"Oh, and the wife 'n' kids, too. Right. I nearly forgot."

Ruth swats her napkin toward him, then starts to stack their dinner-stained plates. "Coffee? Or tea?"

"Hmm . . . Coffee, Ruth. Thanks. Here, let me help you with—"

"—No, no. You sit. Sit. Rest yourself."

Is Ruth Fitzgerald happy, too happy, to escape?

*

Tom and Ellen watch Ruth's silhouette inside the lit-up kitchen as Ruth moves back and forth between the dishwasher and the fridge. Somewhere, out there in the gathering darkness, a cow bellows. A sliver of a pale yellowy sunset lingers at the edge of the fields. Ellen swats at a swarm of midges—these tiny invisible bugs that come out at twilight.

"And there was this dog of his?" she says, not turning toward Tom.

"Rosie!" Tom says. "God, Rosie. Jesus. Yeah! I'd forgotten about that. God, he loved that dog. Entered her for every sheepdog trial for miles around. Here in the secondary school, we'd all have some class of devilment or dancing lined up for the weekend, but if Fintan had a sheepdog trial, you wouldn't see sight of him. Home in the fields training Rosie. God, that dog was his *life.*"

Tom seems more relaxed with his wife not here. He seems released from the choreography, the collusion of whatever it is they're hiding. Could it be the ring that Ellen thinks she's seen in that photograph, the ring on Carmel Cawley's left finger? Carmel Cawley who has two children, a girl and a boy, and is separated or divorced from that angry, menacing man who she met down at the lake, the man she met coming out of the Cawleys' house on the lane?

"And he had a girlfriend?" Ellen prompts. Yes. Yes. No mistaking it. Tom's congenial, raconteur's grin has frozen. He's annoyed. Ellen twirls one hand, mimics trying to remember a name "Carmel? Carmel . . . ?"

"Yes, he . . . um . . . used to go out with a girl, a girl from down in the village. Carmel. Did he tell you that?" He shoots an impatient glance at the house.

Ellen scrapes her chair around, to face him straight on. "It's okay, Tom. I mean, we all come to marriage with some sort of romantic past, right?"

A lie. Big lie. When Ellen met Fintan Dowd, an Irish bartender in that college-hangout pub in Boston, Ellen Boisvert's greatest love affair had been with her schoolbooks. Here, on this backyard patio in Ireland, she glimpses herself back there, when she landed in Boston—timid and self-conscious, convinced she was wearing all the wrong clothes when she crossed from her college dorm to the classrooms and refectory at Saint Bonaventure College. She was afraid to venture past the corner drugstore. Until just after that first, freshman Thanksgiving, she and a few more shy girls finally ventured out, prowling the city and all its smells and noise and the delicious prospect of parties and boys. But outside of some drunken, late-night fumblings at someone's house party, Ellen Boisvert had never been with anyone until Fintan.

Ruth is coming back with a tray and clinking cups, a steaming coffee pot. Tom stands, too quickly, sets their candles jiggling as he rushes toward the open French door. "Here, I'll get that for you, love."

"Tom and I were just chatting about Carmel Cawley, Fintan's old girlfriend," Ellen announces across the table, smiling over her coffee cup.

This time, Ruth doesn't check with her husband. But the voice comes high, forced-casual. "Oh, yeah, right. Carmel."

"She's still living in Gowna? Or close by?"

Tom says, "Ach, no. Actually, she moved to England, a long time ago. I'm not sure where she's actually living over there. Whether it's London or . . . where?" He laughs.

"Doesn't she still have family here? In Gowna?"

Again, Ellen sees that man, the man who came walking out of the little house at Number 10, The Lane.

Ruth draws her lips together. "Actually, we saw her last year. Below in the hotel one night. There was a band, you know. And we were out for a Saturday night meal."

Tom takes the baton. "She was having a drink at the bar. With her brother. Tony. He's still here, around these parts. Moved back in with his mother after his divorce. Then, she saw us, came over to our table. She'd had a few too many, the same night. But you know, to tell you the truth, Ellen, neither of us recognized her first. Did we, love? Of course, once she introduced herself, we knew her straight away. But the accent. It's funny, but even after all that time, you're still shocked to hear such a different accent."

"She sounded English?" Ellen asks, her head swiveling between the two, feeling silly, like a tennis spectator.

Ruth: "Yeah. Very. 'Twas gas, really."

"But she seemed to be doing great, all settled in over there. Well, you would be after . . ." Tom's voice trails off.

"After how long?"

Tom shuffles, then bumps the underside of the glass table with his knee.

Ruth intercedes. "Gosh, I forget now. Sure, everyone was off someplace back then. There was almost nothing here in this country, and what there was, like jobwise, was already spoken for. But sure, Fintan'd have told you all that."

Ellen studies the biggest of their dinner candles, where it sits there in the middle of the table, next to the coffee tray. It's as big as a canning jar. She watches the candle gutter in the night breeze.

But then the breeze dies and the candle flickers bright again.

1985. The year Fintan came to Boston. And the year Carmel Cawley left Gowna for England. Ellen is sure of it.

When Ellen looks up again, she catches Tom and Ruth Fitzgerald eyebrowing each other across the table. She is an object of pity. The stranger among them; the woman who must be protected, kid-gloved from the truth.

"Was she alone? Carmel Cawley? Visiting Gowna on her own?"

"Yes," Ruth answers.

"No," says Tom.

Right, Ellen thinks. So I've got my answer.

*

"Don't be a stranger," Ruth says, leaning against the front doorjamb. "Or listen, if you're in town, Ballinkeady, ask anyone for Lambert and Wells' solicitors' office. It's where I work, part-time, a legal secretary. Hours are perfect, what with the kids and everything. We'll have a bit of lunch. Or if you want to go into Galway some Saturday for a bit of shoppin'."

Ellen glimpses young Lorcan's head dipping over the stair banister, hanging upside down, staring at her standing here in the front door. Ellen calls into the house, "'Bye, you guys. Good to meet you."

"Thanks again."

"And . . . Ellen?" Ruth steps further out onto the front step. The doctor's wife sets her hand on Ellen's arm. "I'm really, really sorry, you know. About Fintan." She gestures her head back into the house. "I mean, that fella in there, well, there's days when I might be ready to choke him. But still, I can't imagine losing your one true love."

27

ON HIS FIRST THANKSGIVING in America, Fintan Dowd said he loved her. He said it on the highway, Route 93 south, from Patterson Falls to Boston.

Two months earlier, September, Ellen had answered an advertisement looking for a roommate in a shared apartment in Brookline, just west of the city. She had started her first, post-college position as an editorial assistant at Rheinhardt Publishers, specialists in foreign-language textbooks for middle and high school students, grades 7 to 9. Dressed in her prim skirts and ironed blouses, Ellen spent her days indexing and photocopying and trafficking text between the authors—foreign-language high school teachers—and Rheinhardt's editorial team.

Early on Thanksgiving morning, she took the T to the triple-decker apartment house in Dorchester, where everything was still in darkness, the curtains drawn. When she tiptoed up the stairs, Fintan was drinking tea in the freezing kitchen, the latest illegal arrival from Ireland sleeping face down and fully dressed on the living room couch.

Everyone in the apartment was working the holiday—picking up restaurant and security and catering shifts for their American colleagues.

From the apartment, they walked to a Rent-a-Wreck place two streets away. Then they set off north on Route 93 in a grey Chevy Impala that reeked of air freshener.

On the phone to her mother the night before, Ellen had agreed to get off the highway just outside Patterson Falls to pick up Aunt Lilly, who lived in a state-funded apartment building for the developmentally disabled and the elderly.

For as long as Ellen could remember, Aunt Lilly had been a fixture at every Christmas, Easter, and Thanksgiving table. Though in fact, Lilly was not a real aunt but her father's first cousin who had never been "quite right."

From Aunt Lilly's building, they drove the back roads to Patterson Falls while Aunt Lilly sat in the huge back seat, folding and refolding her collection of foil candy wrappers. She jabbed a fat little finger at Fintan in his driver's seat, then leaned over and around the passenger's seat to ask Ellen, "Who's that, Ellie? Who's that?"

The Boisvert house smelled of roasting turkey. Donna Boisvert had never been a hugger. In the kitchen, Ellen made introductions above the whine of Thomas Boisvert's woodworking saw from the basement. Donna asked them how the roads were, how busy, how jam-packed. She scolded her daughter for the extravagant gift basket of chutney and cheeses from a Boston delicatessen. Standing there in the kitchen, they all ran out of conversation.

Thomas Boisvert came up the basement steps in his sawdust-flecked workpants and undershirt. Ellen made the introductions again, then watched her father flinch at the Irish accent. He shook Fintan's hand but he didn't meet his daughter's eyes.

Nodding toward the kitchen window and the driveway outside, her father asked Ellen where she'd gotten the Impala, how many highway miles she got on that thing? If gas was still more expensive down there over the border in Massachusetts? Fintan, seizing on this chance for a man-to-man, went to answer. But Thomas went on talking to his daughter, as if the tall, curly-haired stranger weren't standing in their kitchen.

*

The turkey was carved, then they took their seats around the table under the kitchen window. The living room TV and the Macy's parade twittered across their awkward, perfunctory chatter about who would sit where and if Donna had put out milk glasses for everyone.

Ellen saw it all—this family meal with the Tupperware serving bowls and the easy-wipe table cloth—through Fintan's non-American eyes.

As they passed the turkey platter, Donna Boisvert compensated for her husband's sour silences by relaying the latest headlines from the neighborhood—the fact that the Theriaults, their neighbor's daughter, had had another baby, that ShopFast, the town's chain supermarket, was rumored to be changing hands again.

They are not pernicious people, thought Ellen. Surely Fintan can and will see that?

For years and years and years, the Boisverts had survived these high holidays by talking about cars and grocery coupons and the neighbors' new garden fence. All of them making noise—words to while away the hours until everyone retreated back to his or her own world.

Fintan asked Ellen's father, "Mr. Boisvert, what do you drive yourself these days? I didn't actually see your car out there in the driveway."

Again Ellen watched her father flinch at the Irish accent, at this dinner-table voice that evoked too many memories of the town's Irish American mill workers who, according to Thomas and his friends at the Richelieu Franco-American club, had too much lace-curtain cockiness. The Irish who got to keep their own church and pastor while Patterson Falls' French church was closed.

The Boisverts possessed all the pride and prejudices of some postwar, first-generation immigrants to America. Above all, they believed in their own decency. And decency meant paying your taxes and mowing your lawn and keeping your car serviced. Over that Thanksgiving dinner table, there was something too high-minded, too unapologetic about this fresh-off-the-boat Mick with his thick brogue.

"So you an American citizen?" Thomas asked Fintan through a mouthful of mashed potatoes.

"No. No, I'm not. You have to live here for . . . well, longer than I have, Mr. Boisvert."

Spite glittered in Thomas's eyes. "But you got yourself a green card, right?"

Ellen set her knife and fork down. Her mouth had gone dry.

Aunt Lilly fidgeted and blinked around the table, sensing some new, funny game. She jabbed a gravy-smeared finger at Fintan, then asked, with a crackly laugh, "Who's that, Ellie? Who's that?"

Ellen said, "Da-ad. Pl—"

But Fintan beat her to it, a calm and acid voice above Lilly's cackle and the living room TV. "Mr. Boisvert, with all due respect, I'm not sure my immigration status is really any of your business."

Thomas scraped back his chair. He left his turkey and broccoli casserole and potato half eaten. He crossed to the cellar steps again.

Donna Boisvert began to gather plates and to ask who wanted pumpkin or blueberry pie?

Afterward, the four of them ate their dessert and Cool Whip to the whine of Thomas Boisvert's electric wood saw through the kitchen floor.

Ellen and Fintan were washing up when the phone rang. Louise. Calling from an all-day party around her apartment complex pool patio, her voice slurry from margaritas.

Donna took the phone and delivered the same neighborhood news to her Florida daughter as she had, earlier, to Ellen. Watching her mother laughing into the phone and asking Louise for the exact temperature down there in St. Pete, Ellen felt a familiar stab of resentment. This was and always would be Louise—calling or breezing home for a quick visit, and always after the storm had passed.

Fintan and Ellen left for Boston just before the six o'clock news.

Driving back through town to Lilly's apartment and afterward on Route 93 South, Fintan was silent.

Ellen wanted to cry—not just for her father's rudeness or Fintan's silence. But she wanted to weep for the entire ruination of what a Thanksgiving Day was supposed to be. Now she knew that she had wanted Fintan to like it all—to admire her mother's stuffing, to watch the Macy's parade and eat his pie. And above all, she had wanted her own family to live up to her own concoctions of them, to her own storied version of small-town parents—traditional, God fearing, and New England wholesome.

In that drive south, she admitted to herself that, for four years of college it had been this way—the terrible disappointment when you walked in that kitchen and remembered the mismatch between how they were and how she had beheld them from a distance.

The Impala still reeked of cheap air freshener. Now Route 93 was a necklace of headlights all heading south—carfuls of people all harboring their own disappointments or delusions of an American holiday. Fintan drove in that hunch-shouldered way that told Ellen he was lost in thought, needling away at something inside him.

After the last exit for Manchester, he set his hand back on her knee.

"You all right?"

"Yeah. Fine. You? . . . I'm sorry about Dad. He's just—"

Fintan shrugged. In the slithery highway lights, Fintan trapped the huge steering wheel with his knee while he reached over to caress her left cheek. She willed herself not to really cry, not to let the tears come. "Look, Ell, I've been thinking . . ."

Months, years later, Ellen would enter a roadside public bathroom where the air-freshener smell would remind her of the Thanksgiving night when a man—when anyone—first said he loved her.

" . . . I've been thinking that we should get a place, move in together."

Her heart skipped, thrilled.

He took his eyes off the highway to smile across at her. "What do you think?"

She leaned across to hug him. "Yes. *Yes.*" Then, "I love you."

"Me too."

28

THE GIRL TIPTOES from the room and shuts the door. Jo listens to her footsteps in the parlor, then up the stairs. Then the water rushes through the pipes. One of these days, that girl will wash her own flesh off. Her skin and hair will go floating through the house and out to the septic beyond the orchard.

Tonight the Yank girl told her stories again—sitting here next to the bed, the words soft and slow, like someone reciting a prayer. The Yank girl tells her stories of the boy in Boston—how they met in that pub he worked in, how he studied for some sort of American degree, how they once went on their holidays to Mexico or Florida or someplace where it was roasting hot.

The girl has managed to coax Ned back into the house. Coaxed him like a stray cat. But still he never steps past the parlor door. Still he stands there between the china cabinet and the couch, the cap scrunched in his fist as he delivers news of the stock and the fields. *Yes, ma'am,* and *no, ma'am. That's true all right, ma'am.* This week, he's having the usual men in to cut and bale the summer hay.

After the girl leaves the bedroom, Jo listens for her bedtime rituals, the footsteps across the upstairs landing. These sudden sounds in the house, this sudden presence of another person. In the beginning, after the girl moved in, they used to frighten her, jolt her awake. But now they're a strange comfort, a set of noises and rituals before sleep.

Jo doesn't believe the half of her stories, happy little yarns about a young couple in Boston. But what matter now, truth or lies? Swap the truth for the lie, and it's often the same story anyway.

Jo shuts her eyes and there he is again—her boy out there in those streets, serving in a pub, working in that office where the girl says he got a posh job and got promoted twice. Tonight he's in a place with too many cars and buses with their horns blowing and all those exhaust fumes on the freezing winter air. He's walking down the footpath, his back to her in a swanky winter overcoat, a scarf wrapped around his neck and his breath fogging on the icy air. He's holding a little girl by the hand—a blond little girl in a little grey coat with a red scarf and matching red mittens. She's a child from a storybook, a child that has come to Jo in dreams before. In the dream, they're retreating into the distance, disappearing among the crowds of winter people on a city footpath. Just in time they stop and turn, the man and the little girl laughing as they wave at her, the red mittens waving madly. "Say 'hello,'" the man says. "Wave and say 'hello' to your gran." There they are laughing and waving, cocking their heads like people on a television.

*

"Did you hear we got a telly?" Jo asks Kitty. "We got a telly within in the town."

Kitty has teased her hair into a beehive. Across the parlor table, her pointed bosoms press against her polka-dot blouse, which is tucked into white bell-bottom trousers. Next to Kitty sits her new husband, Brian.

Earlier this afternoon, Brian and Kitty drove through the yard gate in a red Volkswagen car. Kitty sprang from the passenger seat in her polka dots and white bell-bottoms, looking ridiculous in the farmyard mud at Knockduff. In her high heels, Kitty picked her way across the yard to the boy standing there in the back doorway. Kitty tousled the boy's curls and said, "Fintan, say hello to your new uncle."

"Brian," she said, turning to the pale, smiling man in his immaculate holiday clothes, "Brian, this is Fintan, the best little boy in Ireland. And he just had a birthday, didn't you, Fintan? He just turned eight."

Now across their white-cloth table, the table set with Jo's own wedding china, they eat a supper of pink ham and sliced-up tomatoes and shop bread, not their usual *caiscín*. Jo has cycled down to the village to buy all this, all this convenience food because she presumes this is the kind of thing they all eat in Dublin City—shop bread and paper-thin ham. Mother, in her black widow's cardigan, has stayed in her fireside armchair, where the sisters have brought her a supper tray.

"It's below in the kitchen," says Jo about the new black-and-white television. "John put up a special shelf for it."

"Oh, isn't that grand!" says Kitty. Brian, seizing on this conversation, turns toward the boy. "And tell me, Fintan, what's *your* favorite telly program?"

The boy flinches from this man's cooing Dublin voice, the obvious shock of being asked a question, a direct question just for a child. He is never addressed by name.

Across the table Jo watches her son sitting there, his young hands callused from farm work. Under his knitted *geansaí,* the boy's arms and neck are marked with bruises where she has lashed out at him, given him the back of her own hand for when he won't leave the cursed telly to go out and do his own share of the milking before dark. Or sometimes, Jo slaps her child simply because he's there—just there between her and the rest of the world.

"Tell Uncle Brian," Jo prompts, in the strange, fluting voice she uses for visitors.

The boy's voice comes as a whisper. "*Wanderly Wagon,*" he says, red-faced with shyness and staring down at his food. "I love *Wanderly Wagon.*"

Brian jabs a fork toward the little boy and winks at him. "Oh now, didn't I *think* that'd be your favorite, for sure. Now don't tell your Auntie Kitty this, but I do have the odd watch of *Wanderly Wagon* myself. On the sly! Sure, it's great fun!"

Then the cutlery becomes loud again. They have run out of things to say. Mother has dozed over her tea tray. The boy swings his Wellington legs under the table—thuck, thuck, thuck. Jo eyes him. *Stop. Stop or I'll kill you.*

Two weeks ago, Kitty announced her marriage by letter. A small affair, she wrote. In a north Dublin church with just a few friends and Brian's mother and sisters.

Ever since the postman brought that letter, the house has been full of wailing and hand-wringing. Night after night Jo has heard it, Mother's words spitting from beside the kitchen range. *Kitty, Kitty, Kitty.* Kitty this and Kitty that. "What kind of daughter?" Mother wailed. "What kind of girl? And sure, we don't know who he is, who his people are, what breeding, what stock."

And yet today, here's all this fuss for Kitty and all of them sitting here like actors around a table, stagestruck and petrified in their own house.

Brian reaches for Kitty's hand and holds it, right there on the tablecloth in plain view. Jo stares at his little hand, not a man's hands at all, but the flesh soft and powdered. The nails are clean and pink. He intertwines his fingers with Kitty's. Embarrassed, Jo looks away. In her mind's eye, she's putting the hot saucepan from the range on there, the hot sizzling pot, right on Brian's little office-boy's fingers. She hears the sizzle of flesh, like branding a bullock.

Then Jo watches her own John, sitting here next to her and munching his ham and bread, his neck scrawny and jiggly with age.

In her letter, Kitty said that Brian was a bank clerk, and that every day, he leaves their new, semidetached house to take the bus to his job in a bank in College Green in the city center.

"Would you believe it, but this is actually my first time in Mayo?" Brian tries again, his voice trumpeting across the parlor. "Been down the country before but never *this* far down!" He smiles around the table, this jaunty little Dublin man, hoping for some responding chatter. That fixed smile, sitting there in a white, short-sleeve shirt and in his beige holiday slacks. Brian Walsh is as different from John Dowd as it's possible for two men, two human species to be.

"That was a gorgeous meal, Jo," says Kitty, setting down her knife and fork. She lowers her voice, glances at their sleeping mother. "Now, any chance of a drink? I'd love a drink; wouldn't you, Brian? We'll all have a drink to bless the nuptials!"

Jo pours them whiskeys, a bottle of stout for John. At Kitty's persuasion, they switch on the new transistor radio on the sideboard. Then, the happy couple coaxes Jo to pour a sherry for herself. "Go, on, it'll just do you good. Pep you up."

They clink their glasses and, with the sherry, Jo feels the air in the parlor lighten. She feels as if they've been released from something.

"Tell me," says Brian in his indulgent child's voice. "Tell me, Fintan, what d'ya think of that oul' dog on there, the dog on *Wanderly Wagon*, what's his name . . . ?'"

"Judge!" shouts the boy. "His name is Judge." A smile flickers across his young features. He looks straight at his new uncle. He thucks his feet against the table leg again. "Judge is only a pretend. But I got a dog—a real dog! She's a pup!"

"Ooooh! Really?" Kitty sets down her whiskey glass. She claps her hands, her red nail lacquer flashing. "Aren't you the lucky boy?"

"Would you *show* me your new puppy?" Brian coaxes.

The boy leads his new uncle through the house and up through the yard where Brian, in his suede shoes, detours around the puddles of *cac bó*. The child stands in the stable doorway, waiting for Brian to catch up. Out of the house, away from his mother's dour and punishing gaze, this is a different child, a child who stands there rocking on his heels and giggling.

He points to a black squirmy pup in the manger, lying there in the straw. "Uncle Brian!" he screeches. "Look at her! Look at my Rosie!"

29

TODAY THE MAN IN THE HAY-BALING MACHINE is working in one of the lower meadows. Ack-ack-ack goes the engine. It grows louder, more raucous through the open bedroom window.

Ellen crosses to the bedside, scoops more crushed ice from a bedside bowl, holds her palm to Jo's lips. Jo tilts the chin to obey. It's like giving a dog a drink of water.

Each ice piece slithers between the toothless gums. They have taken away her dentures. Nurse Ryan said there was too much risk of infection.

Jo sighs loudly. Ellen goes back to the window again, to draw the drapes against the afternoon sun.

"You had no right! None at all," Jo shouts from the bed. "Jesus, Kitty, he's my own son. And you my only sister. The least you could have done was to tell me."

Ellen shivers. For the past few mornings, Ellen has opened the door to this litany of disconnected sentences, words, past events. I am an eavesdropper, thinks Ellen. A stranger eavesdropping on the mismatched pieces of an old woman's life.

"My child. He was still my child!" Jo mutters. She is hallucinating, dreaming out loud. This is the most agitated that Ellen has seen her. "Kitty?" Ellen whispers to the sleeping face.

"You should have told me, rang me down here at the house." Jo says, the lips moving. In. Out. In. Out. Jo makes a little blowhole between her lips. The chest rising, falling rhythmically. The eyes have stopped fluttering.

Ellen tiptoes closer to the bed. "Would you like Kitty to come here? Would you like us to find your sister?"

The lips have stopped moving. Jo is fast asleep.

Ellen checks her watch. She wishes Nurse Ryan would come early today. Should she ring the nurse's mobile phone?

*

Nurse Ryan eats the last of her pink marshmallow cookie, then she takes another sip of tea. Outside the hay baler has moved up the hill, to the far end of the meadow. So the kitchen at Knockduff is silent.

"She's been talking a lot about her younger and only sister. Kitty. Did you know her?" Ellen asks.

Elaine Ryan has short, blond hair. She puzzles her small, pointed features. "Kitty? Sorry. No. I actually thought Jo's all alone with no family left." She shrugs. "I'm not actually from around here, myself." She holds up her left hand, flashes a wedding band. "I was nursing and living in Dublin when I met my husband. He's from Galway, so we moved down here. I retrained for community nursing. Except for the school parents' committee at the kids' school, I don't actually know many local families. But I could certainly ask, ask around for you. Or Tom. Fitzgerald. He'd definitely know."

"I think we should try and find her, the sister. My late husband said she used to live in Dublin." Ellen adds, "Look, I don't want to be alarmist, but judging by Jo's condition the past two days, it might be time."

"Yeah. She's not doing that great, Ellen. Very soon she's going to need more help breathing. A nebulizer to start, at least for short periods, then possibly oxygen." Nurse Ryan surveys Ellen. "We can ask Tom, of course, but, well, that can be quite tough to handle. I mean, I'm not sure how long she can really go on like this." Over her tea cup the nurse widens her eyes. "Or you."

*

"You look tired," says Tom Fitzgerald, standing there in the scullery doorway.

"I'm fine."

"Oh, your boyfriend, our Lorcan. He's been asking when you're coming for dinner again." Tom flashes a wide smile. "I told him soon. I *hope* that's true. Ruth loved meeting you. Get an agency nurse up here a few nights.

This time we'll go down to the hotel for a bite to eat. You need to get out and about. Come down the hill more often and sample our mad, Gowna nightlife." He laughs at his own joke.

Ever since that visit, that dinner in the doctor's house, there's been something extra contrite, effusive about Tom Fitzgerald.

Ellen gives him a wintry smile. "Sounds good. I'll call the agency."

He heads for the back door.

"Oh, Tom? She was mumbling about her sister today, Kitty. Fintan's Aunt Kitty. I think if she's still alive, shouldn't we contact her, find her? Let her come and say her good-byes?"

Tom shrugs. "Last August, when I first came out here, when we were arranging for her admission to Galway Hospital, I asked Jo that. If she wanted me to contact anybody—her son. A sister, even one of the nephew-in-laws. 'No,' says she. 'Nobody that'd give a tinker's curse whether I'm alive or dead. Alive or six feet under the clay.'"

"So did you know her—Kitty?"

"Kitty? No. *I* didn't. But my dad, God rest him, he knew them both—Jo and her sister—in his young days. He used to say that they were like night and day, the two Burke sisters—Little and Large, Pretty and . . . well, Jo was never any beauty. And my dad always said it was a kind of made match—between your in-laws, between Jo and her husband. Common enough in them days, the 1950s, especially where a farm of land was involved. The woman had to have a dowry—or a fortune they called it back then. And the man either had land or, if there were too many brothers, he had to marry into a farm. That or emigrate. Simple as that." He shakes his head. "They were different times."

"Do you think she's still alive?"

"Even if she is, she's no one our Jo wanted at her bedside." Tom shrugs. "Unless she's had a change of heart—which I doubt, to be honest."

Outside, the summer evening has grown chilly. Tomorrow the baling machine is scheduled to do the lower meadows, the fields between the house and the lower gate.

After the doctor leaves, Ellen lingers in the back doorway, listening to the tractor tracking down the upper fields, heading down the slope for the house and the yard.

30

JO WATCHES THE BOY as he strides along the field's newly ploughed ridges—his twelve-year-old's gangly physique as he follows in the tractor's noise and wake.

There's something birdlike about his long, stooping back. With the bucket of seed potatoes, he stoops and stands, stoops and stands. She plants the neighboring ridge, but a hundred yards behind him. Their Wellingtons thuck-thuck in the newly turned earth. Mother and son follow each other's rhythm, their movements synchronized so that one is setting the potato seed while the other is walking, the plastic bucket of seed potatoes over the arm, pacing to the next planting spot. Stoop and stand. Stoop and stand.

The crows are black specks in the grey sky. They compete with the tractor engine noise: curr-curr-curr. The birds seem to mock her woman's stupidity, mock this ridiculous turn of events in the Dowd household.

How will she tell her son, how will she bridge the staid silence between them to actually say the words? "You're going to have a brother or sister."

Since she found out, since Dr. Fitzgerald did his test, she has come to think of the child inside her as a silly little thing, a rowdy, bumbling creature. Jo can't sleep now. At night when she lies awake she wants to whisper to it, to give it fair warning.

John is down in the house, in bed with a spring cold. Nowadays Jo thinks of her husband and her mother in the same breath: each complaining of drafts under the door, grumbling about the wheezes in their chests.

She stops again. She straightens to arch her back. She turns to look back down at their house. From here it's a top-down view of the slate roof, the smoke out of the chimneys, the upstairs windows. *Don't,* she says silently to the child inside her. *Don't bother.*

In the house, Jo has turned from their new gas cooker or from the Formica table under the kitchen window to see her mother watching her. She has seen Mother's knowing smirk—a smirk that vexes Jo, makes her rebellious, determined to somehow change things this time, to reverse the order of their universe.

Next year, Jo Dowd will be forty years of age. Her sickly husband will soon be eligible for the old age pension. Before long, her pregnancy will be obvious to everyone. It'll be a holy show before the whole parish when she travels down the hill to the shop in Gowna, or when they all get the hackney down to Mass of a Sunday. Everyone in the church will see the bulge under her coat. They'll think that it's either pitiful or obscene.

For months, the village has been all talk about the renovations and reopening of the Gowna dance hall. There have been announcements off the Sunday pulpit, collection envelopes and bake sales and raffles to raise funds.

These days, when he's sent out for the evening milking, the boy brings the transistor from the parlor with him to hang from a nail on the stable wall. Down the upper yard in Knockduff come these mad, newfangled songs, "Tie a Yellow Ribbon Round the Old Oak Tree." Or there's a man called Gary Glitter who tells the Dowds' cows that they're his only true love.

There's a business man from the town who's going to bring country music bands and disco outfits to the Gowna Hall again—every Saturday night. The rest of the week, the village hall will be available for parish events, concerts, and fund-raisers.

"I'm going," Jo announces one Sunday evening, after they have all come up the hill from the Easter devotions, where the priest announced the hall's grand-opening night, April 10.

John looks mournfully from his fireside chair. "Ach, no," he says. "It wouldn't be right." *In your condition.* It's what he wants to say, but he, like their son, has grown afraid of Jo. He avoids her long, poisonous silences, he knows to slope and duck from the sudden typhoons of her temper.

There's a polyester trouser suit hanging in an upstairs wardrobe. It's a suit that Kitty left behind last summer. She and Brian were on a flying visit, on their way to their summer holidays in County Kerry. The suit is a daft-looking thing: a turquoise jacket with patch pockets and three huge white buttons down the front, a white plastic belt in fake patent. There are matching turquoise slacks.

That Sunday evening, Jo goes upstairs to try it on, then marches across the landing to the boy's room and the full-length mirror on his wardrobe. The turquoise trousers are too short, and they sag slightly on her still-flat stomach. She turns and twists before the mirror, sucks in her cheeks and squints her eyes like those women on the telly, the women in the American comedy programs. In the mirror she reminds herself of someone's oversized doll, a doll that someone dressed in the wrong clothes. She crosses and recrosses the boy's bedroom, kicking her feet, twirling like a model and listening to the polyester slacks swishing. She almost laughs out loud. Slacks. They'd cover the tracks of her Wellingtons on her calves. Surely they'd be great fun on the bicycle? She smoothes her hand down over her stomach again, takes one more turn before the wardrobe mirror. No. You'd never guess. Never know that Jo and John Dowd are expecting a child.

Every night that week, she sits in the kitchen with her sewing box, taking in the pants waist, letting down the hems and adding on a piece of matching white material to make the pants legs longer.

Look at the height of her. Once, almost fifteen years ago, the woman in the bridal dress shop in Galway said that about Jo. That was a strange, other life. When she was twenty-five years old and about to be married. *She must have a great appetite.*

Pedaling along the lake road, Jo sees the new lit-up sign flashing into the April twilight like an ambulance. Inside, the hall smells of new timber and concrete. In her blue trouser suit, she crosses to the ladies' where the mirrors are all new and shiny, topped with new ceramic tiles and a line of domed lights. In the mirror she checks her new hair color—a deep brown rinse that covers the grey.

The turnout for the grand opening is twice what anyone expected. On stage, a local band plays button accordion and fiddle and a man with a florid face and a crooning voice sings, "There was a wild Colonial boy. Jack Duggan was his name."

Jo sits in her old spot on the bench along the wall. She makes small talk with the other women as she crosses and uncrosses her legs, half terrified and half delighted by this new version of herself.

One by one, the couples take to the floor—the men in pink, shiny faces, their starched shirts and their Sunday shoes. Some of the younger wives are dressed in polyester trouser suits or A-line miniskirts with zipped up, knee-length boots.

Father Monroe asks Jo out to dance, for a stack of barley in which they kick and prance and twirl. But then, the priest is summoned to the tea room because someone has questions about the raffle.

After that, another man asks her to make up a Siege of Ennis. Tonight, it's as if Jo is watching herself there out on the floor, her new shoes clacking, this strange, frenetic version of herself. On the dance floor, she can forget the household she has just pedaled from. And except for this mad energy inside her, she could forget that, eight months from now, she will be delivering another child. As she dances she feels each man's hand on her lower back. It sends ripples of longing through her.

As part of the dance, she's cast into the arms of a waiting man, a man in a pin-stripe suit with his tie loosened. When he twirls her around, his hands are big and strong; he marks the end of each dance movement with a loud, boisterous step.

"D'you not remember me?" the man asks, his eyes glittery with drink. "You were a few classes ahead of me down at the school," he says, through a gust of whiskey breath. "I'm Brendan. Brendan Quinn."

"Of course," she assures him. Of course, she remembers him now, though in fact, she cannot quite distinguish which of the Quinn lads this is.

After the Siege of Ennis is over, Brendan Quinn and Jo stay on the floor. His shirttail has escaped the waist of his trousers. He has a well-shaven, rakish face. They dance the next set, an old-time waltz, for which he makes exaggerated, sweeping steps so that several times, they bump into the older sedate couples.

Brendan Quinn is home on holidays from London. He tells her that London is not what anyone around Gowna would think. That they probably think that London is lonely for men like him, but where he lives, there's a mighty Irish social scene—dances and ceilis and pubs. There are nights, he says, when the *craic* is so good you'd swear you'd never left home at all.

They dance set after set, and Brendan Quinn has the emigrant's over-the-top gusto for old songs and old nostalgic chat. Between their dances, he inquires for other old school classmates who, in Jo's memory, were not friends at all—just half-remembered names from among those grim rows of school desks.

When the dance is nearly over, Jo weaves through the dancers to go to the ladies' cloakroom. There's nobody there, nobody collecting the tickets inside the hatch. When she turns, she almost collides with Brendan Quinn again, standing there just behind her.

"Jo," he says. "Give us an oul' kiss. Just for oul' times. Sure, there's no harm in an oul' kiss."

She lets him follow her across the ladies' toilet, then into the ladies' cloakroom, the farthest corner, where he backs her against the cold wall and jams his thigh between her legs, his tongue into her mouth. While he's kissing her, she thinks of them up at home. Mother is in bed by now. The boy is sitting there gawking up at the telly as usual, the dog asleep at his feet. And John is dozing in his chair by the range, a scarf over his *geansaí* to keep out the chill. She sees them there as she pulls Brendan Quinn back toward her, draws him close for another kiss. She could devour him.

She shows him a back entrance off the cloakroom, where they step out into the pebbled car park, under the dance hall's flashing lights.

As they walk down along the lake road, her mind is a blank of greed, seething greed.

Brendan Quinn opens a farmer's gate and they walk into a marshy, lake-side field.

Behind a copse of furze bushes, he spreads his suit jacket on the ground for her. Then he tugs at her new blue pants as she listens to him unzipping himself in the dark.

When he pushes himself into her, she feels the size of him, a proper size for a grown man, not like John. And there's no harm to be done, no harm, not with the baby already there. She can't get in trouble.

Afterward they cross the wet grass and clank the field gate shut behind them. Her disappointment turns to desperation, a terrible desperation that she has been waiting all her life for something that just went, disappeared, before she had time to really feel, to hold onto it. "When will you be home again?" she asks, watching the whites of his eyes, the collar of his white shirt in the dark.

He says that, with the new ganger he has beyond now, you just never know when you get holidays. Then, as if he can feel her growing panic he says, "Christmas, sure. Maybe Christmas. With the help of God."

Then Brendan leaves quickly, turning down the road for the village. Into the darkness, he calls good-bye and good luck. Alone, Jo walks back up the lake road to the hall where she's just in time to stand with everyone else as the band plays the closing national anthem, *Seo dhaoibh a Cháirde.*

With two other women, she walks back out into the April night, where she rolls up her trouser legs so she can cycle back up the hill home. The women retrieve their bicycles from the side of the hall and wheel them among the last cars left in the new tarmac car park. When they pedal away, the flashing marquee bulbs are finally switched off for the night.

"Goodnight, Mrs. Dowd! Goodnight to you!" the women call to Jo as she turns up the Knockduff road for the hill and home.

On the hill, she doesn't get off to walk the bicycle but pedals madly, her backside jutting from side to side. Her coat flutters behind her, her cheeks burn, even in this dewy April night.

Later, the pain wakens her. Gone. Soon gone, she tells herself. Just stomach gas. Or the size of Brendan Quinn. But the pain travels around her back, bends her in two. Then the bedsheet beneath her is cold, thick. It smells like a disemboweled rabbit.

She tiptoes across the landing to the upstairs toilet while John snores on. The child. The unborn child has leaked from her. It has dislodged itself.

John stands there, teetering sleepily into the light as she bundles the bloody sheets, a white stork's bundle. She stuffs it in a corner until tomorrow and the daylight. Tiptoes back across the landing to the high cupboard for fresh sheets. There's the boy in his bedroom door, wakened by the commotion. In his bare feet and pajamas, he blinks sleepily at his mother. She hears the dog flopping down off his single bed, the nails ticking across the linoleum. The bloody dog, Rosie. He's sneaked her upstairs again.

"Get back in bed," she calls to the boy, a hoarse whisper, her fist raised to threaten a good clout.

Back in their bedroom, John stands there in his long johns, that helpless look, the eyes wondering, asking, blaming. As she tucks and smoothes the clean sheets, she sees that look of his. Blame. Suspicion. What has he read in her face? They say a man knows. Smells another man. So it's her fault. Dancing all night and pedaling the bicycle against the hill, lying with a man who thrilled and filled her. Her fault.

Next afternoon, Jo walks down the avenue to the bottom field. She is heading toward the hazel rock when she sees Ned, young teenage Ned, the farmhand who comes to help on the land. His scythe rasps through the spring day as he cuts thistles in the front paddock. He stops and sets the scythe handle over his young shoulder to wave at her, obediently. Wave to his boss's wife.

Ma'am never waves back. Instead, she hurries across the grass toward the hazel rock and its dark, mossy crevices. In her left hand is what looks like a white bag of rubbish.

31

FATHER NOEL BRADLEY'S front door is set open to a tiled hallway. From a room at the end, what looks like a kitchen, comes music from a radio, a radio program playing Bach.

"Hello?" She steps in out of the afternoon thundershower, calls down the hallway. "Hello? Father Bradley?"

He appears from a bedroom door, wiping his hair with a green towel. He's dressed in the same black spandex bicycle-racing shorts and yellow T-shirt. He's obviously been bicycling in the rain.

From under the towel he gives her a twisted smile. "Oh, hello. Ellen! Were you knocking long? Come in! Or you'll get drenched."

She follows him down the hallway toward a kitchen with white cupboards, a long window that looks onto the garden. "Coffee?" he asks, his voice muffled by the towel.

Inside the doorway Ellen stops. She swallows. Between the priest's shoulder blades, his shirt has a giant sweat stain that she can smell from here. Fintan. Fintan always returned from jogging looking and smelling just like this.

Now, in this kitchen in Ireland, she can smell him—her dead husband, coming pounding up the stairs and into their living room, filling their apartment with a man's sweat smell. She shuts her eyes. But there's only the smell. She cannot conjure the rest of him. Even Fintan's voice is gone. Like a snatch of a radio song that was there, but then faded, gone.

Father Noel drapes the towel over his shoulders, then he stands there with his hair spiked wet. Now he's just a man in a faded yellow T-shirt, the name and date of some road race on the front. He's waiting for something.

Oh, yes. He's waiting for her to accept or decline his offer of coffee. "Yes, Father. Actually, I'd love a cup."

"Noel, please."

"Noel."

He crosses to the sink where he reaches to turn down the radio volume. Then he fills the kettle and sets it on a small electric stove. She sits on a wooden stool at the kitchen counter. He stays standing.

He turns from the stove, gives her that hapless grin. "How are you surviving up there? I was up that way last week, and I was going to call in on you but . . . Well, Tom didn't think that Jo Dowd would want me, though I hear she's failing."

"She's holding her own. Her breathing is getting worse. But she's comfortable at least."

He takes Ellen in. "And how are you doing?"

"I'm all right. It's not so bad up there. Quiet, peaceful." She forces a laugh. "People pay big bucks for summer vacations on a genuine Irish farm!"

"Still . . ." He reaches into a cupboard for a cafetière, calls over his shoulder at her. "Oh, d'you take sugar?"

*

The coffee is strong and scalding hot. The priest sits at the corner of the counter, the stool looking impossibly small under his long, thin frame. He's hung the green towel on the back of the door. "Noel, this isn't totally a social visit. I've come for advice and parish information."

"Yeah?" He raises his eyebrows.

"Jo Dowd had a sister. Kitty. Jo is obviously dreaming about her, their youth. In her sleep, or half awake, she also keeps asking me about a little girl, a child, some child she keeps dreaming about, mumbling to." She raises her eyebrows in a question. Who?

The priest shrugs. "This sister, is she still alive?"

"I don't know. Kitty lived in Dublin. I know Fintan liked her, kind of looked up to her. But Kitty and Jo had a falling out."

"Well, Jo fell out with a lot of . . ." Then he makes that zipping-the-mouth shut sign. "Sorry, shouldn't talk ill of the sick, but I'm not telling you anything you don't already know." Across the counter, Noel's look tells her that Tom Fitzgerald has been talking, confiding in his friend the young priest. The story of the estranged American son, a son who never came home—not even to his mother's hospital bedside. It's not exactly medical-privacy information.

Ellen says, "I'm going to try and find her. Even if they're estranged. A sister should know, at least be given the chance to come and say good-bye. It can't be that hard to find her, can it?"

Father Noel sets his coffee mug down. "You know, I can probably help you there. I can take a rummage through our own church records; send out an e-mail to some of the bigger city parishes in Dublin. Was she married, do you know?"

"Yes. Fintan, my late husband, said she was. So she'd have had a different last name, too."

"Yeah, but if she married in a Dublin parish, she'd have had to get"—he makes quote signs in the air—"'a letter of freedom' from her home parish of Gowna. It's bound to be in the records here. Somewhere. That, and I'll just send out a general interdiocesan e-mail. Her general age, originally from Mayo, the parish of Gowna. But a good place to start would be just our own records. Oh, you have Jo's maiden name?"

"Burke."

"So Kitty—Kathleen—Burke." The priest calculates numbers, years—"Probably married somewhere in the mid- to late sixties, early nineteen-seventies. Right?"

"You're the boss, Father."

"Noel."

They both laugh—a tension-release laugh. He seems glad, eager for her company. He leans closer toward her. "Of course, she could've moved to another place, changed her church, gone to a nursing home or a retirement place. And a lot of priests go away on holidays this time of year; then the rest of us are left driving around between parishes, delivering the instant dial-a-Mass."

Sitting there with Bach still playing softly from the radio, Noel Bradley's voice and face are full of real concern. If she let it, this voice could make her stop and feel the entire weight of it—to step outside the routine of visits to Jo's room and the daily roster of medications and treatments. And the yawning emptiness of her future, a future where she has to fly back to Boston, go hunting for a place to live in Coventry-by-the-Sea.

She has a sudden urge to tell him, to confide in this man in the yellow T-shirt—to tell him about this past year, the months since Fintan died. Yes, and the years before that, how they fought and seethed and, sometimes, kissed and made up and made love. That she's not the do-gooder daughter-in-law that he seems to thinks she is.

"Ellen?" He softens his voice, almost to a whisper. Has he been reading her thoughts? "That day . . . that day you came here, a month back, when we first met. You didn't know, did you? I mean, you'd never met Jo Dowd before?"

She meets his gaze. "No. In fact, I'd been told . . ." Her voice cracks. She feels tears threatening. "Actually, my husband said his mother was long dead. They hadn't spoken since he'd left here. And I don't . . . I don't know why."

He reaches to touch her upper arm, leaving his hand there. Through her cotton shirt, his hand feels good. His hand or his voice have the power to undo her, to make her run out of this house weeping—to run back out into the street to her car and drive away. Forever.

"For whatever reason, no matter what happened between you and him, or him and her, you're doing the right thing now. Staying. It'd have been a shame to just shift her to a nursing home. She wouldn't have lasted the fortnight in a place like that. At least at home she's getting the chance to have all these dreams, fantasies, to have the long good-bye. I wish more of us had your courage."

"I'm not so sure about that, Noel."

He raises one eyebrow, gives her a sad, twisted smile. "Oh, I am."

*

The rain has stopped. The churchyard smells of rain and wet yew hedges. They stand in his doorway. "I'll give a look through the parish books tomorrow. Anything I find, I'll give you a ring up at the house."

She suddenly hugs him. The priest's eyes widen in embarrassed surprise. Then he hugs her back—tightly.

"'Bye. And thanks." She turns to walk back to the village street, leaving him standing there in the doorway. Walking through the churchyard, Ellen feels suddenly lighter, as if she has relieved herself of something, as if something long dead within her might have trembled awake, as if it might have a new possibility.

32

"BUT YOU CAN'T BEAT THE TRAVEL," a woman is saying to Jo. Here, in her bedroom, the sick room off the parlor. First, the woman and her jaunty little voice are the dream, but then suddenly, the woman is right there, standing at the end of Jo's bed. It's that silly little woman in the red winter coat. Then suddenly, Jo and this woman are both standing in a supermarket, trolleys head to head. Maxwell House and Nescafé and Lyons and Barry's along a shelf. Little Red Riding Hood. " . . . I do be always saying to my Mattie above at the house; 'Mattie,' I do say, 'you'll never beat the bit of travel to broaden the mind.' Ach no, I think it's great, I really do. And they're making a blinkin' fortune over there in America, in Boston, the pair of them, your Fintan and my Sheila. Sheila rings every week, Saturday evenings, just before I wash me hair. Of course, *she's* only just up outta the bed at that time, the five hours' time difference. 'Reverse the charges, darling,' I do say to her. 'Reverse the charges because it's worth all the money in Ireland just to hear your voice across the sea.' And she tells me your Fintan's raking it in, too, working in a pub for himself. Of course, Sheila's at the waitressing, too. And the bit of babysitting and she's working for a lovely couple now; they let her drive their car and everything, a spare car they never use. Imagine! But loads of work. Not like here. Lord, Mrs. Dowd, did you hear about the place, the factory below in Castlebar? They're saying that's next. Everyone cut back to half-time already, and some of them already got their lump sum and their 'Cheerio now and thanks for nothing.' Our Sheila says it's nothing to make a hundred dollars in a night's waitressing. Not like here. Ha, ha, ha, God, a week'd be nearer the mark. Well, I'm *delighted* Mrs. Dowd now, that I met you at long last.

'Cos my Sheila does be saying on the phone, 'Oh, I met this grand lad over here, a lad from out Gowna way. Sure you must know the family, Mammy.' 'Well I don't, darling,' says I. 'I'd love to tell you I do, but I don't.' And tell us, had ye a great time over at the wedding? Was that your first time over, in America, I mean? God, ye must've had a great time altogether. Sure they do everything big over there. And a Yank, Sheila told me. Married a Yank for himself an' all."

In her room off the parlor, Jo is trying to open her mouth. Her lips are stuck together. They're dry as sand. And the breath won't come. Puff, puff, puff. Stuck. Then at last it all creaks open, like a vault. The voice is not hers anymore. The voice becomes the man out there in the kitchen on the television advertisement, except someone has slowed the television down, a record caught in the gramophone.

"Oh, yes," Jo is saying across their grocery trolleys. "Oh, yes. 'Twas a lovely wedding."

"But listen, Mrs. Dowd, I'll be telling her now, so I will; she's due to ring again this Saturday coming, just before I go up to wash me hair, the few words with her daddy first, oh, the apple of her father's eye that one, and then we'll be having the chat and I'll be telling her how I met you at long last. Ah, isn't it grand for them though, out there in a strange country? Nearly neighbors' children, you might say. Or neighboring parishes anyways. And your fella after getting married for himself. I'm sure she's a nice girl.

"What? Yeah, what's the name of that pub he's in? Funny names on the pubs over there. Not like here. What? Yeah, oh, Janey now I can't remember it either, though Sheila did mention . . . oh, wait now . . . no, it's on the tip of me tongue . . ."

The television down in the kitchen is clicking, the screen rolling, skipping. Click, click, click. Telly on the blink. Telly on the blink. Then, Mrs. McCormack, the little woman in the little red coat in the supermarket, is clicking her fingers. Click, click, click. "Oh, d'ya know I have it now," she says. "Yeah. Jeez I knew 'twas christened after some man. Yeah, that's a funny one all right. Sure, leave it to the Yanks. 'The Paul Revere Tavern,' whoever *he* is when he's at home."

The Paul Revere Tavern.

*

"What'll you have there?" the boy is saying, leaning in over Jo's sick bed. "What'll you have, Mam?" He's so tall, almost six foot to the ceiling. A white towel over his shoulder, a barman's shirt and tie. "What'll you have, Mammy? Tea? Coffee? Sherry?"

The place is loud with bar voices. The shame. The cursed, deadening shame. My brilliant son serving drinks in America, wiping up tables after drunkards and wastrels.

*

Nighttime. No telly. Extra flavor, extra quality. Above Jo's bed there are the usual noises: footsteps across the landing, water rushing in the pipes. Yes. The American girl. Ellen. The girl he got married to. The girl from the American wedding.

Jo shuts her eyes and there's the boy and this American bride, both of them suddenly here, driving up the avenue toward the house. There's a line of cars—big American cars with strange wings and silver things on the bonnet. The cars stop. The doors bang, and here's her boy and the Yank girl holding hands and walking up toward the house, stepping along in the ice and sliding. They get up again, walk up the hill and fall again, all their wedding guests behind them holding hands, too. The American wedding party trudging and falling up the hill at Knockduff.

33

"A DREAM, ELL," Fintan said over his shoulder from the mirror above the bookshelves in their tiny Brookline apartment. He was fastening his tie—the tie he was wearing with his new suit to his first professional job in Boston.

Two days earlier, he had been appointed project manager at Mahoney Brothers Construction in Quincy.

They have lived together for over six months now in this apartment that they found and moved into after that night, after that Thanksgiving night on Route 93 from New Hampshire. Their bedroom closet was stuffed with his clothes and hers. On Saturday mornings, she climbed down four flights of stairs to the basement laundry, carrying a laundry basket full of his jogging gear and his barman's shirts from the Paul Revere Tavern and her blouses and underwear.

"Back in Ireland," he said, turning back to the mirror and grinning at himself in his white shirt and tie, "back home you'd dream about a job or a chance like this."

Every evening as she walked home from the T station and her editorial assistant's job at Rheinhardt's Publishing, Ellen had a constant feeling that she would turn her key in the apartment door to silence, emptiness, to a live-in boyfriend who had just run away.

Somehow, she could not shake this feeling that they were just playing house, that someday soon it would end. Badly.

His tie knotted, he crossed to the kitchen for his new suit jacket. There was a spring in his step, a joy, a lightness that she hadn't seen before. Last night over their celebratory lasagna dinner, he thumped the kitchen table and said he was finally moving on—no more grubbing for a barman's tips or apologizing for someone's overdone hamburger.

She went to the kitchen door. Stood there watching as he slugged down the last of his morning coffee. Here it was again—her feeling of impending doom. She said, "They do know you're illegal, these guys, right? They realize you have no green card?"

Fintan's dream job offer had come three days ago. The two Mahoney brothers, Bob and Mike, who usually ate lunch at the Paul Revere, waited for the lunchtime crowd to dissipate and then told Fintan to grab himself a coffee from behind the bar and come and join them. They had a proposition for him, their Irish buddy. They wanted Fintan Dowd to join their company as a new project manager. They weren't going to mess with job advertisements and interviews and all that malarkey. They'd just landed two big contracts, and they'd just moved their company into one of their own office buildings in Quincy. Yeah, they had a secretary and all that, but while they were out on the sites, they needed a guy with an education and a gift of the gab. And hey, that brogue of his wouldn't hurt, either.

"But what about your green card?" Ellen asked again from the kitchen doorway. "I mean, these guys *do* know you're illegal?"

"Oh, would you stop?" Fintan laughed at her worry. "Look, it's a known fact that if no American can fill your job, then the company will sponsor you for a green card. No problem. And look, Mike and Bob are more friends than customers. Honest. You hear about it all the time; a pretend-advertisement placed in the paper: 'must speak Gaelic,' 'must bake soda bread,' 'must have experience as a thatcher.' So when nobody—no Yank—applies, then you're home free. Bingo. Apply for work papers. Easy."

Standing there, Ellen Boisvert, the daughter and granddaughter of paper-mill workers, felt a pinch of skepticism. Then she felt envious of her live-in boyfriend and his immigrant's belief that America could still deliver you from illegal alien to corporate prodigy.

After he kissed her and left for his new job, their coffee table was still strewn with the business management textbooks that he'd brought home from the public library. It was the happiest she'd ever seen him. For three nights, instead of watching TV he sat here studying and scribbling notes in the margins, and she thought that it must have been this state of being an educated, well-qualified man who poured beer for a living that had made him so moody and unsettled.

*

After work she stopped at a corner store to pick up a bottle of white wine to have with their special dinner—baked chicken breasts in white wine sauce with a green salad. She climbed the stairs and turned the key in their apartment, crossed to their tiny kitchen with her grocery bags. The trousers of his new suit were draped across the living room armchair. The suit jacket. Where was it? And why was he home so early?

In the bedroom, his running shoes were gone from the closet. His new dress shoes were all wet and rimed with street grit. She smiled to herself. He'd just gone for a quick run before dinner.

*

Eight o'clock and there was no sign of him. The chicken was desiccated on the stove; scum had formed on the white sauce. Nine o'clock and there she was sitting on the couch, the TV switched off so she could immediately hear his footsteps on the landing. Worry gnawed at her. Had he and his new bosses gone for drinks after his first day? Should she call around a few of his friends? Look up Mahoney Brothers Home Builders in the yellow pages?

No. No. He'd be home soon.

He arrived at last. Red-faced, sweating, trekking snow slush across the living room floor.

She rounded on him, furious: "Where the *hell* were you? I made chicken and then I got worried and—"

The look stalled her. Just a look as he crossed to the bathroom and slammed the door shut.

In his bath towel, his curly hair still dripping wet, he came, barefoot, and flopped into the living room armchair.

In an airless voice, he told her what had happened.

After the welcome handshakes and office introductions, Mike Mahoney had teased him about the suit; asked if he was off to a funeral or something. Then Mike had shoved a folder of paperwork at him. "Fill these in," the older man said. "You know, whenever. Then give them to Judy, the secretary, here."

Mike had led Fintan to his new business manager's office, with its venetian blind window, its white desk and a newfangled thing called a Radio Shack computer. The dang contraption was supposed to work wonders—keep track of costing and bids and keep them all in line. But hey, that's why they'd hired Fintan. To figure all that computer stuff out. Keep them all modern and thriving.

Midway through the morning, Fintan, his white shirtsleeves rolled up to the elbow, crossed to Mike's office, a huge room cluttered with surveyors' maps and building permits, boxes of files still unpacked.

"I'll just leave this till . . . well, till later," Fintan said, holding out the I-9 form, verification of employee eligibility, and the part where the employer took a copy of your social security and alien registration number.

Fintan kept his voice low, a collusive glance at the main office where Judy the secretary sat thwack-thwack-thwacking at an electric typewriter.

Mike glanced up from his desk. "Oh yeah, right. You didn't bring your green card with you? Well, no problem. Bring it in tomorrow. Judy can make a copy."

Suddenly, Fintan felt himself blush, a horrible stammering red. "I'm not actually . . . I don't have . . . But I thought you . . ."

Mike's expression puckered. *Holy. Shit. An illegal alien. Not in the goddamn office.* It was different out on the sites—painters, bricklayers, gofers. Ask no questions; get told no lies. But not in the office, not sitting here in his suit at a computer.

In these late-1980s days, there were too many front-page headlines of immigration raids, all those landscape companies, horse stables, and building sites where little brown Mexicans went scrambling, skittering over rooftops. All of it was bad press, bad faith, bad patriotism.

Fintan saw Mike's flicker of rage at having been duped by this off-the-boat Mick. "Well, for God's sake, buddy. What the hell did you think? I mean, you worked how long in that bar?"

So Fintan left his parka and new suit jacket still hanging from the back of his office door. He walked past the small reception desk, the shirt collar choking him, leaving him airless, gasping. He clamored down the stairway, past the first-floor offices, their company names on the doors, the smell of new timber and concrete.

In his shirtsleeves he walked all the way back into the city, through the south Boston neighborhoods, past bars, schools, chain-link fences, a convent, past the pebble-pocked snowbanks. Along the way, he saw nothing of the city and its suburbs and overhead highways. He could just as easily have been walking along the Gowna Road back home, or, for that matter, he could have been strolling through Tokyo. Humiliation had made him deaf and blind to the stop-and-go of a city in its afternoon rush hour.

"It'll be okay," Ellen said to him, sitting there in the armchair with his towel still wrapped and knotted around his waist. His pale freckled arms, his white chest was growing goose-bumped. She felt a new fear rising. "You'll find something else."

His voice came low and scathing. He cursed American naïveté, the fucking national stupidity that thought everything, always, went by the rules. "Rules, rules, and more rules," he screamed. "Yanks never fucking know, never know shit. People half my intelligence sitting on their fat arses in offices across the country."

Standing there, Ellen suddenly remembered that Sunday afternoon, which already felt like half a lifetime ago, when she'd overheard an Irish girl, a girl called Sheila McCormack at that party in Dorchester. *Fintan's Green Card*. Her. Ellen. The girl had called her that.

"But . . . ?" she began. Now he stood up and screamed right into her face. "Shut the fuck up! Shut fucking *up!*"

"Not my fault," she screamed back. "And I damn well warned you."

Thunk!

First there was the sound. A strange, distant sound. Then her jaw throbbed. *He hit me*. The pain and the truth came, one trailing the other, like an aftershock. He just hit me.

He stood there staring at the red welt on her cheek. Stared in horror as if he had just walked in upon this, upon someone else—a stranger's violence.

"Oh Jesus!" he said. "Oh, Jesus, Ell!"

*

On the 12th of April, 1988, Fintan Dowd and Ellen Boisvert got married at Boston's City Hall. It was exactly two months since his botched job, two months of him being unemployed and both of them being extra polite and contrite with each other.

At night Ellen woke to a ghost pain in her cheek, to the memory of his fist coming at her. But in the mornings when he stood there by their bed, holding out a mug of fresh coffee for her, she told herself that it was his one bad day, his one slipup.

By their wedding morning, the thick file of INS paperwork, his affidavits and chest x-rays and testimonials—everything except the marriage certificate—were completed, the responses written in black ink. Parents: John Patrick and Josephine Mary Dowd. Deceased.

They were living together anyway, they'd reasoned. They were in love, planned on living together forever. So why spend money on an immigration lawyer, spend money they didn't have, only to have to wait, to be disappointed anyway? It was time, Ellen assured him, time he went back to night school and got a job that fitted his skills. Time they both got started on a real life.

Liam from County Offally, Fintan's old roommate from the Dorchester days, was his best man. Louise Boisvert, who had flown north from St. Petersburg, was the bridesmaid, shivering inside a clingy, nylon dress with matching high-heeled sandals and dark, flesh-toned stockings. Fintan wore his new white shirt and his new suit trousers with a sports coat they bought on a menswear clearance. Ellen, petite, pretty, her hair scooped into a jaunty ponytail, wore a cream-colored blazer over navy blue slacks—both of which could and would be worn to work for future job interviews.

That morning, Donna and Thomas Boisvert had driven south from Patterson Falls. They would drive back again that evening.

After their city-hall nuptials, five of them went for lunch to DiSienna's, an Italian restaurant on Boston's North End, where Ellen and Fintan had reserved a table. Liam was working on the buildings now, so he said he'd love to come for the bit of grub, but he had to get back to the building site. He'd only just run over to City Hall on his lunch break.

Across the table in DiSienna's, Thomas Boisvert avoided his new son-in-law's eyes. After their fish and pasta lunch, the waiter brought a small white cake, on the house—an Italian rum cake. The other waiters left their tables, the other lunch customers watched and clinked their forks against their water glasses.

Then the bride and groom, Fintan and Ellen, kissed and cut their cake.

34

AFTER THE VISIT to Father Bradley's and the village, Ellen gets back late to the house in Knockduff. As she drives in through the farmyard gates, she sees only Ned's mud-spattered car in its usual spot. Nurse Ryan's blue car is already gone. It will be fine, she assures herself. After Nurse Ryan's visit, Jo is usually exhausted, usually fast asleep.

She drops her bag of groceries in the scullery, then walks up through the house to check on Jo.

Empty. Jo's bed is empty. The walking cane is gone. The bedding is rolled back and there's Jo's head imprint on the stacked pillows. It's impossible.

"Jo." Ellen rushes through the parlor, the hallway, toward the downstairs bathroom.

She runs up through the scullery, back out into the yard. Has someone come? Has Tom Fitzgerald summoned an ambulance?

This is crazy. A sick old woman doesn't just go missing, go walkabout. Ellen stands there, feeling useless and stupid. Then she turns back for the house and the phone.

Voices. From beyond the upper yard and the line of sheds. First Ned. Then . . . Jo? Ellen rushes to the five-bar gate to the upper paddocks.

Ned and Jo stand on a grassy path, just a hundred yards past the gate, their backs to the house and the yard. Jo leans on her cane. She's dressed in an old winter coat with her nightgown peeping from underneath. She's in a pair of pair of old boots; a bobble hat on her head. Ned's hand flutters around her elbow, her back.

For the past two days, ever since the men and the baling machine have finished, the sloping fields are dotted with cylindrical hay bales inside their black plastic wrappings.

Jo lifts the walking cane, jabs it high into the air, to the right, then the left, the bobble hat following her movements.

Ellen walks to the gate and stands there, awkwardly, wondering if she's not an intrusion, a voyeur. But still, Ned might need help.

Jo jabs the walking cane again. "Didn't he leave too much stubble?" The voice is high and quavering. "He should've cut closer up along the wall here."

"Ach no, ma'am," says Ned. "Sure, they're all leaving a bit behind them now. The new machines are all—"

"—I don't pay that fella to be only skirting the tops and the sides," Jo interrupts.

Ned doesn't answer.

They turn back for the house. Just over a hundred yards to the gate, but their approach is so slow, tap-tap-tap. And Ned, cap on his head and the cigarette trapped under the moustache, keeps pace. Stopping, starting, that perpetually impassive face.

Tap-tap-tap. Jo's toothless face is set with determination. From here, Ellen can see that her patient is winded, panting. Ellen opens the gate and rushes up the path to meet them. "Is she all right?" Ellen asks.

"Ach, she's grand. Just out for a bit of a walk, isn't that right, ma'am? Out getting a bit of air and having an oul' look at this year's hay." He looks at Ellen. It's the closest that Ned has come to a smile.

He nods to Ellen to walk along the other side, ready, waiting in case the cane slips, in case Jo grows more winded and falters.

They cross the yard toward the house like this, one of them on each side of her. Stop. Start. Stop again. Jo's raspy breaths compete with the pigeons in the orchard.

A jerk of the elbow tells them that it's time to stop again.

The air and the birds are suddenly silent, time suspended, as Jo Dowd leans on her walking cane and takes in her yard, her house, the avenue down the hill. "I remember," she whispers. "I remember the first time Mother brought me down there. I was only four years of age, and she strapped me onto the carrier of the bike and she brought me down the hill to the village." She shakes her head.

"I'll go to the gate," Jo whispers, her breath wasting. "I want to see the front fields."

So they're off again. Step. Step.

On the way, Jo nods toward the orchard. "The beauty of baths should be ripe soon. But you know, they drop a lot. Ned, you'll spread the straw under the trees?"

"I will, ma'am. Sure, we'll do that now for sure."

"And you pruned the Bramleys?"

"Pruned, ma'am. All pruned."

At the gate, Ned disengages himself, nods Ellen toward the stone stile to the left of the gate. Then he disengages himself as Ellen stands in front for their practiced ritual of Ellen and Jo standing together, chest to chest, while Ellen lowers the older woman into onto the stone slab. They wait for her to catch her breath. The bobble hat pushes forward on Jo's forehead.

"There. Is that good?" Ellen settles the hat back on Jo's head, back to where it's not quite so ridiculous looking. Ned stands there, his eyes darting nervously. Embarrassed by this women's intimacy, he doesn't know whether to retreat or stay.

Jo nods, heaving, panting.

Madness. Complete madness, letting her come out here. But Ellen doesn't know how to protest, how to make her patient get back into the house and to bed.

Jo keeps looking into the distance, down the avenue past the hazel rock. The pigeons have started again. The silence stretches between the three of them. At last, Ned turns away for the upper yard.

Jo's voice startles Ellen. "Down there in them fields he used to train her, the dog. Hours he spent at it, hours and hours of a Saturday and Sunday. He'd be whistling and training her and then carting her off to every sheepdog trial in the country."

"He loved her," Ellen whispers. "Loved that dog."

Jo shifts around in her spot to stare at a spot behind them, into the shadows under the apple trees, the highest of the crab apple trees inside the orchard wall.

At last Jo turns to her. "He *was* fond of her. Shockin' fond. But a man should love his wife, not a bloody dog. A girl like you, he should've treated you like a queen."

"He did," Ellen says. She believes it. Out here in the cool, summer evening, among the fields where he once ran and laughed and called his dog, she believes what she just told Fintan's mother.

Jo sniffs. Then she steadies her toothless gaze on the younger woman. "No," she says. The voice is low but steadfast. "I see it in your eyes, *a leana*. I see what he, my son Fintan did."

Jo watches, follows the path of Ellen's hand as the younger woman touches her jaw. Jo shakes her head slowly. Her eyes are stricken. "I knew. I knew all along."

After that first night, after the night of his botched Boston job interview and when he actually hit her, there had been the almost times. There were the other times when she saw the fury in his face and watched in a strange, laughable disbelief as she watched the fists clenching, his body closing in on her, the eyes lit with fury. And sometimes, there was the fist rising, coming toward her again. Except that he always stopped just before, just in time. After that first occasion, he learned not to spook himself.

But here's his voice in her head, the half-Irish, half-American accent, the words spitting in her face. That first time when she drove excitedly home from her new academy room and job. There he is ducking out from under their leaking kitchen sink. *Stupid bitch. Stupid fucking bitch.* And yes, there's the fist rising except that time—and all the other times—he just keeps screaming her all the way into a corner of the kitchen until she's trapped there, with his voice and spit in her face.

"They're weak," Jo says, as if the old woman has been watching the movie inside Ellen's head. "They're all as weak as bloody kittens. His father was the same way—all moods and huffs and temper. But no bloody balls."

Ellen says, "They're both gone now. It's all in the p—"

"Not yet," says Jo. "Not in the past yet. But it will. Soon. I hope—for your sake."

"It's—" Ellen starts.

"—I wrote, you know. Oh, yes, once that woman in the town told me where he worked, I wrote, sent him money in case he was hungry or lost. Then I heard he was after getting married, so I sent him money again, to start his married life and put a deposit on a house. Begged him to ring or write. Just one line. Just to let me know he was alive. It's a terrible thing to have to get news of your own son from a stranger, a stupid little woman in a supermarket."

"I didn't know," Ellen says, reaching to touch Jo's shoulder. "You have to believe that. I never knew."

Jo cocks her face at her. She masticates her toothless mouth. "I know you didn't."

*

Jo says, "At the end, the real end, they say it's like drowning. The dying. They say that's what it's like—for everyone. So don't let them cart me off anyplace, hospice or one of them dying places. I won't have any of those rosaries and a funeral mass and every old *fánach* below in the village coming with their sympathizing and their handshakes. They're just coming for a gawk, and to gloat that it's not themselves in that coffin."

"So, what *do* you want?"

"Cremated. I want to be cremated."

"And the ashes?"

"Whatever you think yourself. Pitch them under that big crab apple. Or put them on the ridges of carrots. Don't even bother getting them back from the undertaker if you'd prefer that."

"Let's get you back inside," Ellen says.

Jo clutches Ellen's forearm. Then, slowly, she raises the younger woman's arm, presses Ellen's hand to her own cheek. The touch brings a little toothless smile. "You'll do that for me, won't you? I know you will. No masses or any of that malarkey."

"All right," Ellen whispers. "I promise." Then she stands in front of Jo again. She reaches her arms out to lift the older woman up, this shrunken, emaciated woman with the knitted hat on her head. For just this split second, Ellen imagines that she is the mother, standing there waiting to gather a child into her arms.

*

Jo's face is in shadow, just out of the glow of the night light from the night stand. She's tucked into bed again, propped against the pillows. Lying here like this, Jo Dowd's eyes are fluttery with exhaustion. She is a sick old woman again. It's as if this afternoon, as if their little walkabout never happened.

"What you said earlier," Ellen whispers. "About being alone . . . at the end . . . Wouldn't you like your sister? You sister Kitty?"

Jo turns, follows the sound of her sister's name.

"I could . . . find her, let her know about you," Ellen says. "If that's what you want."

Jo winces. Then a tear trickles, one tear over the sunken features.

She smoothes her hand over Jo's forehead. "I'm sorry," she says. "Honest."

Another tear comes, then another. Jo's silent tears.

Ellen pulls the chair up to the bedside. When Jo reaches, she takes the older woman's hand, holds it tight in hers.

It's dark when Ellen wakes. She feels the rough bedspread under her forehead, the crick in her neck. Stiff. All down her back, stiff. From the bedside chair, she's keeled over and fallen asleep on the end of Jo's bed.

Ellen shifts in the chair quietly not to waken Jo.

She feels the fingers in her hair, long nails scratching, scrabbling, stroking her head. She lifts her head, peeks sideways at the old face on the pillow.

"Sleep," Jo whispers, the hand still stroking Ellen's head. "Go on, love. Sleep."

35

SHE WATCHES THE BOY SLEEPING, his cheek resting against the heifer's belly. The lantern sends shadows leaping and creeping across the stable walls. The cows shift in their manager. The milk hisses into the galvanized buckets: hss-hss-hss. He's sporting a teenage boy's fuzz on his chin, on his cheeks. Soon it will be time for him to bring the milk in and get ready for the school bus that takes him to the secondary school down in the village. This year, at seventeen years old, he's studying for his final exams, his leaving certificate.

John is dead now. Mother is dead, too. For six years, it's been just her and the boy.

This morning she had to waken him again, beg and threaten him out of bed for the morning milking.

In the evenings, he tells her he's staying down in the village to study after school. He says he's getting tutorials in Irish and English from a Christian Brother who wants Fintan Dowd, brainy Fintan, to get good marks in his exams. But Jo knows he's telling her lies. Sometimes she goes up to his room and opens his door to the poster faces staring down at her from around the walls and over his bed—Rod Stewart and ABBA and Van Morrison. From his bedside chair, she picks up and smells his discarded clothes—sniffs some girl's musk perfume on his school-uniform jerseys. Some girl from the village, a girl he's met at school who causes him to miss the school bus home, makes him hitch a lift home so he's late for his evening jobs on the farm.

Tonight Jo's going to wait for him. Tonight she'll put down her foot and forbid him to linger down there making himself stupid and cheap. No more gallivanting down the village until his schooling is finished and he's off in college.

But for now, Jo follows her boy's example. She rests her head against her own cow, a strawberry cow that they bought in the mart in Ballinamore.

The winter dark lingers. The stable shadows deepen. The cow chews her cud while Jo and her boy sleep.

*

"Hello, Mrs. Dowd," a girl is calling to her from the yard gate, shouting out an open car window at her. It's a yellow car. The girl has driven up here herself. Jo, coming in from the bottom fields, stands there on the avenue, squinting into the evening sunlight. "Brilliant weather, isn't it?" says the girl, sitting there as bold as brass and smoking a cigarette. Music comes from a car radio.

No, Jo thinks. This can't be the girl he's courting down in the village. Can't be the girl with the cheap musk perfume. This isn't a schoolgirl at all, but a young woman—a cheap, tarty little thing.

"I'm just waitin' for Fintan," says the girl, tapping her left hand on the steering wheel and puffing her fag as Jo walks up to the car.

"Who are you?" Jo asks her, this girl with the pasty little face. "Who?"

"Cawley," she says, laughing. "I'm one of the Cawleys. You know, from the Lane." Then, the girl nods toward the house. "Ach, here he is now." Then she laughs and waves through the windscreen at him, at the boy running across the yard in his new bell-bottoms and a shirt with a ridiculous collar. She leans across to open the passenger door and revs the car engine. "Right. Well, we're off. Enjoy yourself, Mrs. Dowd."

Jo crosses to the house. Cawley. Cawley. Oh, yes, she knows the family. She remembers the father, dead now, but she remembers him from her own dancing days. He had Brylcreem hair and Clark Gable eyes. He worked as a chimney sweep, going from house to house like a beggar. And Jo has seen the mother at Mass. A chattery little woman, with little for doing except rambling around the village like a stray dog, gossiping. The pound of sausages and loaf of shop bread for their dinner. Cheap people. No breeding.

A girl in a car. A girl who had the cheek, the bloody gall to talk to Jo like that. *Right, well enjoy yourself.* And not a school girl at all, but a young clip with a yellow car.

It's been a hot summer. He's finished school at last, his school uniform hanging in his wardrobe upstairs. Next month, August, he'll have his leaving cert exam results and start making plans for college. There's something maddening about him lately, as if he's in a world of his own, a wayward world where he seems to think he's above his own mother. He's off dancing at the hall to these mad discos and bands, trudging down the stairs on Saturday mornings with his eyes like piss holes.

*

By the second Sunday in August, the sunshine has given way to heavy, mussel-grey clouds. This morning, the man comes as usual to collect the boy for the sheepdog trials. He drives up the avenue and stops outside the yard gate. But today there's an extra person, a passenger sitting in the front. It's the musk girl, Carmel. She springs from the passenger's seat, stands there shading her eyes to look up at the house, to wait for Fintan and the dog.

She wears denim jeans plastered to her backside, painted toenails in platform sandals.

The boy is in the scullery making noise. Jo hears him pouring the tea into a thermos flask. He's making a picnic for the Cawley girl.

The girl unlatches the gate and walks across the yard to meet them, clapping her hands at the sight of the dog. Then, laughing, they walk to the waiting car.

That Sunday afternoon, the clouds collide. The wind rises, and Jo goes out to fasten the shed doors. She patrols the house to shut the windows, to unplug the telly and the fridge and the transistor he keeps up by his bedside. Then she finds the candles in a drawer in the scullery.

Bedtime and he hasn't come home yet. When she goes upstairs to bed, the candle bears her own shadow up the stairs ahead of her. She stops at the boy's room again. Stupidly, she expects him to be there asleep, the dog at the foot of the bed.

He was down at the dance hall again last night. His room reeks of sweat and . . . something else. She crosses to his bedside, bends to pick up his discarded underpants, sniffs at the crotch. She recognizes the salty smell. Suddenly, though it seems a long time ago now, this smell reminds her of Brendan Quinn, the man she met at the dance on the night she lost her child. In the six years since that night, the night she lay in a lakeside field with him, she has come to think of sex and death in the same breath. One makes just as big a fool out of you—a stupid, whinging fool—as the other. Just like the boy is being made a fool out of now—lured and besotted by that girl from the village.

The thunder rumbles. The pop stars stare down at her from the posters on his wall. In the candlelight, she imagines that they, too, are smirking at her.

From the landing window, she watches the treetops wave and thrash. A streak of lightning lights up the avenue and the front paddocks, where the cattle have gone to shelter in the hazel rock.

Lightning again. It turns Knockduff Hill to sudden daylight. Then it's dark and silent.

She crosses the landing to her own room, where she watches for the headlights on the avenue.

Of course, she tells herself. The dogs grew frantic with the thunder, then the older man with the car stopped along the way at a hotel or a roadside pub where the owner let them bring in the two frantic sheepdogs.

The rain lashes against the windowpanes.

Still no sign. So they've taken shelter. Jo blows out the candle and curls up on her bed, fully dressed. She falls asleep to the rain-drum on the roof, drumming across her dreams. She dreams of the boy in the rain, so much rain that he drowns in it, his face blue and bloated.

When she wakes, the room smells of candle grease. The rain has stopped. There's someone in the house. She tiptoes across the dark landing, down the stairs and toward the distant sound of jazzy music from the kitchen.

The boy is standing there naked, his buttocks shiny in the candlelight, his back is to the door. He is toweling the musk girl dry, moving slowly down her body. "Finney, Finney!" The girl screeches. "Ah, Jesus! You're tickling!"

Over the boy's shoulder, the girl sees Jo standing there. They face each other across the shadows, the Cawley girl and Jo Dowd. The girl cocks her chin in a jeer.

I'll kill her before she kills him, Jo thinks.

36

THE BOY IS PUMPING UP the front wheel of his bicycle, propped against the gable wall. These days he has grown even more secretive. He resents her every intrusion.

Two days ago, the school exam results came. Fintan Dowd was top of his Gowna class. The local newspaper, the *Mayo Journal,* rang the house to interview this brilliant local boy, Gowna's star pupil.

So he feels confident of getting his first college choice: a new, European Union–funded degree program in international business offered at University College Galway. Long before he took his exams this past June, he has talked of nothing else. International business. It's what he wants.

Since that night of the thunder storm, Jo Dowd has made inquiries. The Cawley girl is already turned twenty-one. For three years, she has worked at the hospital in Galway as a hospital aide—one of those girls who wheels the tea trolleys around, doles out bowls of porridge to the sick and infirm. She lives in a staff room behind the hospital but now, with her younger boyfriend moving to the city, she wants to set up house and live like a whore with Jo Dowd's son.

Now Jo walks toward the gable wall. She forces her gait, her voice to stay calm, even-tempered, like approaching a skittish foal.

"Where are you off to now?"

He doesn't answer. She listens to the air filling the tire, hss-hss-hsss. "I'm going out," he says, without looking up at her. "Down the village. Carmel and I have things to arrange."

Earlier, Jo heard him on the phone in the hall, making plans with that girl—plans to look for a flat together for when he moves to Galway City and the university.

"At your age, things change. Things come and then they go again. You've your whole life ahead of you." She forces the words out. And the other words are there, just there in her head, but she cannot say them aloud to him: And I'm proud of you, my child so bursting with brains, escaping to the city, leaving this cursed parish, where all my life I have been a laughing stock—the woman married off just to keep the family farm. They have all been laughing. But who's laughing now? My boy the top of the school? Who's laughing now?

Oh yes, how strange those words would be now, spoken out loud to a boy who seems to resent her very existence. Spoken between a mother and her son for whom things have somehow escaped, gone. Died.

He tightens the cap on the bicycle valve, then turns from the bicycle with his arms folded. He pushes his spectacles up the bridge of his nose. Since he finished secondary school he's bought himself new spectacles with little gold rims that make him look like a young professor. He has that know-it-all look. Like she's some busybody maiden aunt—harmless, but definitely needing to be put in her place. "Mam, why don't you say what you actually mean? And no, sorry to disappoint you, but your little speech changes nothing between Carmel and me."

Then he wheels his bike across the yard, the spokes tick-tick-tick.

By September, Jo has grown demented with the vision of them tucked up in some student flat together, like rats in a nest, like tinkers in a caravan.

On the Saturday night *Late Late Show,* some woman is bellyaching for the right to live with her boyfriend and claim herself as a tax dependent, to be put on his health insurance. "We are a country with our own, government-sanctioned apartheid," the woman bawls into the camera. "Apartheid against the thousands of couples who want a divorce. Against the thousands of Irish girls who have to travel to England every year for an abortion—and all because of some church *we* don't even believe in."

Jo switches off the telly and goes to bed.

In bed, the woman's words echo. *Some church we don't believe in.* Laughable, so laughable. There are people—in the towns, in the cities—with all this blathering and jabbing your finger at your fellow panel members on a television program. *A church we don't believe in.* As if believing had a thing to do with it. The church is the building down in the village, opposite the newsagent's shop. It's where you get married and bring your child to be baptized. For years and years, it's where you go every Sunday, a hackney car driving up the avenue, on the dot, to collect yourself and your husband and your young boy dressed in your Sunday best. It's where they brought your husband's and your parents' coffins. Church is like your Saturday-night bath.

So why give a hoot? Why begrudge the boy and that girl their fornicating? Like dogs in heat? She doesn't. She wouldn't grudge it. If it was some other girl.

She sees Carmel Cawley on that stormy night, down in the kitchen, naked and laughing at her.

*

On Tuesday afternoon, the postman comes in his green van, brings a letter with an official university stamp. Yes, the boy has been accepted to the university program of his choice—international business studies at University College Galway. His second choice was a bachelor of commerce degree in Dublin. "Congratulations," says the letter with the official stamp. Then, "Please accept or decline."

They must send a fee to secure his place. So her son has the brains and she is asked to send along the check or a postal order. With a hundred acres, the Dowds don't qualify for a student grant. Which makes Jo proud. The Dowds are not scroungers, not for government handouts. She can well afford it.

Jo sits at the kitchen table, lights a cigarette.

Since this summer, this last year of his at school, he has become two boys—at least in her mind's eye. He is the little communion boy who blushed red when he was asked to show his new pup to Kitty's new husband. And now, just this summer, here is this wayward young man. The swagger and the condescending, professor's voice. *And no, sorry to disappoint you, but it changes nothing between us, between Carmel and me.*

Outside the light is already mellowing in these late August days. The apples in the orchard are ripening. This year, when he's off in college, she'll pick the apple crop alone, hunt through the grass after crab apples by herself.

The boy and Rosie the dog come in from the fields. He sits at the table for his late lunch. She takes the university letter from her cardigan pocket, drops it on the table in front of him.

He grins at that first "Congratulations" line. His eyes glitter. "Great! Well, that's *that* sorted."

"Ring them tomorrow and tell them you've changed your mind. That you're taking Dublin instead, not that international thing. Not Galway."

He's peeling a freshly boiled potato, holding it high above his plate on his fork.

Then it registers with him, her steely tone, exactly what she's telling him: that she's refusing to pay, to send in the fees. He drops the peeled spud on his plate, reaches for the salt with that smug smile, that maddening voice. He can make her see, change her mind. "No, Mam, you're not going to bully—"

The rage surges into her throat. The bloody gall of him! And of her, that girl. Then her fury explodes across the table at him. "Not our type, not our class. Making a show of yourself, of me, of our family before the whole parish. So if you think you're spending my and your dead father's money, well, you've another think coming." She reaches across. *Thwack, thwack.* Across his face. His man's face with the hippie spectacles and the stubble of whisker along his jawbone.

He sits there, stunned. There, on his cheek, are the imprints of her fingers. The sight goads her. She wants to slap him again. Hah! Where's all his smug bravado now? Where's his little girlfriend with the cheeky puss on her?

His lower lip trembles. Good. Let him cry and whinge, just like he did when he was a small boy.

"Please, Mam," he whispers. "Please don't do this. I . . . I really want to do that course. All year . . . all my studies; it was for this. It's what I wanted." His voice falters. He clears his throat to try again. "I just wanted . . ." He looks around the kitchen with its small windows, the dishcloths drying on the clothesline strung above the range. He glances toward the ceiling and the bedrooms—the bedroom where his father died, where he himself was conceived. "I wanted something different, something happy."

*

In those early winter months, he arrives home from his Dublin university on the train, then the bus to Gowna. On Fridays, it turns six o'clock and Rosie the dog goes to wait for him by the kitchen window, ears pricked as if the dog knows the time, the hour. From Gowna he thumbs a lift, then walks up the hill to the yard and the house where Rosie is already scratching at the back door. His green knapsack bounces on his back as he races across the yard to her. "Rosie, Rosie, Rosie. God, my little Rosie. How I've missed you, missed you."

In the house, he stays in his room or he's gone off with the dog. When Jo and him are together, he watches television or he keeps up a strange, staged conversation, as if she's a person that he's just met on a bus. He says nothing about his Dublin university and little about his Auntie Kitty or her house in a housing estate on the north side of Dublin. This is where he lives now, with his aunt and her husband, Brian. In exchange for his room rent, he mows Kitty's lawn and trims the hedges in a garden that Jo has come to imagine as something out of a child's storybook—everything doll-like and frilly.

After Christmas, there are no sheepdog trials for the winter. The weather turns bitter; there are bus strikes in Dublin. So he says he can't get a bus across the city to the train. When the bus strike ends, he says he has a Saturday morning tutorial in a professor's office.

On those absentee weekends, Jo rings Kitty's house, long-distance, to inquire for her son. They are not used to telephoning across the country, from sister to sister. As Jo dials the number, she has a creeping suspicion that he might not really be there, that she'll catch him out in some lie or charade. Always, there's something extra trilling about her sister's voice, which Jo attributes to the telephone. Kitty was always one for putting on airs.

"Hold on and I'll get him for you," Kitty says. Jo listens to the high heels down a hallway. "Fintan, darling, it's your mother." Standing there, still in her Wellington boots from the evening jobs or the fields, Jo hears their distant whispers. When her son takes the phone, she swears she hears some mischief in his voice.

37

SOMETHING SKITTERS through the grass, straight across Ellen's path. Rabbit? Field mouse? It's the 27th of July already—so just a few weeks until Fintan's one-year death anniversary. The way things look, she'll be already landed back home then by mid-August. *Home.* The word stalls.

Except for a few packed-up storage boxes, she has no home.

The very minute she gets back, she'll look for a rental near the academy—a short-term lease to buy her time until she finds and buys something permanent—something suitable for a thirty-nine-year-old widowed teacher.

In a month, it will be time for all those new-semester committee meetings and new-student orientation. Then, just after Labor Day, here comes that sudden return to classes and tutorials and the campus suddenly alive with the students walking between the quads in the still-warm September days. Now, striding through these summer meadows, the thought of her life, her old life, makes Ellen stop along her path. From up here in this high meadow, Ellen has a top-down view of Jo Dowd's house—its slate roof and the twin chimneys set against the backdrop of Jo's front paddocks and the evening sky.

She won't be needed here much longer. The thought should cheer her, make her feel some blessed release. It could be a week or even less. Nurse Ryan and Dr. Fitzgerald have said so.

She walks on down the hill, onward through the sloping fields. The elderberry trees are overripe and drooping. Here and there, the freshly mown stubble grass is stained purple from their fruit.

Tom Fitzgerald's Volvo is already gone from the yard. An hour ago, when he came to check on Jo, Ellen grabbed her cardigan and set out for some fresh air.

There's a sudden hum, a noise on the still air. It's something in the telephone wires. No. She scans the yard, then the avenue. Someone is coming up the front avenue on a motorcycle. Ellen watches the black speck speeding among the green fields and stone walls. Just before the yard gate, the driver does a wide, arching turn and then stops.

A nephew? Jo said that her late husband had nephews that were "thick as double-ditches"—avaricious men she wouldn't tolerate near the house or her death bed.

A man in a black jacket gets off, sets the bike on its kickstand. Dark hair, no helmet. He unlatches the gate, clanks it shut, then he strides across the yard to the house. Even from up here, the man's gait is familiar.

She watches him glance around him toward the orchard, the upper yard, then he knocks on the back door. He waits a minute, then disappears into the house.

*

They stand staring at each other across the back scullery. He's standing by the kitchen sink, arms folded, as if waiting for someone to show up. It's him again, Carmel Cawley's brother, the man she met at the lake, the man who lives in the tiny house down in the village. "Hi there!" she says.

He looks annoyed, dismayed to find her here in Knockduff.

"Hi?" she says again. Ned, she thinks. Ned's car is already gone from along the orchard wall. She wishes that it wasn't, that he'd stayed late.

Tony. That's his name. Tony Cawley, who is standing here staring at her, where she's standing inside the back doorway. She watches the truth dawn, his look of annoyance as he adds up the facts in his head.

"So you're the feckin' wife?" He glances around him, at the back window, the line of winter coats and hats hanging from their wooden pegs behind the door. He's looking for someone to blame, someone who never told him who Ellen actually is. "The bloody wife!" He says it again. Standing here in his black leather jacket, his crumpled jeans, he seems to crowd the narrow space between the sink and the door to the inside kitchen.

"Yes. I'm Fintan's wife—widow, actually. He died."

"Yeah. I'm only after hearing that part—about him being dead. Only a few days ago. In town."

"How . . . ?"

"Friend of mine in Ballinkeady. We used to play football together; still play the odd match from time to time—Seán. Seán McCormack. He has a sister beyond?"

"Sheila?"

"Yeah. Nice looking, that wan. Had a few goes at her myself in my time, back before she went off to Boston for herself. Married now. The money, of course. Kids, the whole works. They come home in the summers, swanking around." He nods his head toward the kitchen door. "So . . . ah . . . how's the ould wan anyways?"

"Mrs. Dowd's not well."

"Well, yeah, I *know that,* but how's she doing? Like, now?" He shifts from one foot to the other. Is she supposed to invite him in? No. No, answers the voice in her head.

She folds her arms. "Does your sister know about Fintan's death?"

"Yeah. I texted her. Not . . ." He gives Ellen a twisted smile. "Not that our Carmel'd actually give a shite."

"What do you want, Mr. Cawley?"

He takes a few steps toward her, where she's standing inside the still-open back door. His eyes are spiteful. And yes, here's that flirtatious smirk again. "I'll tell you what I want. I want to know the minute, the very second that oul' bitch kicks the bucket. Because we've some business for doing, my sister and me. We want what should've been ours years ago. I want my sister not to have to slog away in some dirty kitchen in a posh school for little rich English bitches, half of them feckin' Arabs that don't even speak English and that'd blow us all up faster than they'd ate their breakfast. And I want her to stop living in the school's dump of a flat because she's had to bring up a child, our Catherine, on her own. Slogging away while your wanker of a husband got off free as a bird. Promised her the world and then took off to America for himself."

A child. A girl. A daughter. Fintan had a child named Catherine. She watches him rant on, a litany of wrongs. She watches his right hand rising. He makes jerky, furious movements. Stop. I must stop him, she thinks. He'll waken Jo. He'll frighten her.

Catherine. Fintan *has* a daughter. A girl who lives with her mother in an apartment in England. The kid that was here, in Gowna, last summer. She was with Carmel that night that Tom and Ruth Fitzgerald met them down in the village. Ellen is sure of it.

In her mind, Ellen hears Jo's voice, the out-loud dreams in that darkened bedroom, the morphine ravings when the old woman's voice turned crooning, cajoling. Jo was obviously seeing, talking to a child. A little girl. Her granddaughter. She listens for movements inside the house, listens for the call bell attached to the bed.

Nothing except for Tony Cawley's voice booming through the scullery.

Ellen raises her palm, traffic-cop style, to stall him. "Please lower your voice. Now!"

He stops in mid-rant. His voice drops to a loud, seething whisper.

"This time," says Tony Cawley. "This time we're getting what's coming to us."

I've it all taken care of with my solicitor. Jo said that once. A long time ago now, when Ellen first got here, when Jo Dowd believed, assumed that her daughter-in-law had come from America for one thing only: inheritance, land, a family's hilltop farm.

"So you're here for your or your niece's inheritance?" Ellen asks. "But she's . . . Jo is still alive. Sounds like that's an inconvenience for you."

He steps closer, towering above her. He jabs his forefinger at her. "Sure, don't I know bloody well she's still alive? Otherwise, Fitzgerald wouldn't be still coming up here, would he? I watch his car leaving the house, turning up along the lake road. Every bloody evening. He'd hardly be coming to see a dead woman, would he? Not even Fitzgerald'd charge the government for treating a corpse—though I wouldn't put it past him. But we've a solicitor got. And the minute that oul' wan snuffs it, you'll get a letter. That'll tell you what's what. They've told us you can do it with a grandparent's DNA. The grandmother is the best. So we're ready to get a paternity test. No more schemes or fast ones."

His black leather jacket smells moldy. He's eyeing her breasts.

He reaches above her head and pushes the back door shut. Ned, she thinks. Ned. This man watches the doctor come and go. So he watches Ned McHugh, too.

She forces a steady, inquisitive voice. "Has Jo met this girl? Your niece? Her granddaughter?"

"Oh, *please.* If that oul' bitch'd had her way, our Catherine wouldn't be around at all. There's *be* no Catherine. An' if she thought she could get away with it, she'd have had my poor sister done away with, too."

Done away with? No.

Just an hour ago, before she went off for her walk, Ellen sat by Jo's bed, the old woman propped against the pillows, their hands clasped on the white bedspread—the only acknowledgment, only awareness that there was someone still there, except for those people in her dreams, the people Jo muttered and called out to. Then, when Dr. Fitzgerald came tiptoeing in, he looked from his patient to Ellen and smiled wincingly at the younger woman. It was the kind of smile that said the end was near, that nothing could be done.

"But Jo wouldn't—" she starts.

Suddenly, he touches her right breast, lightly first, as if he's just discovered that it's there and available to him. His eyes glitter. Through her T-shirt, she can feel his forefinger moving around her nipple. She steps backward, collides with the back door.

"Oh, now, sweetie pie." His words keep a rhythm with his moving, circling finger. "You'd find out a lot if you just asked your little mate there, our so-called doctor. You'd find out exactly what the Dowd bitch would or wouldn't do."

She angles into the corner, between the doorjamb and the line of coats. He steps closer. His left hand grabs her left shoulder. Then she feels his fingers along her neck, his thumb cradling her head. "Yeah, ask him. Fitzgerald was fucking there. He was her right-hand man, Mister Genius young doctor himself. Yeah, ask Fitzgerald. He'll tell y—"

Jo's old woolen coat. It's hanging right in the middle of all the others. Ellen hung it up in a hurry on that day, Jo's last good day when she went walkabout, inspecting her meadows and her land one more time. When

Ellen got Jo back into the house, Jo was so weak that Ellen carried her back to bed.

And Jo's walking cane. Please. It should be there, hanging from the same wooden hook, out of sight.

"Jayzus, Fintan'd love to see us now, hah?" Tony says. The musty smell of the jacket as he moves in for a kiss. But she smiles at him, musters a teasing look, as if his mentioning her dead husband titillates her. Then she moves a little to the left.

"I knew, you know," he says. "That first day I met ya. At the lake. I knew you'd take whatever was goin', that you'd enjoy th'oul ride as much as anyone else."

She musters a befuddled look, as if she is battling between her own guilt and desire. Then, she edges further along the wall, until she feels it, right there beneath her left elbow: Jo's walking cane.

"We should go upstairs," she says, forcing her voice steady, full of lust and guilt and compulsion. "Where she won't hear us."

He drops his grip to step backward. He makes a little bow in a parody of gentlemanly chivalry. "Right. Well, after you. Lead the way, ma'am."

She whacks the left knee first, then the right. "Fuck!" His legs buckle. The fury drives her. Gives her vicious strength. He holds up his hands to stall her next assault. She whacks his arms, his waist. He squeals and yelps. "Fuck! Fuck!" With Jo's cane, she flocks and angles him into the corner, the corner between the kitchen counter and the back door. His black hair has fallen all the way across his forehead. Whack! Whack! Whack! He keeps his hands up, jabs them left and right in a boxer's maneuver. He's trying to protect his face.

Stop. A voice tells her inside her head. Stop or you'll kill this man.

But rage drives her on—his thighs, his waist again. Tony is whimpering. He lowers his hands from his face and bends over to protect his crotch. "Please! Aw, Jesus, fucking Christ!"

She is about to hit one more blow, the last, good blow to the balls. But she stops herself, the cane held above her head.

"Get out! You have two minutes to get the hell out of this house."

He straightens up. He stands creakily, his face creased with pain. He limps toward the back door.

"Fuck you!" He hisses at her from the yard.

She calls after him. "Yeah, you wish you had."

*

Tom Fitzgerald answers his cell phone on the first ring. The voice is flat. He is expecting the worst and final news of Jo. "Hello?" he says, then pauses.

Ellen says, "I need to talk to you. Tomorrow."

"Ha? What's wrong? Did she take a turn?"

"No. No. I just checked on her. Jo's resting. Fine."

Something in her voice alarms him. "Ellen, are you all right?"

"Tony Cawley was here." She swallows, forces her voice on. "He says that he and his sister have a lawyer. They want a DNA sample, a paternity test." She stops. "For Catherine. For my husband's daughter."

Silence again. Down the phone, in the Fitzgerald household, Ellen listens to a TV twitter in the background. "He says that you can tell me. Tell me what happened. He says that Jo tried to get rid of Carmel—and their baby."

Someone turns the TV volume down. Then the phone reception crackles slightly, as if he has moved into another room of his house. "Are you all right? Did Tony frighten you? Do anything? He was always a bit of a hot-head. He didn't?"

Ellen pictures Tony Cawley limping across the yard to his motorcycle, cursing her to hell and back. "I'm fine," she says. "I'm fine. Or I will be once you tell me what happened. Seventeen years ago."

He sighs heavily. "Yes. No. I mean . . . Ellen, it's not what you think."

Ellen is sitting at Jo's kitchen table, the receiver from the black telephone cradled between her ear and her shoulder. The windowsill has been cleared of its clutter of magazines and ashtrays and cigarettes. Tonight, she has a clear view across the backyard. She watches the half moon that sits, half-hidden beyond two crab apple trees in the orchard.

"My husband had a kid. For our entire marriage. He had a kid in England. I was married to man who didn't give a shit. About his own child."

"He did c—" Tom starts.

"—Yeah, I want to believe that. But I wanted to believe a lot of things. The problem with that is that they just weren't true. So I want to know now."

There's Fintan. She can see him now, at their kitchen counter in their Boston apartment. He's drinking his morning coffee and scanning the front-page headlines on his folded-up copy of the *Boston Globe* while absently taking bites from his morning English muffin. All this ordinary life while there, lurking behind him, hidden in the sleeves of his overcoat, dancing through his head while he read the morning headlines, was this whole other part of him. Another existence.

"Ellen, you're doing a great thing for a sick old woman. But if you'll take my advice, when this is all over, you'll just go back to Boston and your life and—"

Now, in his mother's kitchen, Ellen's voice comes screechy. "No! I'll go back to Boston when I'm good and ready. Or when all of you stop screwing around and tell me what happened. When you tell me who the hell I married!"

And loved, she thinks. Because she's there, too, in that image in her head. In that breakfast scene where her hair is still wet from the shower, padding across the tiled kitchen as they mumbled their good mornings. Now she tells that younger version of herself: "Pitiful. You were stupid and pitiful. You loved him—or at least, you loved the part you were allowed to see or know."

"I need to talk to you—and I'll do what needs to be done to force you, even if I have to get some local police records."

There's a long silence on the other end. Outside Jo's kitchen window, the moon has slipped most of the way behind a night cloud.

"I'll see what Ruth and the kids are doing. And I've a full day's surg—"

"—Tomorrow evening," Ellen interrupts. "Unless one of your other patients is actually dead or dying, you'll make it tomorrow. Evening. Seven o'clock. I'm calling the nursing agency for a replacement. Seven. I'll be at your house."

38

IT'S ALMOST THE END OF JUNE and the boy has been home for a fortnight, arrived home from college after completing his final exams.

Jo winces at the sudden voice in the house, this intrusion on her solitude. She has come to think of him as an upstairs lodger, someone who carries that air of another world, a city world full of noise and traffic and voices.

Since his first leaving she has grown used to it, this silence, the tick-tock of the wall clock, the quiet, secret rhythm of her days. Even Rosie the dog seems to have muted her mad, barking ways. In the winters, especially this last winter when, except for Christmas, he has found reasons not to come from Dublin.

In October, he goes back to Dublin for his graduation, a ceremony with a cap and gown and a dinner for parents. Jo has already decided not to go.

He startles her, the height of him suddenly there, as if she's forgotten that he's come home. Or sometimes, she passes the parlor door and, just for a second, she wonders who that man is, this man who is suddenly sitting there in one of the good parlor armchairs, his nose stuck in a book.

He is avoiding her. She is avoiding him. She's up and out and working by the time he comes downstairs in the morning. In the evenings, he doesn't sit for supper but clomps upstairs to wash and change, then leaves the house by the front door to stride around the house for his racing bicycle.

It's late afternoon, the 21st of June, St. John's Night. Down in the village, the kids are collecting for the St. John's bonfire.

They used to come up here, running up the avenue with their wheelbarrows and their cheeky faces, knocking on her front door and giggling at the sight of the old woman as they asked, "Have you any ould tires or timber for the bonfire, missus?"

But for years they've stopped coming. No village child is brave or foolhardy enough to make it all the way up Knockduff Hill to knock on old Mrs. Dowd's door.

In his two weeks home, he has managed to colonize her parlor. He has spread his books and his newspapers across her dining table. He leaves his dirty teacups along the hearth or the mantel. In the late afternoons, she comes in from the fields to the clack-clack of his portable typewriter, one of the items he unpacked from his Dublin boxes.

"Could you come in here a sec?" He calls to her from the parlor table, where he's sitting typing up another CV and letter of application.

"Mam, I got engaged," he says, over his sheet of typing paper. "And the wedding'll be soon. We don't want to wait. And we're not having anything big. Just a few friends."

Engaged? We? A girl, yes, some college girl, someone he knows in Dublin. But married? At his age? Ridiculous. "Who's the girl?" she asks.

He gives her a weary look. "Ma-am. You know damn well who 'the girl' is. It's Carmel. Always was."

Carmel. Carmel. Carmel who stood naked and smirking at her, here in this house, here in Jo's own kitchen.

"Is she pregnant?"

"Yes."

The air stops inside her. She swallows. Swallows back this killing rage.

"Look, we'd have been getting married anyways, so what's the difference?"

Her hand twitches. She wants to walk over there and batter his face. "Is it yours?"

He levels his gaze on her—a slow, poison look, a look filled with every bitter thing that has passed between them. "Look, Mam. *We're* getting married. We're making it the same weekend as my graduation, when our friends will already be in Dublin. Auntie Kitty and Uncle Brian are coming. So you can attend or not. Up to you."

He shoots the typewriter's carriage home. Then he starts reading his typed paper, his head swiveling to review the lines he has typed.

Kitty knows. *Knows*. Her own sister, and she never told her. So Jo, his mother, is the last little detail in his plans.

She watches him sit all the way back in the dining chair, its mahogany frame creaking beneath him. He has a malicious little smirk. "We've it all sorted. I'm actually filling out forms now, typing my letter of acceptance for this job. It's an insurance company in Galway. Selling life insurance. It's part salary and part commission, flexible hours, so it'll still leave me time to work here."

Jo pats her cardigan pockets, then her trousers. Jesus, where are her fags?

He's still talking as she walks away, across the hall to the kitchen. There are her Bensons in the window. She folds a piece of newspaper, lights it in the grate of the range. Then she stands there puffing, watching the swatch of sky framed in the kitchen window.

Clack-clack-clack from the parlor. She puffs impatiently. My son is going to be a father. Trapped.

She walks back to the parlor. "What are you talking about, work here?"

"We're going to build a house," he says. "In that bottom field below at the road. I mean, it'd only be a half-acre. I had a chat with Seamus Ryan—Ryans the builders. He says we could start the foundation before the winter and then the builders could really get moving."

His words ping off the parlor walls, the mantel, the china cabinet. Her mind can't grasp them, what he's proposing. They keep escaping her. She has to relay them to herself. He's talking of building a house. My boy and his pregnant girlfriend, a man and a woman and a child in a house.

" . . . and I could take over and work the land now, not later; you're not getting any younger, Mam."

She sees her boy's life reeling backward. No longer her bright boy—the boy the newspaper wrote about after his school exams. In her mind's eye, he is one of the local Gowna men, the jokers who spend their Saturdays sitting along the counter in Flanagan's. Then there he is, with that jaunty, *eegit's* walk, crossing Gowna's main street. He's puffed up with porter and bravado chat. He's carrying an armful of Tayto crisps to quiet the carload of wailing kids.

At home, the little wife is waiting and grumbling. With each baby she has grown fatter and sourer. She's waiting in a house built on her, Jo Dowd's, land. And after all his education, he's back home working this land and with a half-arsed job selling insurance, going door to door like a knacker.

"No," she says, pushing aside his forms and papers to lean across, her face level with his. "No."

He pushes back his chair, stands there opposite her, taller by almost an inch. "We'll do it with or without you," he says. He spreads his hands to take in the parlor, the yard outside the two curtained windows. "It's all half mine anyways. All those bloody years out there mucking out stables and up before school for the milking when I should've been like any other kid? It was my father's and now . . . until . . . well, it'll be half mine."

"Half your *father's?*" Stupidly, she wonders if he'll burst out laughing. Laugh at his own mad joke. Or while he's been away living that city life, has he somehow forgotten who he is? No, who *they* are. Has he somehow forgotten the sufferance, the bitter sacrifice that forms the core, the credo of Jo Dowd's very existence?

She reaches to hit him. But this time he holds her wrist in midair. He tightens his grip, his strong, man's fingers squeezing until his mother whimpers in pain.

39

"THEY'RE GONE TO THE PICTURES," Tom Fitzgerald says, as he shows Ellen into a huge living room set with cream leather couches and russet-colored walls. "In Castlebar. Dinner in a burger place first, then some action flick Lorcan's been going on about for weeks. The kids were thrilled." Then, "How's our patient been today?"

"Okay. The same. Slept most of the day."

"The agency nurse turned up on time?"

"She was early. When I left, she was already settled in for the evening. She brought her knitting. Seemed like a nice girl."

"Sit. Sit!" he says, nodding her toward a cream armchair to the right side of the hearth. Ellen's armchair makes a puff sound as she sits on the cushiony leather. He says, "With the agency nurses, it's kind of potluck. Sometimes, they're just in it for a job, the fantastic hours and pay, but sure you can't blame—"

Her look stops him, interrupts his usual village-doctor small talk. "So I've got a stepdaughter," Ellen says.

Tom flops on the couch. In his sweatpants and T-shirt and stocking feet, he looks younger. He also looks exhausted as he passes a hand over his chin, across a gingery five o'clock shadow. "Yeah. Catherine. She was home with the mother here last summer, that night we met her down in Flanagan's."

"What's she like?"

Tom smiles. "Oh, you know, like every young teenager. A big streel of jet-black hair down over one eye, the black eyeliner or whatever you call that stuff they have nowadays. And it probably all costs a fortune to make it like that. And she certainly wasn't happy to be stuck in Gowna, or down in Flanagan's with her mother and her uncle. Actually, the only thing that got a smile out of her was our Riona. First, they did the usual thing: sniffing around each other like two strange dogs. Then, next thing we look, they're thick as thieves and giggling and talking about their music and dance classes."

"Dance?"

"Our Riona's been taking ballet after school. Oh, yeah, and Carmel's girl—Cat she insists on calling herself, which, of course, our Riona thought was *way cool*—is mad into some sort of modern dance, too. So they hit it off, our girl and the little cockney kid."

"That was the only time you saw her—Cat?"

"No, we saw her around the village after that—down at the shop, swishing around the street. Hard to miss a kid like that—the *gimp* of her, tall as a telegraph pole and all dressed in black and always looking like she'd love to kill you. But sure, they're all like that nowadays. Can't be easy for Carmel. And there was no mention of a boyfriend, a partner or husband."

"So your daughter liked her?"

"Oh, yeah. The whole week after they rang and texted and texted more, and Riona pestered her mother to be let down to the house on her own on her bike. But . . ." Tom pulls a theatrical face. "'Twas a bit . . . awkward."

You're lying, thinks Ellen. You just didn't want your blond, clean-cut daughter hanging out with a kid like that.

Tom leans over to grab one of the couch pillows. It's a pretty, tapestry cushion of deep russets and yellow in a Tex-Mex design. "But I know they're still in touch—e-mail or instant messaging or whatever. And they exchanged photos of themselves—each all done up in her dance gear."

"Tony said they were poor, making ends meet. That Carmel just worked menial jobs there—in London."

Tom shrugs. "Possibly. Carmel left school early, never did her leaving cert—unless she took some Open University thing over in London." He gestures his head. "Have you actually seen the house above? In the Lane?"

"Yes. Tony lives there now?"

"He moved in with the mother. His kids come on weekends sometimes. He had his own house out the Galway road, but he sold it after the divorce."

Tom cradles the cushion against his crotch, then leans all the way back against the leather couch. He's watching, gauging Ellen's reactions. The doctor suspects that something ugly passed between Tony and Ellen. "Carmel Cawley always had notions of herself. Even last year, even that night in the hotel, the way she'd tell it, you'd think her life was going fantastic. And long before she went off to England, she'd a job as an aide above in the hospital in Galway, wheeling the trolleys and doling out tea to the patients. But to hear her tell it, you'd think she was the head matron—the nurse in charge."

"Where did they meet, her and Fintan?"

"Oh, at the dance hall back the road here. 'Twas the only place you met anyone back then, twenty years ago. This was the tail end of the show bands and the start of the whole disco thing." Tom smiles nostalgically. "It was great, when I think about it. Really kept an oul' buzz around the village."

"He was in love with her." Ellen conjures that photo of Carmel and Fintan at the house, in the closet in his old room.

Tom is obviously wondering whether to confirm or contradict. "I don't know. I think he was obsessed with her, like, he could never believe his luck that she'd actually picked him. She was at least three years older—out of school, working, driving her brother's car around the place. Back then, a woman with a driver's license and a job and a room away from home seemed really exotic."

"So what happened with the baby—with Catherine? Tony said that Jo tried to get rid of it—the kid."

He runs his palm across the cushion's tasseled edges. His voice turns low and mournful. It's as if he's speaking to himself. "We were all really naïve and stupid. We thought we were smart, sophisticated, but even after four years of college, we were as green as the grass."

"We. We—who?" Ellen whispers as pieces of this story propose themselves in her mind. "What did you have to do with it?"

"We had no legal abortion here in Ireland then. We still don't. There was one referendum, but it was defeated. So girls went to England—stayed with friends or a cheap guest house, checked themselves into an English hospital, paid their money and came back with the damage undone. Nobody the wiser. Their mothers or fathers or the boss in their office jobs knew nothing. Nobody knew how many girls went. But some said it was nearly 20,000 a year."

"So that's why Carmel moved to England? Fintan sent her to get rid of the baby, but she decided to keep it?"

He tilts his chin at her. "Oh, Christ, no. No. Fintan *wanted* that kid. He was finished his degree, top of his class. And that's what fellas said back then, that she got pregnant on purpose, to make sure she'd keep him here, in Ireland at least, before he emigrated with his diploma under his arm like half of the rest of the country. Look, we were only twenty-one. And Jo wouldn't have the . . . the termination done in England. Oh, no. That wasn't Jo Dowd. She wanted it done where she could make sure it *was* done, make sure she got what she paid for."

"You. You—were—a—medical—student."

He holds the patterned cushion to his chest like a shield. His voice is monotone, barely above a whisper. "Me and a mate of mine from college." He swallows. "She paid us 2,000 quid apiece—a fortune to a student."

"And you agreed?"

"Yeah. My father wanted me to take over the practice here the minute I qualified, though I had high-falutin' dreams of taking off to Australia. I even applied and got a residency in a hospital in Melbourne. Then, my father got wind of it, and for the last few months of my studies, he started traveling to Dublin, ringing on the doorbell of my flat and insisting that I remember who'd paid for me, what my family duty was. But with 2,000 quid of Jo Dowd's money I could've taken off, free and clear."

"But it never worked."

"It was supposed to."

"What, Tom? What the hell happened?"

He props one foot on his knee. "She was clever, Jo was. I'll say that for her. She left no detail uncovered. We needed a place where we wouldn't be seen, where nobody from Gowna would see or tell. It was her came up with it—the dance hall on a Sunday night. A Sunday evening when it was all boarded up and empty, and when nearly everyone in the village was at a Sunday evening devotions down in the church.

"She knew there was an entrance around the back. And there was this cloak room behind the stage, just off the ladies' toilets. It was perfect." His voice trails off. His expression is tortured.

"And Carmel actually went there—of her own free will?"

"Oh, yeah. Well, no, not at first. But Jo took care of that, too. She offered them—the Cawleys—even more money than myself and Vinnie, my friend from college. I don't know how much, but either way, a woman like Jo Dowd comes along, offering a large check. So Carmel went along with it. Tony drove her up there, up the road on a Sunday evening, the 30th of June. I remember," Tom says to Ellen. "I've forgotten anniversaries and birthdays, but I've always remembered that date; 30th of June, 1985."

"So you and this other medical student were ready, waiting."

"Yeah. Had everything from my Dad's surgery. Carmel was only six weeks pregnant, so it was going to be easy. To be honest, we thought of it as a kind of a lark, something that us fellas could do for each other—get poor Fintan off the hook. I even remember thinking how cool, how level-headed Jo was, that she was just paying to get her son out of trouble. Cool and broad-minded and not said and led by the Catholic church, the way everyone else was."

"And Fintan went along with it, too."

"Afterwards. We found it all out afterward. It never crossed our minds that Jo was only acting on her own behalf—not his. And we never dreamed that he actually wanted to have a kid—but afterward." Tom's rakes his fingers through his thinning red hair. "He didn't know. His mother had set it all up, behind his back. Part of Carmel's bribe was to pretend, say she'd had a miscarriage. It was an easy lie. Easy money for everyone."

"Except it didn't work?"

"Obviously not." He reaches a hand toward her, as if, in fact, he could magically stretch that far, across the space between them, from his couch to her chair. "With all Jo's smartness, all her little well-thought-out operations, it all backfired on her, on us. We were up there at the appointed time, me and my friend Vinnie; Vinnie had a car. We found an old table in the hall's ticket office. We scrubbed it down, laid a sheet over it. The day before, we'd bought two cheap desk lamps in Woolworths in Galway. We plugged them in, set them on each end of the table and angled them to keep the light focused but low. We were like kids, stupid kids playing in our own episode of *Trapper John, MD*. I even remember what was hanging from the hooks in that old cloakroom—stuff that people had left behind. There was a dark blue blazer with glittery lapels. And there was a woman's winter coat, off-white with fur along the collar and cuffs.

"I had stuffed two plastic bags with antiseptics and a speculum and swabs and all the gear that the textbook told me I'd need. We'd even brought a six-pack of beer to have when it was over, when we were finished and Jo came with our money.

"Tony and Carmel arrived. At first, Tony came striding in, all cock-of-the-walk, but when he saw our setup, saw the actual table and the sheet, the speculum and all the rest laid out on a towel, he mumbled that he'd just wait for his sister out in the car.

"So it was just Carmel and me and Vinnie. And I introduced them 'n' all. Like, 'Vinnie, this is Carmel,' as if we'd all met at a party. And she was flirty with him, all smiling and jokey.

"I handed her a hospital gown and I said we'd just ramble around, us boys, that we'd walk out into the main hall while she got undressed.

"Vinnie and I were standing out on the dance floor. We both lit a cigarette. We'd shared a flat and med classes, hospital rounds and pubs and parties in Dublin. But now, there we were standing in that oul' hall with the smell of stale cigarettes and Jeyes Fluid from the toilets and the floor still sticky and filthy from the dance the night before. We were like an old couple that were supposed to dance or talk or make a move, but neither of us had a word to say to each other. So we went back to the cloakroom to go and play doctor.

"Carmel was lying there in her hospital gown, just staring at the smoky ceiling, just staring straight up as if she just wanted it to be all over and let her know when to look down at herself, at the rest of the world again.

"When we heard the car we thought it was just Tony, deciding to drive away for a while, to kill the time by taking a drive out along Lough Gowna. But then we listened to the car parking. A door banged shut, but the engine was still running.

"Fintan. He'd found out. He ran across the room and then stopped, stood there as if he'd collided with something. He just stood there staring down at her under those cheap lamplights. Then he started screeching, terrible screeching.

"First we thought it was just temper, or shock, or both, but then, we saw that he was actually crying. Crying and fell to his knees and sobbed and cursed us all to hell."

A telephone rings somewhere in the Fitzgeralds' house. It rings six times, then an answering machine picks it up. Through the sitting room door, Ellen listens to Ruth's recorded voice from the hallway. "Hello! You've reached Tom, Ruth, Lorcan, and Riona. We're not here at the moment. But leave us a message!"

"So Carmel never got Jo's money?"

"I don't know. But I doubt it. Jo was to arrive on her bike when it was all done. She was supposed to pay us all then."

"Where . . ." Ellen starts to ask, but the words falter. She sees that vision of her husband again, sitting there at their kitchen counter, eating his breakfast and reading the American headlines before he rushed off to his Boston job.

Tom replaces the cushion and reaches past the arm of the couch to switch on a lamp on an end table. The light is soft and buttery in the big, comfortable room. "See, unlike the rest of us, Fintan was the only one without a plan, a trick up his sleeve, a financial gain. He'd actually convinced himself that he could make it all work—marriage, a kid, living on his parents' land. Carmel was supposed to tell him she miscarried. But then, she was suddenly just gone. Of course, we all assumed that it was to get a legal abortion, to finish what we were supposed to do. And then, last summer, here's Carmel back in town with a teenage girl in tow." He shakes his head, gives a dry little laugh. "It was terrible that night last summer. When we met her in the hotel. I thought she'd avoid us, pretend not to know or see, but she seemed to actually enjoy introducing her daughter while watching the expression on our faces."

"So Ruth didn't know? About you?"

He shakes his head.

"So Jo doesn't know she has a grandchild?"

Tom shrugs. "I don't know that. But I doubt it."

"But Tom, even if Fintan believed that his girlfriend was going to lie about a miscarriage, why did he take off to the States, in the opposite direction?"

The doctor shrugs. "You tell me. You were his wife."

Should she tell this doctor, this relative stranger, why she abandoned her life in Coventry-by-the-Sea to come here?

She thinks of it now, that day in the Risen Planet Café, the day after the end of school term. It would have been easy, so easy to have missed this: if Ellen had eaten lunch someplace else, if she had decided to clear out her faculty room instead of walking up to town, if Sheila McCormack hadn't recognized her across those lunch tables. Any of these and Ellen Boisvert would not be sitting here now. She would never have known Jo Dowd. She would have let her husband die in peace. Then, a strident voice rises inside Ellen's head. "The dead have their own peace. But what about us, the living. What about me? Shouldn't I have some peace, too?"

Suddenly, she tells Tom Fitzgerald the story, how she believed—was told—that her husband was an orphan. How, on an otherwise ordinary day, through a chance meeting, she'd discovered Jo's existence. She says, "When I met him, I was even younger and even stupider than you were. I was attracted to that idea, the idea of someone so far from home, so adventurous, so untethered to a family or tradition or expectations. I *wanted* him to be an orphan." She tells it all in a quiet, even voice, while watching the soft lamplight fall across the Fitzgeralds' polished-wood floor. She tells how she was just about to go away, to fly back to Boston when Jo called her in the middle of the night ranting about grandchildren in America.

Tom gets up from the couch to stand before the unlit fireplace. He takes a framed photo from the mantel. It's a photo of him and Ruth and the kids somewhere on vacation. Ruth is in a blue sundress. The kids are each in shorts. Riona wears denim cut-offs and a red, strapless bikini top. There are palm trees and white lounge chairs in the photo's background. In the snapshot, Tom, in sunglasses and a pale, bare chest, stands behind his daughter, his right hand set protectively on her bare shoulder.

He stares at the framed photo so long that Ellen wonders if she should tiptoe away, up the hallway and out the front door. He doesn't turn toward her when he speaks. "We fight like blazes, you know. Me and Riona. It's a constant battle between us. She's one of the most headstrong kids I've ever met. Or maybe I expect more—more *gratitude* than I get. We're just constantly at loggerheads lately, especially in the last six months. If I suggest she take piano, she wants to take violin. If I suggest Spain for a holiday, she suddenly wants Italy. It's her age. And we're too alike, the pair of us."

He faces Ellen, looking down at her in her armchair. His expression is stripped of his usual congenial-doctor persona. He looks as if he might cry. "Even in a small place like this, I've seen terrible things in my practice—negligent, abusive parents, men who torture their partners or wives. You know, Ellen, I thought when my own parents died that I'd never get over it." He jabs the framed photo toward her, as if he's showing it to her for the first time. "But the thing I'd never, ever get over would be if one of these guys just cut me off, denied my very existence. If they ever told the rest of the world that they'd no father."

He places the framed photo back on the mantel. "What would I have to do to make them do that? What terrible, awful thing? I hope I never find out—but in a way, I have. I . . ." His voice catches. "I know. You just . . . Christ! You just told me. And I was actually part of it."

"She wrote, she said. Wrote him letters and he never wrote back. She said there was a falling out; she assumed that I, his wife, was part of that estrangement." Ellen gives a wry laugh.

*

They are standing in the doctor's front hallway, between the hall table and the blond-wood staircase. The phone's red message light is blinking—the person who called an hour ago. Tom's face is lighter. His voice is almost recovered, almost returned to that bustling, I'm-the-nice-doctor voice. He nods toward their kitchen door. "I never even offered you anything—a drink, a cup of tea. Don't tell Ruth. She a devil for them kind of things—strict on hospitality, protocols."

"I'm fine. It wasn't a social visit. But thanks—for everything."

"Ach, for nothing. I'm just sorry it couldn't be an easier, nicer story—something that made us all look a bit less savage or greedy. But they were different times back then. An' people forget now, how limited, constricted everything really was. Everyone scrabbling for the same few shillings, for the few jobs there were. That's not an excuse, just a—"

"—That photo," Ellen interrupts. She suddenly remembers it. "The photo that you said Carmel's daughter sent. You still got it?"

"*Prob*-ably. I know Riona tried to use it as a sort of bribe to get us to let her drop ballet and change her classes for some mad hip-hop thing."

"Can I take a look?"

He passes his hand over his chin again. "D'you think that's a good idea?"

"No. But I'd still like to just see her. I'd like to see Fintan's kid. Please."

Over the polished-wood stair banister, Tom hands her the printout of a digital photo. He glances toward the front door, nervous of his family's return. "'Twas easy enough to find—clipped to Riona's dressing-table mirror."

Ellen studies the photo of eight girls in a dance studio, four in front; four in the back. Some are willowy and sophisticated; others are plump and still childlike in their dance tights and leotards and strappy tops. The girls in back are standing with their palms up, in a parody of theatrical fright. The four girls in front are kneeling on a polished-wood floor, their eyes wide and ferocious; their arms and hands crooked in an attacking-bear pose.

Back row, center. There's Fintan's girl. She stands an inch or more above the others. Her black bangs are cut at a crazy angle. She's wearing a puzzled frown for the camera. Fintan's frown.

Above the girls' heads is a white banner draped across a wall, "Jarkowski Dance Studio."

"Catherine." Ellen says the name aloud in the doctor's house. She studies the eyes, the bony little shoulders inside the strappy dance top.

40

"LIE DOWN," the little girl says to her. "Lie down in the grass and we'll tickle you."

So Jo, laughing, kneels and then flops down in the overgrown summer meadow in front of the house. She stretches out, her hands above her head. There is a smell, a musky smell. It's wild honeysuckle—the wild honeysuckle that grows all over the hazel rock.

"No peeping," says the little girl. "No, no peeping." The girl giggles. Her brother joins in, screeching, laughing at the sight of their mother lying there in the long grass. Through her summer skirt, the grass is prickly. She hears them plucking the buttercups, the wild barley they'll use to tickle her. She listens to their whispery voices. The boy, always, the more cautious of the two, watching out for his sister, pointing out what she shouldn't pick—what might prick or sting her. "No. Not that," the boy says. "Here, you just do the buttercups."

Jo opens her eyes. Through the long, wild grasses, there are her children hunkered in the meadow, the boy in his summer short pants; the girl in a pink floral dress. The boy's curly hair is silhouetted against the summer sky, the midday sun. The girl is blond, an angel-blond. Above her the sky is a pure summer blue. From Jo's spot in the field, the whole world has shifted. The trees are monstrous. They're the trees in a fairy tale. The house is way up there on the hill, just a blob on the horizon, a dark spot on the sun.

The children's voices grow louder as they cross the distance between them and her. And just before she shuts her eyes again, she sees that they are holding hands. To oblige them, to play along in their game, she shuts her eyes and lies still, lies here in the summer smell of wild honeysuckle as the kids come again, kneel in the grass over their mother.

*

Ellen opens in the bedroom door slowly. The agency nurse startles awake from where she's nodded off in the bedside chair. A swatch of lemon yellow knitting flops from the nurse's lap onto the bedroom floor. Both women watch Jo's sleeping face. The old woman is muttering and giggling.

"She's been laughing," whispers the agency nurse. "Off and on all night. She's been giggling like this to herself."

Ellen bends to pick up the nurse's piece of knitting. She follows the trail of yellow yarn across the white bedspread to the big ball of fuzzy yellow yarn clutched in Jo's hand.

"She seems to like it," the nurse whispers. "Once I put it in her hand at all, she wouldn't let go. She just kept laughing and kneading my ball of baby wool." Then the nurse glances down at herself, pats the rise of her pregnant tummy. "We're not bothering to find out if we're havin' a girl or a boy, so I stuck with yellow—safer." She flashes a smile at Ellen, then checks her watch. "I'm supposed to be on till 12, if you want to get a bit of a rest for yourself."

"No. No, that's okay."

Jo keeps giggling and kneading the ball of yellow yarn.

"I can just start another ball," the nurse says, gently breaking off the yarn from the piece of finished knitting. "I've plenty more at home. I bought too much anyways."

They walk to the kitchen together, where Ellen switches on the light to read the chart in its folder, the nurse's initials opposite the dosages and temperature and blood pressure.

"Her temperature is up a bit," the nurse says from behind Ellen as she zips up a jacket over her scrubs. "But that could really be anything. I mean, at this stage. I changed her nightie and bathed her as best I could."

"She seems comfortable," Ellen says. "I'll sit a while with her and take it from there."

The nurse jingles her car keys, takes her purse and knitting bag and crosses to the scullery. "I left my mobile number there," she says to Ellen. "Just in case."

When Ellen returns to the bedroom, Jo is no longer giggling. Her small, shriveled face is turned sideways on the pillow, the toothless mouth set slightly open. Now she's clutching and stroking the big ball of yellow yarn in both hands. For one split second, Ellen thinks it looks like she's going to throw it, toss it like someone playing a game.

Ellen sits on the bedside chair, studying the sideways face against the pillow. This is the woman who rode her bicycle down the hill, parked her bicycle behind the Gowna dance hall to check on the young Tom Fitzgerald's work, to pay him for a job done. No. Ellen shakes the thought away. Not tonight. Tonight, there is only this sick old woman. The face is slightly pinker than usual. Jo's forehead is glistening with sweat.

From the nightstand, Ellen tears off a piece of cotton wool, dips it in a glass of water, and leans in to dab at Jo's forehead, then down the bridge of her nose to her cheeks. The lightest touch, light enough not to wake or frighten.

Jo parts her lips and sighs. Then she mewls like a cat and giggles aloud.

*

"This one!" says the boy. "How d'ya like this one, Mam?" He's trailing a sheaf of wild barley over her forehead, down the bridge of her nose, over her cheeks. "Is it tickly? Tickly?"

"Yes! Oh, yes!" She giggles. "But it's lovely and feathery! Lovely."

The girl squeals. "Me next! Me next!"

The girl has something softer. It's a strand of bog cotton. The girl trails it down Jo's cheeks, down along her neck. The bog cotton is damp and dewy.

*

This time his room seems sadder. Ellen stands there under the harsh, unshaded lightbulb, looks again at the arc of prize-winning ribbons over his bed. She opens the wardrobe again, touches his plaid shirt, the corduroys still hanging from the wire hanger. The detritus of his young life, the last shreds of innocence—of belief.

She bends to pick up the yellow envelope from where it peeps from the pages of the textbook. She takes out that photo of Fintan and Carmel at that university dance. This time, Carmel looks even prettier to Ellen. Both of them are the picture of young romance. Both of them are the picture of blissful naïveté.

Then Ellen conjures that printed photo of their daughter in her dancer's pose. Standing here in his old room, Ellen inserts the girl here between her parents, superimposes the tall, pouting girl into the photo. Catherine right there between them. They all fit, all three of them, the way that Ellen never did. Their marriage might have been happy then unhappy, difficult and then suddenly easier. But it would have survived, been fed and renewed by this aged and deep conviction that they were meant to be.

In Boston or in Patterson Falls, when Ellen Boisvert saw other people's children, when she went to a friend or colleague's baby shower, she never dreamed up a child for her and Fintan. She sees it now, how their marriage was one of playing house, counting time until something happened, something got resolved, fixed, moved on. But it never would have. Never. Even if he'd stayed alive.

She crosses the room to sit on his bed. For the first time since her husband's death, Ellen Boisvert weeps—great, body-heaving sobs. She takes his uncovered pillow and hugs it to her left cheek. She weeps until the pillow is wet and warm. On this summer night, Ellen's weeping is the only sound in the Dowds' silent house.

*

She wakes freezing. Her eyes are dry and tight. Daylight streams through the small bedroom window.

She fell asleep on the narrow single bed, on Fintan's old, teenage bed. She fell asleep holding, hugging the still-damp pillow.

Rain ticks against the window pane. Ellen gets up, fully dressed still, and stiff with cold from the bed.

Ned's car is parked along the orchard wall. When Ellen plugs in the kettle, the electric clock on the wall over the scullery sink says nine o'clock. Ellen has overslept.

In Jo's bedroom, a damp breeze sends the curtains ballooning over the windowsill. The curtains' damp edges suction and then lift from the painted wood. The sound overlays the hiss of the oxygen machine. Slap-slap-slap.

Ellen crosses to pull the window shut.

The ball of yellow yarn has rolled down Jo's bed, lodged there on the white bedspread, somewhere between the twin ridges of Jo's legs. No. *No.* Ellen stands and watches for the breath, the rise and fall. Then she crosses to the bed, feels for a pulse.

Nothing.

Jo's dead eyes stare at the open window. Her lips are set together in a smile.

"Ach, she's gone, the creature." Ellen jumps at the man's voice from the parlor doorway. Ned. The shoulders of his checked sports coat are wet from the rain. He stands there with his tweed cap scrunched in his hand.

"Ned. You knew?" Ellen whispers.

For the first time, Ned McHugh almost meets the American woman's eyes. "I was above in one of the top sheds. The calves turned awful giddy in themselves. I knew 'twas time, then."

"How long?" Ellen asks, panicked, picturing herself up there, asleep in the wrong bed, asleep and out of earshot from Jo's downstairs room. Had the poor woman called out? Screamed? Needed her?

Ned steps into the room, closer to the bed. "Ah, not long, ma'am. An hour at the very most. Less, I'd say. God go with her."

Ellen

41

THERE'S A LIGHT out there on the lake, appearing and disappearing in the dark and through the trees along the headland. Then Ellen hears voices—a woman's first, then a man's, both amplified by the waters of Lough Gowna. They sound so close that they could be standing right next to her, standing here on the pier. Smack-smack-smack. The boat is anchored out there, rising and slapping against the lake's dark, lacquered surface. The woman laughs. Then Ellen hears some jazzy music from the motor boat.

The night sky is dark and starless.

Since Jo's death, a week ago now, she has moved back down to Flanagan's hotel, where Gerry Flanagan and other assorted strangers have stopped her along Gowna's main street to sympathize, to offer their condolences. Every day she has driven out to the house at Knockduff, parking her car in the old spot, then wandering through the silent, ghostly rooms.

The people from the health department came and took away the invalid bed, the bedpans, the assortment of stainless steel trays and medical accoutrements. The undertakers and Dr. Fitzgerald said they'd take care of the rest, of the cremation and the death certificate. And for Tony Cawley's lawyer, the required swab of the cheek for the DNA sample that he and his sister need to prove paternity, to get their money for his daughter.

She spent an afternoon clearing out Fintan's old room—the clothes in the closet, the greeting card and photo of him and Carmel Cawley at that dance.

She stacked his old textbooks and the newspaper clippings together, put them in a cardboard box to carry down to the village and the hotel's dumpster.

She was almost done carting his things to her car when, with a surge of hope, she reread the address that Fintan had listed in his textbooks' flyleaf pages. 23 Oak Grove Avenue, Whitehall, Dublin. She went back into the house and called directory assistance for a number for that address.

"Um . . . I'm looking for a woman named Kitty," she said to the man who answered the Dublin phone number. He had picked up on the first ring; he sounded young. A son? Ellen wondered—hoped. Auntie Kitty's son?

"*Kitty?* Look, is this some kinda joke? Who is this?"

"She . . . lived there. I think. Once. A woman named Kitty."

"Aw, for fuck's sake!" the young man said. Then he hung up.

After the phone call, there was nothing for Ellen to do but to tiptoe back up through the house, up through the scullery, past the line of old coats and Wellington boots. She closed the scullery door behind her. Ned's car was still there, parked in its usual spot along the orchard wall.

Since Jo's death, he had come faithfully to work in the fields or the sheds. But since that morning, he'd never come back into the house. Ellen drove out through the yard gates and down the sloping avenue. Halfway down the hill, she got out to unlatch and then latch the second gate, standing there to take one last look at the stone grey house. It looked shuttered. A house alone on a hill.

Then she drove away toward the Gowna road; left it all for Jo's and the Cawleys' lawyers to handle, to battle it out with letters and legal fees and probates.

Now Ellen watches the white motorboat light nudge out from behind the trees along the point. The man and woman's tittery voices compete with the sudden purr of the engine. She can smell the boat's diesel exhaust. The strains of jazzy violin music have grown louder.

She takes the small paper bag from her jacket pocket. One by one, she takes out satiny prize ribbons, each with its white satin center, the faded gold embroidery. *First prize. Fintan & Rosie Dowd.*

Today when she cleared out his childhood room, she took them down from the wall, the display above his single bed.

The ribbons tail on the night breeze. She watches them, the reds and the blues, one by one, as they drift away on the dark lake.

42

"NOW. THE ROAST LAMB. Which of ye has the lamb?" A waitress is standing at the top of their dinner table, two steaming dinner plates in her hand.

"Oh, yeah," says Father Bradley, pushing back his chair slightly. "That's me. I'm the lamb!"

"The lamb o' God," quips Tom Fitzgerald. Ruth shoots him a shushing look as the doctor chortles at his own joke.

"And the cod?" asks the waitress again, holding forth the second plate. "Someone ordered codfish."

"Here," Ellen says. "I had cod."

Behind this older waitress stands the younger Latvian girl who usually serves at breakfast time. The younger girl passes the remaining plates to the older, florid-faced waitress. Beef, roast chicken, poached salmon. And a large green salad for Riona Fitzgerald who has announced that, now that she's back from her summer holidays in Portugal, she's going to turn vegetarian for the rest of the year.

The two waitresses lean past and over their heads again to place large platters of steamed broccoli, a bowl of carrots, huge bowls of French fries and boiled new potatoes at intervals down their table.

It's a Friday night and the Fitzgeralds and Father Bradley have taken Ellen to dinner at Flanagan's hotel. It's her good-bye dinner—last meal in Gowna.

Upstairs in her small, second-floor hotel room, her suitcase sits unzipped and open on the bedroom floor, waiting for the last few items, waiting to be packed up for tomorrow's flight to Boston.

There are four other occupied tables. Two tables have local-looking couples—faces that Ellen recognizes from her visit to the supermarket or from walking around the village. At one table sit three French tourists, their hair drenched, their rain slickers draped across the backs of their chairs.

Earlier, just after the waitress brought their appetizers, Gerry Flanagan came bustling across the dining room followed by six American tourists who he seated around a large, round table near the door. They're a group of men and women in V-neck sweaters and pressed jeans who made a great, theatrical fuss about who would sit where, and where they might hang their wet raincoats.

Now, as Ellen half listens to more reports from the Fitzgerald family's summer holiday in the Algarve, she watches the American women's faces at the other table. A woman with highlighted hair and a lipstick smile is listening with feigned interest as her husband tells a loud story about an argument with the airport personnel in Shannon.

They seem so foreign, their voices and demeanors so overblown for this country hotel. For this village of Gowna. It's as if they're playing their parts in some stage play where they assume there's a listening audience.

"But sure, that's the thing, isn't it?" Ruth Fitzgerald says, her voice vying with the American man's hooting laugh. Ruth is sitting opposite Ellen. She's leaning toward Ellen now, her pretty face tanned and smiling.

"Hmmm?" Ellen starts from her thoughts. What thing? What part of the Portugal conversation has Ellen missed?

Ruth nods to the rainy evening outside the dining room windows. "If you could even get a few decent weeks of weather here, you wouldn't need to go abroad."

Ellen says, "You got a really great tan."

"Ach," says Ruth, stretching out her bronzed forearm. "And that's with a factor 25 on every day!" She dips her head toward her husband and children. "This shower went running around the place—every day a full timetable of snorkeling and swimming and the devil knows what. Not me. I got a chair at the pool and didn't stir from there until I was called for meals. Getting rid of them for a week was my holiday!"

Father Bradley sits next to Ellen. He's wearing worn Levi's jeans and a faded dress shirt with the sleeves rolled up. Earlier, when they all met in the hotel bar for pre-dinner drinks, there was something extra solemn about him. He says, "Ellen, I'm sure you're off back to great sunshine out there in Boston. Saw on the news there that ye're getting a real roaster of a summer."

"Supposed to hit 90 by the middle of the week," Ellen says. "At least, that's what my mom said on the phone last night. My sister won't be happy. She lives in Florida and she's flying up to New Hampshire the end of next week—her annual trip home to escape the Florida heat."

Lorcan and Riona Fitzgerald are seated between their parents. Lorcan gazes across the table at Ellen, a fork of roast chicken held in midair. His hair is blonder; his pert little nose is sunburned pink. Riona, like her mother, has turned a deep tan under her low-necked T-shirt. She's abandoned her salad to fidget with her cell phone, playing some game that makes a chirping sound. Riona who hit it off and exchanged dance photos with Fintan's daughter.

Jarkowski. Ellen suddenly remembers the name, the large printed letters on the banner that hung above Catherine Cawley's dance troupe. Jarkowski Dance Studio.

"We went snorkeling, me and Dad. Did you ever try snorkeling, Ellen?" Lorcan asks, mustering a grown-up voice.

"Lorcan," Tom says. "Ellen was actually *talking* to Father Bradley. What've I said about interrupting?"

"Dad, I was just ask—"

"Chirp-chirp!" It's Riona's cell phone.

Cat? Ellen wonders. Does she still text her little friend in London?

Ruth says, "Riona, I've asked you three times now . . ."

"Both of you," says Tom. "Both of you agreed that if you were brought out for this meal that you wouldn't carry on. That's what we talked about and what you agreed. Remember?"

Father Bradley sets his fork down and crooks his body away from their table and the squabbling Fitzgerald family. He drops his voice. "Tom said it went all right in the end. With Jo. The undertakers, the cremation and everything? I still felt like I should've been there, but . . ." He shrugs.

"It was fine. Everything . . . everything was the way she wanted."

"Did anyone turn up in the end, a niece or a nephew or that sister of hers?"

Ellen shakes her head. No. "Oh, Noel. I forgot. I actually made a call. An address I found in one of Fintan's old textbooks. A house in Dublin. Thought it might've been the sister, Kitty's."

"And?"

"Just some guy who seemed really pissed off at me for asking for a woman named Kitty."

"I've had no luck with the interparish search," Father Bradley says. "At least not yet. You'd never think the country's that big. You'd never think there'd be that many young girls or women left the parish of Gowna for Dublin—and Dublin when it was small and nearly as parochial as Ballinkeady anyways."

"Maybe she remarried," Ellen says. "I mean, after the first husband died or whatever." She nods toward his plate and the slices of pink, succulent roast lamb. "You should eat your dinner before it gets cold. It looks great!"

"Want a bit? A taste?" He cuts a piece of meat and holds his fork out for her, like someone feeding a child. When she leans closer to eat it, the intimacy of the act makes her blush a deep pink. She swallows the meat and glances guiltily across the table to see Tom Fitzgerald studying both of them. "Gerry Flanagan buys it local," the priest says, his words rushed and flustered. "He's actually known for his good lamb."

Father Bradley leans across the table for some more potatoes, his profile turned from her. Tom says, "So what happens with everything now, Ellen—I mean, the entire house and land and everything up there?" He lowers his voice. "She always told me she'd it taken care of with her solicitor. But of course, that's *all* she'd tell me."

Since that day at his house, the days he confessed his own, youthful part in the end of Fintan and Carmel Cawley's romance, the doctor has been softer around the edges, less of the staged, congenial small-town doctor.

Ellen says, "It's between her solicitor and the Cawleys'. Probate. I guess. Too soon to hear yet."

Tom gives her a wincing look, and then shakes his head. "I dunno. It's a pity. With all Jo's faults—and God knows she had plenty—she *did* work hard. She and Ned kept that place immaculate. I'd hate to see it all just get divided up or sold to the lowest bidder for some cheap, slapped up housing estate. Or sold over the telephone and fax from a London firm of solicitors to some cowboy developer."

In her mind's eye, Ellen glimpses a development of cookie-cutter houses on Knockduff Hill—the sort of housing estates she's seen outside Galway and Ballinkeedy and all the way up here from Shannon Airport. Jo's perfect orchard is erased, as are the front paddocks and the hazel rock, the sloping avenue and the double set of farm gates—all of it replaced with white, look-alike houses with their bright-colored front doors and tiny gardens.

"Then buy it!" Ellen says, raising her voice above the clatter and chatter of the hotel dining room. "You could fit in some farming along with your practice."

Tom rolls his eyes. "Oh, yeah, in my spare time."

She turns to Father Bradley. "Or you, Noel. Isn't there room around here for a spiritual retreat place? Hilltop views? Peace and quiet? Surely the church has the cash?"

The doctor and the priest look across the table at each other and laugh. Father Bradley says, "Right, we could invite everyone and have them pay admission and they'd all drive all the way down here to Gowna, all delighted to be getting in touch with their inner spiritual selves. Until, of course, they ran smack into Jo's ghost, shaking her stick at them and cursing them out of it for bringing any kind of religion onto her land!" This time, Ruth laughs with them. Then they all stop abruptly, embarrassed. It hasn't even been two weeks since her death, since that morning when Ellen walked into her room and saw that face on the pillow.

"Excuse me," says Ellen, setting down her linen napkin. "If the waitress comes back while I'm gone, order me some tea and the apple crumble." She pushes back her chair and walks across the dining room toward the hotel lobby and the ladies' room.

The Americans have just gotten their dinners, and the two waitresses are setting the bowls of vegetables and potatoes down along the table. "Spuds!" proclaims that same man again—obviously the jokester of their group. "Gotta have them spuds when we're in Ireland!"

In the lobby, there's a man coming up the back hallway from the parking lot, laden down with two huge black vinyl bags—obviously a set of drums. He nods to the bar door. "You wouldn't get the door for us?" he asks her.

She opens in the bar door to a gust of voices and clinking glasses and background music from the bar stereo. "Thanks a million," the man says as he edges through. In the corner, on the side of the bar near the village street, another band member is testing the sound equipment.

Ellen starts back down the narrow hallway past the stairs. Tony Cawley is coming out of the gents' toilet, zipping up his fly. He looks up to see her there in the darkened hallway that smells of antiseptic cleaner from the bathrooms. "I thought you'd be gone off back by now." He's wearing a stained grey sweatshirt over his loose, oil-stained jeans. The usual lock of dark hair falls across his forehead. "Why don't you feckin' stay around? You'd have no problem with a job. I heard Gerry's looking for a bouncer here. A heavy to work the door, go beating the shite outta people! You'd be dead suited."

"It's my last night," she says. "I'm having some dinner."

"Must be nice."

"Yes. I recommend the lamb."

He sneers at her. His voice is petulant. "You get anything yet? From the solicitor?"

"Nothing I know of. It could be waiting for me back home—back in Boston. That's my legal address."

"Testing!" calls an amplified voice from the bar. "Testing, one-two-three."

They wait until the noise has stopped. Tony says, "I suppose I'm meant to be thanking you."

"For . . . ?"

"Well, for not making it any more difficult than it has to be. With the undertaker, the DNA sample. You know all that costs money—more money if you have to get a court order to do it. So . . . ah . . . thanks." He shrugs.

Again, Ellen thinks of Tom Fitzgerald standing in his hallway, waiting while she, Ellen, studied that photograph of Fintan's daughter—the photo of the teenage girls at a dance studio. She sees the tall, pouting girl who, unless there's been some strange happenstance of genetics, is definitely Fintan's daughter.

Tony nods toward the front of the hotel, the lobby and the glass doors to the dining room. "I presume you're with Fitzgerald and the wife?"

The electric guitar starts up a song. The drums thump along. Then the music stops. The band is still setting up and doing sound check.

"Yes. Tom and Ruth and their kids. Father Bradley, too."

"And I presume Fitzgerald's filled you in on things?"

"That's none of your business."

Tony shrugs again. "Fine."

There's a gust of voices as someone opens the bar door and walks out toward the front of the hotel.

Tony salutes her. "Well, have a nice life as the Yanks say."

She turns toward the ladies' bathroom.

"Oh, and hey!" he calls after her. "I never asked you," says Tony. "Have you kids yourself? I mean, over there? In Boston."

"No. Now, if you'll excuse me, I need to . . ." She's already reached the ladies' room door. From the hallway he eyes her tummy. "I don't know why you haven't any kids. We know Fintan had no problems in *that* department. But don't think you can ever go acting the little long-lost stepmother with our Catherine." He narrows his eyes at her.

She pushes open the toilet door. She lets it slap shut on his face and beery breath.

He opens in the door with the beveled glass and shouts into the cold, tiled interior. "If you ever make contact with my niece, my sister and me'll have a barring order on you so fast you'll wish you were never born."

*

In her bedroom mirror, she watches herself pack the last of her things into the suitcase. The downstairs band has just started up its second set. She can hear the bar voices, the twangy sound of an electric guitar, the lead singer's voice through her bedroom floor.

Her cell phone bleeps from her nightstand. Who? She leans across the bed to read her text message. It's Viktor, her downstairs neighbor from the Academy apartments. He's returned to Coventry-by-the-Sea early for the fall semester. Managed to finagle another six months of the freebie pad. So it's gonna be the same for her. Six months gratis. Would his little *Ellenita* be heading back soon? Either way, give him a call.

She checks the bedside clock's digital numbers. 10:30. So just 5:30 over there. She sits on her hotel bed and dials Viktor's land line from the wall phone above her headboard. She listens to it ring, brr-brr-brr in his living room across the Atlantic—just the other side of the clapboard wall from her own living room. In fact, if she were there now, sitting in one of her armchairs, she would hear his phone ringing through the wall. She always does.

She inserts herself back there: among her armchairs, bookshelves, her framed posters of Paris and Québec. But she keeps slipping out of her own picture. After her summer in Ireland, after a year of widowhood, there is too much of her now, too much to fit back into its old narrow slot.

Viktor's machine clicks on. "*Hola*. This is Viktor Ortiz. I'm not here right now, but please leave . . ."

She prepares to leave a funny, breezy message. But at the sound of that voice, that life, she feels something hard and sour catching in her throat, the weight of knowing, learning. "Hey Viktor. It's me, *Ellenita*. I'm ah . . . well, I'm still in Ireland. Flying back tomorrow. I'm at a hotel. So if you get in later, I'd love a chat. I'll give you the number . . ." She recites the number from the hotel phone.

Then she slides off the edge of the bed onto the carpet, sits there with her knees to her chin. She watches Gowna's silent main street, the night rain in a halo around the streetlights.

An hour ago, she stood out there in the rain hugging the Fitzgeralds and Father Bradley good-bye. "Maybe we'll come over skiing," Tom said. "Next winter. We'll definitely give you a shout."

"Look after yourself," Ruth said, gripping Ellen by the forearms. "And don't be a stranger. For God's sake, send us an e-mail and tell us how you're getting on."

"I'll be in touch, Ellen," Father Bradley said. "The minute I hear anything about Jo's sister. Good or bad." He had a wistful look.

Then she stood there waving as Tom Fitzgerald's Volvo drove out the hotel gateway and turned up the Main Street toward the priest's house. The Fitzgeralds were giving him a ride home.

Downstairs now, the band's singer finishes up his song. "Thanks," he says. "Thanks very much folks for dancing. We'll take another break and then see ye back for the last set of the night."

A car passes underneath her window, the wipers thwacking, the streetlights glistening on the rooftop. "Hello!" It's a man's voice. Ellen scoots on her bottom closer to the window to peer down. The man is standing directly underneath, just outside the bar door and shouting into his cell phone. "No. No, I'm down here at Flanagan's. Yeah. No. Sure, chance it. They're serving another while anyways. Oh, now, you know how Gerry is."

She looks behind her at the wall phone above the bed, the cord dangling down the wallpapered wall. *Call back, Viktor.* She longs to hear a voice, any voice that will take away this loneliness.

43

THE TUBE FROM HEATHROW AIRPORT speeds into the sunlight, past the upstairs windows and the red-brick gables of south London houses. Ellen checks her cell phone again. No missed calls. Damn.

From her train seat, Ellen eyes the other Friday afternoon passengers—business commuters with their briefcases and newspapers; a flight attendant in a navy blue uniform and a black wheelie suitcase. Further down the train sits a large, loud family—mother, father, kids, and grandparents—all wearing white cotton sun hats. From her seat, Ellen can smell their suntan oil.

The woman's voice announces the next station: "Hounslow Central."

This evening, Saturday, Ellen will take the train back to Heathrow to fly British Airways back to Boston's Logan.

The train is slowing again. The flight attendant steps off, and Ellen watches her crossing the station platform. The vacationing family has turned noisier, the three children fidgety and petulant while the young mother promises that they'll all soon be home soon, all back home and their holiday over.

On the telephone this morning, Miss Daniela Jarkowski said that the dance studio would be easy to find. "Get off at—you're taking the tube, yes?—well, get off at Camden Town or Chalk Farm. Walk from there. You have the address? From the web site? With the Saturday market crowds, you should begin your journey early."

At the station, Ellen carries her suitcase amid the Saturday morning rush, that crisscross of voices and the patter of footsteps, the volley of voices in the underground corridors. How can it be just a short flight away? This city and what she's just left—the quiet, sleepy village of Gowna or the road she just drove to Shannon Airport with its overgrown hedgerows and the stretches of fields and limestone?

Now, standing on the escalator and balancing her suitcase as she scans the framed posters for movies, summer festivals, theater productions, Ellen wonders if this sudden flight change, this extra day and the diversion to London was a stupid idea.

On the telephone from Flanagan's hotel, she told Miss Jarkowski that she and her husband were moving to north London, where Ellen's husband has a fictitious contract job with a multinational. So their fifteen-year-old daughter needed a dance studio. Could they come and check it out?

The sun is suddenly bright on the London sidewalk. The street smells of coffee. Techno-music blasts from a store. At another store, a man is unlocking, rattling up a security shutter.

More techno. Then reggae.

A flashing neon signs offers Tattoos and Body Piercing.

A woman is stacking leather boots on a set of street-side wooden shelves: "Doc Martens. Best Price," says the cardboard sign.

Ellen would need a week to take it all in—the voices and movement and crisscross of languages. At another market stall, a man stands on a step stool to hang a line of black T-shirts along a railing. He winks at her as she walks past. "Some nice shirts here, darling; cheapie, cheapie."

She turns into the side street, to another line of just-opening stalls and food vendors setting up their pans and woks and crepe makers. The smell makes her hungry, reminds her that she hasn't eaten breakfast. There's a blast of Elvis singing, "Love me tender." Another security shutter rattles open.

*

The stairway of the Red Dragon Chinese restaurant smells of frying grease and duck sauce. At the top of the stairs, taped to the white stucco wall, is a homemade, computer-printed sign with an arrow pointing toward the front of the building: "Jarkowski Dance Studio. Day & Hourly Studio Rentals."

Ellen opens the studio door to thumping music and a huge painted room with red-painted walls and three rows of girls who are dancing in front of a large, room-length mirror. Between the grimy front windows, under a white floodlight, music blasts from a laptop set up on a narrow, high table, the two speakers on the floor: *Love me, love me / Say that you love me.* "Arc! Arc! Hip!" A woman's voice above the music. "Right! Left! Triangle! Mira. Excuse me, Mira! Mira! You're turning your whole body, sweetheart. Just that shoulder, then slo-ooowly lifting your chin. Good!"

Ellen studies the teacher, who is standing in the opposite corner, left of the laptop setup. She's a wiry little woman in a white, oversized T-shirt and black leggings. Daniela Jarkowski is older and smaller than her phone voice.

At last, Miss Jarkowski sees Ellen standing there inside the door. Unsmiling, the dance teacher holds up both hands. *Ten. Ten more minutes until the girls' break.* She nods Ellen to a plastic chair set against the side wall.

"Okay, now hop step. Hop. Step. Beautiful. Now get ready for the next . . ."

Cat Cawley is the girl in the middle row. There she is: the center row, second from the end. She has a goth-black fringe pinned back off her face, the rest of her hair in a wispy little ponytail. Her skin is ghostly white against her black shorts and knee socks, a black strappy top. Oh, yes. That's Fintan's daughter.

The music revs up. "Kiss me, kiss me."

The young girls dance in a distracted, fidgety way, watching each other's reflection in the mirror, whispering over their shoulders. A few girls are downright clumsy and out of sync with the music. But Catherine Cawley's eyes are shut, her face serene. Her whole body is graceful, in perfect rhythm. She's by far the best dancer here.

"Now, girls, get ready for the turn. Turn!" The girls all turn in almost unison, facing the door and Ellen's plastic chair. They dance to the right, arms high, together, the thump-thump-thump of stockinged feet on the polished-wood floor.

Fintan's daughter is right there, less than ten feet away. She keeps her eyes closed as she dances.

"You have five, six, seven, eight. Throw! Throw! Jump!" calls Miss Jarkowski.

Then, in unison with the other girls, Cat Cawley turns toward their teacher behind the laptop.

*

In her tiny office, Daniela Jarkowski lights a cigarette. Across the desk from the dance teacher is an old wooden chair with a half-used packet of printer paper, but she doesn't invite Ellen to remove it, to take a seat.

"So your daughter, what kind of dance is she doing now?"

"Tap," Ellen lies across the small metal desk.

"She's good, yeah?" The tone is skeptical.

"Okay," Ellen says. "Not as *good* as she could be. She needs practice."

Miss Jarkowski exhales smoke through her nose. "Ach, they all need practice. You see those girls out there? Each one, they arrive on Saturday. 'Oh, Miss J, I've had to go here, pop over there. Time for everything but I haven't had time to practice.'"

"What . . . what about that tall girl? The girl with the black hair? She seems good."

Miss Jarkowski frowns across the desk at Ellen.

"The tall girl in the second row. The jet-black hair."

"Ah, yes. Catherine. Best student I have. Very, very good. But the poor kid, you know. She misses too many classes. And now she travels from some bloody place, from out in the home counties or . . ." Miss Jarkowski twirls her cigarette hand. "And the mother sends my money late. Always late. Once, she telephones me, this mother, stupid woman, and she says that Catherine's not coming. No more dance. She says—"

"—But she is here. She's trying."

Something in Ellen's voice stops the dance teacher in her rant. She levels a quizzical gaze on Ellen. "You know this kid, this Catherine?"

"No. But you can't help noticing her, how talented she is."

Miss Jarkowski gives a theatrical shrug. "Usually they pay. Must pay. But a kid like that . . ." She gives Ellen a twisted smile. "Hey, maybe one day, she's gonna make me famous, right? Make me famous and I can sleep late on Saturday mornings and not take two tubes to come and teach these girls with no talent." The teacher gives a high, forced laugh—"Oh, except your kid. Hah! Your American daughter, I'm sure, is very good. Very good. Now, when are you and your family moving to London?"

"Next month."

Another cigarette puff, then Miss Jarkowski glances at her watch. She pushes a sheet of printed paper across the desk. "So your daughter can read this. On your airplane tonight when you fly back to America. If she wants Saturday mornings, contemporary dance, maybe we can find a place, hah? Maybe something? Maybe it becomes sixteen girls? Why not?"

Crossing back across the mirrored studio, Ellen weaves among the clusters of dancers, the girls, standing there in their little cliques of three and four girls.

No Cat. She's noplace to be seen.

On the landing, Cat Cawley doesn't turn to the sound of Ellen closing the studio door behind her. Cat is standing alone, eating a candy bar and watching the street from the front landing window.

Ellen creaks along the landing toward the stairs. She starts down, then stops on the third step. "Hey. You were great in there. Really great."

Cat turns. There's a tiny chocolate stain on her upper lip. They face each other through the white stair rails. Cat flashes a small, shy smile. "Oh, d'you actually *think* so?"

"Yes."

"Oh. Oh, *thanks*."

Through the studio door the music starts again. "I like the way you move!" Then Miss Jarkowski's voice: "Okay, change lines this time. New girls, change to the front. Same formation as last time."

Ellen says, "Your break's up. Maybe you'd better get back in there."

Cat gives a little hand flap, the teenage approximation of a wave. "Yeah. 'Bye."

44

December 2002

ELLEN SLIDES two crisp dollar bills under the park ranger's Plexiglas window. He passes her a tiny green ticket and points her toward the open parking spots along the fence. She rolls up the car window and bumps across the packed-mud parking lot, past the wooden sign with the white lettering: "Welcome to the Santa Madera National Forest. No firearms, fireworks, alcohol. Leash law. Please lock your vehicle."

On this Saturday afternoon, the lot is already half-full. It's shady and cooler up here in the park. Under the piñon trees and along the low fences, the parking lot and trailhead are rimmed with watery, glittery snow.

Ellen's red Nissan with its Massachusetts license plate is the only non–New Mexico car.

She grabs her fanny pack and sweatshirt from the passenger seat, then reaches into the back for her water bottle. In all the guidebooks, they warn newcomers and tourists about elevation headaches.

Now Ellen starts up the first part of the trail or *arroyo*.

On Saturdays, she teaches two morning classes at the Santa Madera Community College. Otherwise, she would have made it out here for her Saturday hike much earlier, when the sun was still high in the blue New Mexico sky, and when there was time to climb to the top of the park and back down again before the park rangers come looking for her.

Today, if she walks fast, she'll make it to the first lookout halfway up the mountain.

Sometimes on her Saturday hike, Ellen conjures the town park in Coventry-by-the-Sea, its white bandstand and its statue memorial to Nathaniel Lunt, died 1872, a British-born town father, shipbuilder and antislavery advocate in his new country of America. She pictures his statue amid the clipped lawns and well-tended begonia beds.

A town park. Just like this. Except that New England park is already fading in her mind.

Yesterday, Ellen woke to a snow-covered skylight above her bed. She rolled back the covers and thumped across to her second-floor window to see the year's first snowfall. Outside, under a blue December sky, the snow had blanketed the apartment buildings and the benches in the courtyard.

Noel the cat flopped down from the end of the bed and crossed to the window, too. He set his front paws on the windowsill. Together, they stared at that blinding blue against white. She scratched behind his ears and he purred—this New Mexico cat named for an Irish priest.

In her e-mails to Ireland and Gowna, Ellen has told Father Noel Bradley about his American namesake. But she hasn't told him that, the second she saw this kitten at the animal shelter northwest of town, its sleek black fur reminded her of Father Noel's bicycling shorts.

Now she pulls to the side of the trail to let an approaching woman and her black Labrador pass. The dog strains at its leash, forcing the woman in her swishy Gortex coat to hurry down the slope.

"Hi there!" the woman calls.

"Hi," Ellen answers, inwardly smiling at the red ear muffs and winter jacket. Three months living out here and she's still amused at these people all muffled up for Arctic weather, when this, she's been told, is about as cold as it gets out here, in this spot just east of the Rio Grande, in the lower peaks of the Santa Maderas.

She pictures those twenty-below-zero days in Patterson Falls, New Hampshire, when she and Louise waddled down their street to school in snowsuits and boots. Here in the New Mexico forest, she can hear them now—all the kids from all the houses along River Road, Patterson. For months at a time. Swish, swish, swish.

Her sweatshirt is too hot and heavy draped around her shoulders. She unknots it, ties it around her waist. Then she takes a long drink from her water bottle and steps around a hole in the steep path. Up here, not yet quarter-way up the trail, there's more snow under the undergrowth.

The Santa Madera Community College sits just off Highway 85, heading south out of town. The college is all spaceship white except for its rows of dark-tinted windows to block the perpetual sun.

Last September, Ellen Boisvert arrived there in her interview suit and stockings on a 105-degree day. Amid their interview questions about pedagogical approaches and cross-curricular integrations, the interview panel members couldn't keep a tone of incredulity from their voices. Why would a preppy-school girl from New England want a job teaching teenagers from the county's surrounding towns and Indian reservations?

At the interview, they boasted about the college's well-published study on first-generation college students—Latina and native kids who betray their own family by signing up for college classes.

When they called her with a job offer, Ellen gave a two-week notice at Coventry Academy. In one long weekend, she packed up her belongings and drove, pioneer style, across the country. When she woke in highway motels with rattling air conditioners, she still started awake with that sense of duty, as if Jo Dowd were waiting for her breakfast and medications in a downstairs sickroom.

Her students at the community college can only be assigned papers or assignments that can be completed during class time or study-support labs. At home, her students have neither space nor time to write short comprehension paragraphs, nor to practice the reading and writing exercises from their GED prep classes on Saturday mornings.

She has, of course, driven out to see where they live, Native American and Latina and Caucasian, each in their separate-race trailer parks. The trailers are placed at odd angles from each other, most without shade or vegetation, as if someone had just spat them from the sky.

At the college, her fellow teachers invite her for potluck dinners or to join them for lunch in the cafeteria. But so far, there is an unspoken caution toward Ellen Boisvert, the petite, self-contained woman from back east who rarely speaks of a family, a relationship, a reason for being here. People like Ellen Boisvert have nearly always come here *from* something.

She pulls aside again for a man with his toddler hoisted into a baby backpack. The blond child bops with his father's steps. When they pass, the kid stares, slack-jawed, at her. Up here, the trail is bordered by sapling Ponderosa pines. She steps off the trail to a gap in the trees, a spot from which she can see the whole town down there—the clusters of houses and gas stations and roadside casinos—all of it cast in pink by the evening sun.

After her first week in a downtown motel, she called the number on a "for rent" sign. The estate agent led her through the Paso Robles model apartment, opening the white built-in closets and directing her to the view of the *Paseo* out front. But Ellen never ventured past the living room and its white stucco walls and its vaulted ceilings.

"I'll take it. How much do you need for the deposit?"

At least once a week, her friend Viktor Ortiz sends her newsy updates from the Academy and its faculty; he says he might come out here to visit on Christmas break. Ellen hopes he doesn't. Already, Ellen finds herself being bored by the Coventry Academy gossip. She feels her and Viktor's friendship stretching apart, losing its elasticity.

"Where you from?" someone often asks when they overhear her accent in a downtown café where she sometimes sits with a cappuccino and her piles of student tests to grade. These people tell how they visited Boston once, had a beer in the *Cheers* pub; how even the local cab driver got lost in the ridiculous traffic in those unfathomable streets.

During these disposable conversations, Ellen waits for that nod of the head, that mental ranking of New England alma maters, professions, Boston suburbs. But there is none.

For the first time in her life, Ellen Boisvert is just another woman alone in a town. She's nobody's daughter. Nobody's wife.

On these winter weekends, when Santa Madera's downtown smells of the piñon that burns in the outdoor cafés' *chimineas,* local Indian and immigrant Guatemalan women sit under the wooden eaves, their turquoise and silver jewelry set out on colored blankets. They never meet her eye. She never meets theirs. Perhaps each woman fears that she will see a mirror of her own displacement, the same resolve to eschew a past life, to abandon a previous existence and place.

Ellen pulls to the left for a young, twenty-something couple who have been climbing the trail behind her, their voices loud on the still, afternoon air. Their golden retriever strains on its leash. "Thanks," the man says, breathlessly, as he and his girlfriend hurry past and up this steepest part of the *arroyo*.

Up here, Knockduff Hill, or that house at the top of the sloping avenue could be in another place, another galaxy—that house and the hundred-acre farm that Jo somehow, secretly, willed to Ellen Boisvert, her dead son's wife. When?

Over and over, Ellen has tried to pinpoint the day, the time when Jo managed to change her will. It must have been the day when she found Jo and Ned out walking on the avenue, that sudden, lively day when the old woman had a reprieve of wellness. The damn woman could get Ned to do anything for her. She left Ellen her 100 acres and house. She left Ned her money.

The Ballinkeady lawyer's letter arrived, certified delivery, two days after Ellen arrived back in Boston from London.

Dear Ms. Boisvert:

As the legal representatives for the property and cash assets of the late Josephine Dowd, nee Burke, we wish to inform you . . .

The young couple is sitting on one of the three rough-hewn benches that are set in a semicircle on the western edge of the lookout. The benches are angled toward the opposite mesa and the sunset over the valley. The man is testing his camera's lens setting, lifting, pointing the camera toward the mountain, then fiddling with the lens again. Set for the perfect sunset shot.

On her own bench, Ellen unfolds the Irish airmail envelope from her fanny pack.

November 24, 2002
Unit 4, The Willows
Malahide,
County Dublin
Ireland.

Dear Ellen,

I have tried this letter many times. I would have e-mailed you, but that would have been rude, wouldn't it?

First, a sincere "thank you" for caring for my sister in her final days. You must know by now that Father Bradley, the Gowna priest, has come to see me. I rang him, not the other way around, though he had been looking for me. I rang him because I knew, dreamed that she was gone. After that phone call, he came to visit me.

All last summer I had been dreaming of my sister. Every night, I'd wake up and there she was, lying in the bed beside me. We shared a bed as children, as young girls. Did she mention that? Happy times. Sometimes, her voice in the room was so real that I thought she really was here, that she'd come, finally, to make up friends.

The night she died, I dreamed of her again, the two of us sitting on the wall in the front of the house, chattering away and swinging our legs in the sunshine. In that dream, she smiled and said good-bye to me.

First I made a phone call down there, to the house at Knockduff, because I was sure poor little Fintan would be home. But the phone just rang and rang. After that, a Telecom voice said it was disconnected. For days I scanned the death notices in the daily paper. Then at last, I forced myself to ring down there, to Gowna's presbytery.

Even when you've fallen out with someone, you still miss them. Three, four times a day, you catch yourself thinking that they're still there, that Knockduff is all still there—all the noise and the cattle and the apple blossoms in the orchard.

And then Father Bradley told me the news of Fintan. My dear Ellen, I just couldn't believe it, couldn't, wouldn't accept it. I don't still. I think that he's there, over there in Boston working away, being important and brainy.

I wish that we'd met when you were here. She should have told you where I was. Should have let you ring and bring me to her bedside to say good-bye in person. Or afterward, you could have come and visited me here. But that's all gone now and I hope there will be a next time. Next time you're in Ireland. Or would you come specially?

It's a nice place here at the Willows. My husband Brian died five years ago, and I sent my sister a letter with the news, but heard nothing in return.

I had to sell our old house in Whitehall. Brian's niece Caroline and her husband helped me move in here. I have my own small flat. When the weather is fine (we've had terrible rain and storms the last week), I sit out on the patio and I can smell Dublin Bay.

They've taught all of us residents how to use computers and the Internet and e-mail. I told them I was writing to my niece in America and one of the attendants, a lovely Polish girl, took this photo of me and put it on a screen and then printed it up for me to send to you. Honest to God, I think they teach us all this in the hope that it helps us to remember how to put on our own shoes and not grow more doddery than we already are.

Anyway, I'm including the e-mail and the photo in this letter. It's always nice to learn something new. And then there's the online catalogs—lovely style and shoes. I just order them and they deliver them straight to the door. Do you shop with them yourself?

There's a van that brings us out to the shopping centre every week, but with the walking stick it's just a bother, an embarrassment.

Carmel Cawley e-mails or rings me now and again. A few summers back, they were both home here for a visit. I keep Catherine's photos on my fridge. She's grown up so fast, that child. It seems only the other day since my husband and I flew to London for her first birthday party, and she was even jigging and dancing in her playpen back then! Carmel told me what you did for them. May God reward you a hundredfold.

Ellen, I hope this isn't our last correspondence. I hope you come over and visit again. All I can say to you is that we should let the dead rest in peace. There were times when my sister Jo seemed like the devil incarnate. But we all do things we regret, wish that we'd never done or said. Since hearing about my sister's death, I am sorry, so sorry for taking heed of her and her old huffs and tempers. I wish now that I had defied her, that I had forced her to talk to me.

That last Sunday I'll never forget the rage in her face and eyes. Maybe my sister was always full of that temper, that silent resentment. You don't see it when you're young. I hope for your sake that old age softened her.

Ellen stops reading to remember her first sighting of Jo Dowd in that house in Knockduff—a tall old woman with her cane held above her head, ready to murder or attack the intruder. No, Kitty, Aunt Kitty. No, old age didn't soften your sister Jo—not really, not until the very end.

You know, Jo always believed that I'd been the pet down at home, that I got away with everything, and later, that I had the perfect life up here in Dublin. As if, without land and cattle, life was all a bed of roses. God, if she only knew the half!

I still dream of that last Sunday morning in Knockduff.

After Father Bradley's visit last month, the attendants here wanted me to see a grief counselor. They brought a woman to see me. But with all her degrees and qualifications, I thought she had very bad manners. She slugged her tea and was far too nosy. So I stopped after a few weeks. But I did ask her about the dream I've been having for years now. Told her how sometimes, it goes away, but then it comes back again, five or six nights in a row. She said that our minds get trapped like that, keep going back over the things that frighten us.

I told her it would frighten anyone to see my only nephew, a grown man on his knees, down on his knees in the orchard and cradling his poor dog in his arms. Awake or dreaming, I still hear Fintan crying. Still hear him screaming out that poor dog's name. Rosie.

When Brian and I got there, he'd already been kneeling there for over an hour, in the damp afternoon, dressed in nothing but an old T-shirt. He was crying and crying and the rope dangling from the apple tree above them.

I say forgive, I pray to forgive, but what kind of a woman would try to get rid of her own grandchild? And then, as if that wasn't bad enough, to hang a dog?

When he was a young fellow, that dog was the one thing that he loved after all his years of hard work, all his years of being up there in that house alone with the pair of them and his grandmother, every day working as hard as they did.

That Sunday, we only drove down there after she rang the house, ranting and raving that it was all my fault, all my fault to let himself and his girlfriend stay here like that, let them carry on like that under my own roof. And now look at the fix he was in—trapped with a pregnant girlfriend. My fault, my fault, my fault. It was all name-calling and accusations and how it had always been easy for me, so easy with my posh house and no children.

Brian insisted that we drive down there. To tell you the truth, I didn't want to. I was so vexed I said to just let her stew in her own venom. But he talked me into it. Said we could make a weekend of it, stay someplace nice on Saturday night, then drive on to Mayo first thing on Sunday morning. A chat, he said. A chat would get her to see a bit of sense.

I knew. I knew the minute we opened that first gate and drove up the avenue. Knew something was bad, wrong. You always do, don't you? And then, there they were—Fintan and his poor dog.

Lord, here I am again—writing it down this time, as if dreaming it weren't enough! But he screamed at her, screamed that he hated her, that she'd never be happy until she made him as miserable as her; so miserable she was even refusing to come to his own wedding.

She stood over her weeping son and said if he really wanted to know what was what, if he really wanted to go ahead and marry that girl, maybe he should just take his bike and pedal off down to the village hall for himself, around seven o'clock. Take a little trip down there and see for himself what sort of girl he was insisting he'd marry.

So he did. We drove him down. And you know the rest.

After the hall, he came back with us to Dublin. We drove off the three of us. Fintan with only the clothes on his back but insisting we had to bring him away, away. For Christ's sake bring him away or he'd go back up to Knockduff and kill her.

We stopped at a chemist shop in a town where Brian went and knocked on the private hall door and begged the man to give us something, something to sedate the boy so we could drive him back to our house in Whitehall, Dublin.

He stayed with us for a fortnight that summer. I tried to cheer him up. I got him an appointment with a doctor. I even went into town to a pet shop and bought him a pup and brought it home on the bus.

He'd be gone running and jogging for hours, out in the dark. I'd be just about to ring the guards, frantic he was mugged or half dead someplace, when here he'd finally turn up, exhausted and fit to drop.

That day we drove him out to the airport, he told us he was flying to London, to follow Carmel, to make it up with her. We'd given him the money for the ticket and to get them started in a place to live.

Then we never heard from him. Only from Carmel. She rang our house one night looking for him, wondering why he hadn't turned up. Then she wrote me a letter saying that her brother had found out, that her brother had a friend who knew him over there in Boston. That she never wanted to hear the name "Dowd" again.

I didn't even know he was married, but hoped that he was. I hoped and prayed that he had found a nice girl that could make him happy. I'm sure you did.

They tell me it's better not to dwell. To keep busy, to force myself to think of happy things. So I do, at least until I fall asleep and dream.

Ellen, dear, this is a much, much longer letter than I had intended. It's getting dark outside now, and it's only just after four o'clock here. They already have the place decorated for Christmas, so here I am sitting at my little kitchen table, looking out at the garden and shrubs all lit-up with little white lights.

I'll look forward to hearing back from you, to hearing all about your life out there. I will remember you in my prayers.

Love, Auntie Kitty.
01-356978
KitWalsh@eircom.net.

Ellen studies the computer-printed photo of the pretty little woman dwarfed by the wing-backed armchair she's sitting in. The photographer has snapped her from the waist up. Kitty is facing the camera with a wistful smile. Her hair is dyed a butterscotch blond. Her eyebrows are penciled in. She's wearing large pearl earrings and a silky scarf knotted over a pink sweater set. Behind her rimless spectacles, the eyes are bright and inquisitive. She reminds Ellen of a dainty, aging doll.

In the Santa Madera National Park, the young man and his girlfriend are standing at the very edge of the lookout, their backs silhouetted against the pinking sky. Snap, snap, snap, goes his camera.

The retriever's nose startles Ellen, nuzzling at her hand. Then the dog rests its head on her lap, the sad, limpid eyes looking up at her.

"Sorry," the man calls back over his shoulder. "But she is friendly."

"Oh, she's fine," Ellen answers, then bends to kiss the dog's golden head.

Epilogue

"GIRLS, GIRLS, GIRLS!" Mrs. Pritchard shouts up at them on stage. Her voice is all echoey in the empty theater. "Start again. Please. From the top. Gerda, let's start right back to the roses again. And you, yes, Catherine, let's drop the ax-murderer look, darling, okay? You're supposed to be Gerda in *The Snow Queen,* not Jack the Ripper, all right?"

Crap, Cat thinks. But then, Cat Cawley forces herself to smile down there into the lit-up theater where Mrs. Pritchard stands and paces in front of the rows and rows of empty seats.

It's November 12. So Christmas is still more than a month away. And anyway, this is just their first week's practice away from Mrs. Pritchard's studio, at real stage rehearsals.

At the studio, over a month ago now, Mrs. Pritchard asked all interested students to audition for the part of Gerda. Even two of the boys tried out, and maybe Cat had got it wrong, but she was sure this guy, Franklin, was going to get the lead part. On audition night, they were all dead nervous.

For nights and nights before that night, Cat practiced every single afternoon after school. She rented the DVD, of course, and just watched and practiced in their living room, until Mum said that if she ever heard one of those bloody songs again she'd put the sodding telly out on the footpath for someone to just take away.

And then it happened. Mrs. Pritchard chose sixteen-year-old Cat Cawley to be Gerda. Mrs. Pritchard said that she, Cat, could hold the part longer.

When Treacy Atchinson-Radcliffe heard the news she said—out loud so everyone could really hear—"How come the new girl gets picked? She hasn't even come here from a proper dance school."

Treacy Atchinson-Radcliffe is on stage now, standing behind Cat in the chorus, playing the hyacinth. Cat really hates her. One of the other girls said that Treacy even had her mum call Mrs. P to make a formal complaint and threaten to reenroll her daughter in a different dance studio. That girl told Cat that Mrs. P only made Treacy the hyacinth to shut Treacy's mum up.

Now Cat moves slowly across the stage like she's supposed to, but one eye on Mrs. P down there, gauging the dance teacher's reaction, if she's pleased with Cat's moves or not. Okay, Cat, she reminds herself, keep the smiley sweetie face.

Mum has a bet on with Cat. Mum reckons that her daughter just can't keep it up, all this looking innocent and nice. Not even now that Cat's got the lead part.

It's funny how it all started, really.

They were living way out in Cripton, in that academy. Really getting on each other's nerves in that tiny flat. And everyone getting on everyone's nerves in the one-story building where all the workers lived for free and shared bathrooms and the big kitchen. They had been already living there for eight months on that evening when everything changed.

It was a nice sunny evening, so Cat had brought a chair out the back, set it on the strip of pebbles underneath their window, sat there with her new *Kiss* magazine and she'd just lit up a fag when the phone rang. Not her mobile, but the big pay phone in the corridor, which, like, only rang in the middle of the night, usually. It used to wake them up at all hours, her and Mum. Then one of their neighbors would answer it, a bloke with a foreign accent, standing out there in the corridor and shouting down the receiver like he was in a train station, not a staff residence hall.

So that evening, Cat let it just ring. But then, it just didn't stop, so Cat went back around and in the front door. "Yeah," she said, into the phone. "Who do you want?"

And there was this woman on the other end, with a poshed-up voice. "Hello. I'm looking for a Carmel Cawley, please."

Cat said, "She's at work. Can I take a message?"

"Are you Catherine?" asked the woman.

Cat felt dead nervous then, wondering why she didn't recognize the voice, if it was a teacher's voice, one of her teachers up at the academy, calling to complain about Cat again. "Yeah. What do you want?"

"Actually, I'm calling from the Pritchard School of Dance up here in London, Covent Gardens. We've had an inquiry on your behalf. We hear you're quite good, that we should let you audit—"

"—If you're taking the piss, this isn't very funny." Then Cat hung up, and she was just going back outside again, back to her *Kiss* magazine, when it started ringing again.

This time, the woman said, "Could we have a better contact number for your mum, please? I think that would be best."

So Cat thought she shouldn't but she did it anyway. She gave her mum's mobile number.

*

"Good, good," Mrs. Pritchard's shouting at the stage again. "A little better this time. Now you! Gerda or Catherine . . ."

"It's Cat, miss."

"If you could just come up a little faster there on that last one. And you need to do that final curtsy toward your buttercup, but also try and turn a little more toward the audience. Toward me. Yeah. Look, we'll come back to that one later. Okay. Where's my hyacinth? Hyacinth? You should be already swaying. When our friend Gerda here finishes that last curtsy, you need to be ready."

Mum came home from work and poured her usual wine and said that she really was going to swing for one of those boarding school bitches soon—all their questions and bloody food allergies and vegan shit.

Mum always drank the first glass fast. Then, Mum lit a fag and poured her second glass and said, "Oh, by the way, babes, some woman rang me this afternoon. Yeah. From some place, some dance school up in Covent Gardens."

"Oh, yeah? What'd she want, then?" Cat turned from the telly, trying to keep her voice casual.

"Says they want you to audition. And I think you should, babes. Can't do any harm to try, right?"

Across the living room, Mum had that secretive look, like she was thinking really hard about something, but it was something she wasn't going to tell her daughter about. Something big.

"We can't afford a dance school," Cat said. But of course, she only said it because she really wanted Mum to contradict her, to say, "Of course we can. No bother."

So Mum blew her cigarette smoke out and gave Cat that sly, secret look again. She said, "Hey, maybe we can babes. Maybe we really can."

Mum rang in sick the following Friday, and they got the van to drive them to the Cripton train station. All the way up to London on the train, Mum kept telling Cat to sit still and for Christ's sake, to stop biting her nails. "Once we get there," said Mum. "Once we get there, I'm gonna find a Boots and get some nail-polish remover for you. That black shit looks like rubbish on your nails, what's left of them."

The Pritchard School of Dance had all these big windows and a pointy ceiling like a church or something. And just before the audition, Cat kept thinking, What about Miss Jarkowski? Won't she be pissed off if I just leave?

But then, Cat forced herself to stop thinking about anything, 'cos she wasn't going to get into Mrs. Pritchard's anyways, and it was all just a joke, 'cos not in a million years could her and Mum afford a place like that.

There were three of them—three teachers just sitting there in the studio gawking up at her as she requested her song, then she started her best hip-hop number.

Afterward, Mum said she had to go in the office and talk to Mrs. Pritchard for a while, so why didn't Cat just walk around a bit or go look in the shops and she'd just text her when it was time to go back to the train?

"A trust," Mum said a week later, when the letter came saying they were accepting Catherine Cawley to the Pritchard School of Dance. "For once, we don't have to worry about the money, babes. Not anymore. It's all paid for by a trust."

And then, just a week later, Mum announced they were going up to London again, this time to visit a friend. They got off at the Russell Square station. They walked along and turned down these streets and then they stopped in front of this old house with railings and steps and a big white door.

Cat asked, "Is there a party here?" Even though it was the middle of the day. Then this woman appeared in the open doorway, dressed in a blue suit. "Oh, *there* you are, Ms. Cawley," said the woman, who was really gawking at Mum. The woman seemed surprised at something, like how Mum or both of the Cawleys looked. Then the woman looked like she was going to laugh as she said, "Well, do come inside. At least you'll learn a little about the housing market in this area."

The maisonette was really fab. It had these big windows and two bathrooms. As Mum followed the woman through the rooms, Cat kept thinking, No, Mum. Stop arsing about. We can't buy this place. You're just making yourself sad and stupid.

"We have no money, Mum," Cat whispered to her, when she got her alone in the gorgeous kitchen and the estate agent woman was out of earshot.

Mum just had that secretive look again.

*

For over seven months now, they've been living in that place—a two-bedroom. Mum said they could've got a house, easily got a house, but she couldn't be bothered with a garden.

And the maisonette is near Cat's new school, Brantley Independent, where some of the guys are actually quite hot and one of them, Richard, seems to like Cat. But Cat hates him. But she doesn't hate him as much as she hates Treacy Atchinson-Radcliffe, the fat hyacinth that can't dance.

"Are we, like, rich now?" Cat asked Mum one day. Mum had just hung up the phone after calling the uni, the university, asking all about this course where you start learning how to be a nurse. Though Mum's actually *way* too old to go to a uni or to learn anything new.

"So are we like, rich or something?" Cat asked Carmel again. They were sitting at the kitchen table having a coffee, and Mum had all this printed-up stuff on the table about her uni course and how she could enroll.

"No," Mum said, "Well, no, not rich but . . ."

"But what, then?" Cat asked, trying not to sound too worried. Because all along, this little voice inside Cat kept saying, "Oh, no, not some other bloke again, some bloke who's letting us stay in his maisonette, but then he'll turn out to be a total wanker in the end."

Mum leaned across toward Cat and went, "You know that time last year when we went to visit your gran?"

"Yeah, 'course. Gowna, Ireland. Where Uncle Tony and my friend Riona live."

"Well, I once had this old friend there, babes. An old lady, you know, very old."

"What she look like? Did I meet her?"

"No. No, you never met this woman. But anyway, she was really old and she died and left me . . ." Mum took another sip of her coffee, and for a minute, Cat thought her mum might start crying or something. But then she went, "Well, she died and she was such a good friend that she left me her money. For me and for you."

"Wow! Wow! That's a really good friend. So why didn't I meet her?"

"Catherine, you don't always have to know everything, do you?"

"Well, yeah, actually I do."

Mum pushed Cat's hair back off her forehead and said, "You know, before your opening night for the *Snow Queen,* you've really got to do something about that hair. There's this stuff that will totally take dye out."

Mrs. Pritchard is shouting again: "Gerda, darling. Keep that last movement a little tighter, please! Again. Start again. And concentrate this time. You've really got to concentrate."

Mum said that for every dance practice, Cat should just look out into the theater and pretend that the rows of seats are already full, like, rows and rows of people all eating their chocolates and gawking up at the stage to watch Cat Cawley dance.